The Deliverance of

Barker McRae

MERCER
UNIVERSITY

MERCER UNIVERSITY PRESS

Endowed by

TOM WATSON BROWN
and
THE WATSON-BROWN FOUNDATION, INC.

The Deliverance of Barker McRae

A Novel

STACIA PELLETIER

MERCER UNIVERSITY PRESS
Macon, Georgia

MUP/ H1038

Published by Mercer University Press
1501 Mercer University Drive
Macon, Georgia 31207

29 28 27 26 25 5 4 3 2 1

Books published by Mercer University Press are printed on acid-free paper that meets the requirements of the American National Standard for Information Sciences—Permanence of Paper for Printed Library Materials.

Printed and bound in CANADA.

This book is set in Adobe Caslon.

Cover/jacket design by Burt&Burt.

ISBN 978-0-88146-972-1 (print)
978-0-88146-973-8 (eBook)
Cataloging-in-Publication Data is available from the Library of Congress

Trespass, *verb*

1. Literally, to pass beyond; to pass over the boundary line of another's land
2. To intrude; to go too far
3. To violate any known rule of duty

Deliverance, *noun*

1. Rescue from danger or any evil
2. The act of speaking or pronouncing; utterance

—*Webster's Dictionary*, 1828

Author's Note

The Deliverance of Barker McRae is fiction that borrows from history. Barker's story takes place at the height of the Cherokee land lottery and the Georgia gold rush, two intertwined events that have not received sufficient attention in our collective understanding of the United States in the early nineteenth century. When the State of Georgia began illegally distributing plots of gold-rich Cherokee land to white settlers in 1832, one of the biggest land grabs in US history quickly and tragically ensued. In some instances, white orphans were eligible to receive land rights in the lottery, though their guardians often took charge of any acreage the children received. Property claims were disputed on all sides throughout the gold rush and often had to be settled by attorneys.

While Barker is a fictional character, her story takes place against the backdrop of these important—and underrecognized—historical events. More information about this period of Georgia history is available at the end of the book.

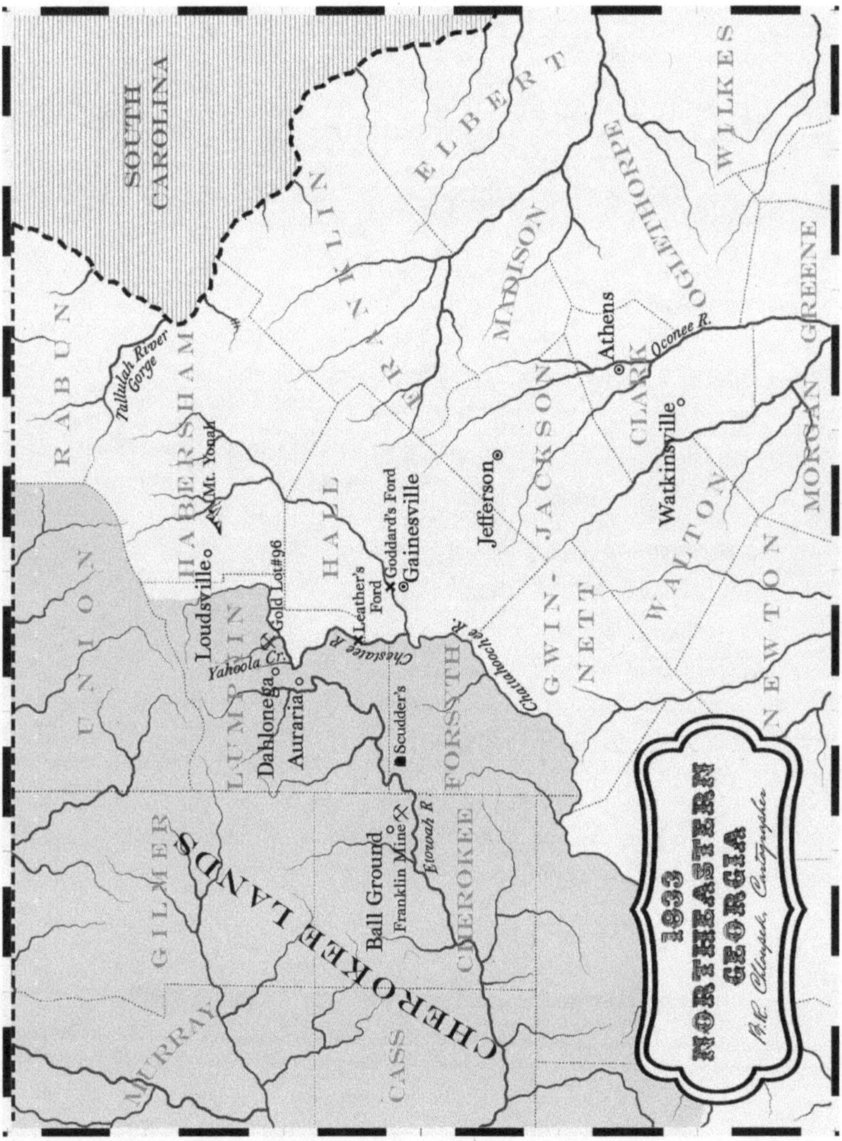

Northeast Georgia, 1833.

Map by Brett Chloupek

Prologue

THIS IS WHAT it means to be the ward of Wiley Wood.

You creep in and out of bed every night and every morning, perfecting the art of soundless movement. Your goal is to avoid waking him, avoid baiting the bear. Your uncle sleeps on a feather mattress in the main room while you sleep on a straw mattress in the loft above him. Your aunt comes and goes half the night, drifting, floating.

There's one room in this dogtrot cabin for sleeping and another, across the covered passageway, for cooking and eating, and Wiley's not about to let you spend the night on a pallet in the kitchen, much as you have asked him, much as you have tried. Sleeping's for sleeping and cooking's for cooking, and the two halves of this hewn-log house survive by way of their separation; he won't have it otherwise. He's a humble man, your uncle, but he's worked hard all his life; he deserves a little order and respect. Everything you see—this farm, those hogs, that big bay colt you call Birdie—he has earned by the toil and labor of his own two hands. At night, before sleep, he'll untie his eye patch and lay it on the bedside table, where it looks up and watches all three of you. He'll eat a hunk of the cinnamon bread your aunt has baked him, devouring it with a boy's eagerness before brushing the crumbs from his nightshirt onto the floor, the same rough planks you'll sweep for him in the morning.

Your uncle likes to tell stories about his maiming days, how he lost that eye only after taking a hundred from his opponents—gouging being the sport of the day for a young man growing up in north Georgia, the brutal credo of the frontiersman. He'll position his thumb and index finger to show you how he used to do it, how he would angle that thumb and push it into his adversary's eye socket, curling his other fingers around a lock of his enemy's hair, cinching him tight so the poor fellow couldn't escape.

—Back in those days, he'll say, holding forth as Aunt Elma in her calico and apron exchanges a look with you across the table. —We fought with nothing but strength and cunning. And a good pair of spurs on the boots, if we was lucky enough to have some.

He'll wiggle his fingers for this part of his tale, brag about how he used to keep his thumbnails an inch long or more, filed to points and hardened with tallow. One time, your uncle Wiley and his brother were driving hogs from Jacksonborough for sale and slaughter when they stopped to quench their thirst at a "torn-down place," as the locals call it, and wound up in a brawl with a dozen riled-up settlers. Not a chair or table was left unsplintered in that tavern by night's end. Your uncle and his brother successfully took on so many combatants, or so he claims, that in the morning, the proprietor's children circled the dining room with saucers in hand, collecting all the torn ear bits and gouged-out eyes they could find amid the shattered cutlery.

Most of the time, you look the other way, feign uninterest or busyness when your uncle shares these tales. Or you'll swap another glance with Aunt Elma, who will shrug her shoulders at you, keep to whatever chore she's pursuing. *What can we do,* her shoulders will say.

For her part, Elma Wood is unwell, silent by day, restive by night, some mornings incapable of cracking an egg into a pan without getting bits of the shell in too. Harvesttimes, she spends her days at Armstrong's Mill, which is no mill at all but the bruising endeavor of grating bushels of corn ear by ear against a tin grater. She's old-fashioned that way, or obstinate, take your pick; your aunt won't haul her corn to the local water mill like other women. One year she lost the tip of her pinkie from grating so hard, impossible to find among all those kernels; she had to throw that batch to the hogs and start over. In winter, she'll stand for hours, days, grinding the grated corn in a mortar, beating it down with her pestle until it's meal-fine, ready for baking or boiling. Then, spent, in the moonlit hours, she'll slip outside the cabin wearing just her nightdress and a coat over it.

Your aunt will stand out there, alone, in the passageway between the two halves of the dogtrot, the same dogtrot her husband swears he built by hand even though Elma distinctly remembers neighbors hauling logs and chinking cracks with clay for him, even though what Clarke County militia captain Wiley Wood says never matches what happened in his wife's recollection. Under the moon, she'll walk into the waiting field, making her way through her pumpkin patch, the shriveled cornstalks. There she'll spend an hour or more keeping company with the dirt, contemplating the night sky, removed from whatever might be underway back inside.

You admire your aunt, and you also despise her—for that ability to separate herself out, for her remotion, for her refusal to return indoors. Elma has swapped out the moon for Wiley; her vigilance has gone lunar, not spousal. She'll spend those nights convinced that the slightest nodding off on her part, the slightest lessening of female attention, will cause the moon to forget itself and plunge downward, fall straight to bedlam.

Barker McRae is twelve years old when she goes to live with Wiley and Elma Wood on their subsistence farm outside Watkinsville, Georgia, eight miles south of the college town called Athens, one mile from the Eagle Tavern that her uncle adores, and by the time she turns thirteen she understands death is not the worst thing that can happen to a person. This is not some grand statement on her part. The realization comes in some ways as a blessing.

She doesn't complain about her lot, doesn't have time to complain, lacks the energy for it. Every ounce of fight must be reserved for thinking. Because by her mind only will she find a way out.

By the time she turns fourteen, Barker understands that her father did not know who he was leaving her with the day he said goodbye, that he focused only on Elma Wood when he dropped Barker off at the farm with nothing more than a suitcase and a Bible that he expected her to read while he was gone. He didn't pay sufficient heed to his daughter's new surroundings. He didn't take note of the uncle. And what he found in Barker's aunt reminded him just enough of her sister, his own dear wife, Sarah, dead just that summer, to justify the handoff—a tendency toward introspection, callused hands and gentle shoulders, a penchant for quiet.

Lorenzo McRae blames himself for his wife's death; he has come to regard Sarah McRae's passing as a punishment. He fell too deeply in love with her—that was his sin: his selfishness. He caused God to sit up and take notice. He dared place earthly loves before heavenly; he made the mistake of enjoying the curve of his wife's lips too much, her graceful throat, her low, sweet voice when she said his name, the pet name that only Sarah was allowed to use for him: Laurie.

Lorenzo missed delivering a sermon once, in Macon, of all places, because he was making love to his wife at the travelers' rest where they were staying. The innkeeper had given them two rooms without charging them for the second. *For the preacher,* he had said.

Two rooms! Two rooms made a mansion. Barker was sent off to read in solitude and marvel at the miracle awaiting her, an entire night without either of her parents telling her what to do. Laurie and Sarah went off to their four-poster retreat next door, a high oaken bed with blue-and-white quilts piled on top. There they would steal an hour together, try to remember who they were when they weren't being a preacher and a preacher's wife, riders on an evangelistic circuit that never ended.

When he realized his oversight, his failure to show up at the chapel for the service he was supposed to administer, Lorenzo wasn't sorry. He laughed. Yes, he laughed with delight that day—fool!—when he realized his mistake. Never before had time scrambled away from him so beautifully. He pulled the quilt over Sarah's tumbled brown curls and joined her under its canopy, burrowing in. Under that quilt, Lorenzo confessed to his wife that he was trying to repent of his forgetfulness but could not find it in himself to be sufficiently abject. After all, if God was omniscient, as He surely must be, then He was aware of Sarah's admirable qualities, and He would have to forgive Lorenzo his momentary carelessness.

—*Laurie,* Sarah said to him, and kissed his eyebrows. —He'll forgive you as Laurie. Not as Preacher Lorenzo.

But within a month of that afternoon in the four-poster bed, Sarah was gone, dead of a malignant fever. Some black-cloaked women came, Methodist wives whose names Lorenzo and Barker didn't know. They laid the body out, clothed Sarah in her finest meeting dress, the dark green one with the white collar. They prepared her for the coffin, draped woolen blankets over her, not shrouded sheets, for wool does not rot the same way sheets do. Lorenzo was stricken, incapacitated by grief, unable to do anything but muscle out a brief word of thanks to these women before he departed, fleeing the room.

A week after the burial, Lorenzo—no longer Laurie; the pet name died when Sarah did—dropped his only child off at her aunt and uncle's farm, deposited her with kin he had never met before that morning. Alone, he could return to the road, conduct his circuit rider's penance, go back to God breathing down his neck every mile of every day again.

When Barker asked if she could go with him, he said not this time.

—But we always go with you, she said.

—What we did before isn't what we do now, Lorenzo said. —Following Christ requires adaptation.

His child traveling with him worked only when Sarah was alive, when Barker's mother rode beside him in the wagon. Lorenzo didn't know what to do with a motherless daughter, especially not one nearing womanhood herself. No, Barker must be off, and he must proceed in his separate mission; he must do his heavy breather's bidding, go back to being the preacher the Methodists had dismissed for being "irregular" and "uncertain." They complained about his penchant for dancing and cursing, his pacing when he preached, that long red hair he let hang down his shoulders, his radical teachings. Was it possible to be too much a Christian, too intensely in love with Gospel freedoms? It appeared it was. The Methodists didn't know what to do with him.

And the day he dropped Barker off, Lorenzo trusted his daughter would be safe, well kept by Elma Wood's hardworking hands until he had completed the duties to which God had called him. When Elma asked how long he would be away, posing that question with a curiously strained expression, Lorenzo replied with confidence: —Three months. I'll be back in three months.

Privately, he had his doubts about the timing. After all, if God has walked away from a man, how will that man know when God is no longer angry with him? How will he discern the divine disposition if he cannot see God's face?

But the point is, Lorenzo never saw the uncle coming.

Within days Barker had learned to be vigilant. Within weeks she had become a sentinel of Wiley's comings and goings. She taught herself to read her uncle's moods, guess his thoughts, interrupt his frowns, his rumblings.

Are you hungry, Uncle Wiley? I'll fetch a bowl of stew.

Are you tired? Take your boots off—here, I'll do it for you.

Are you thirsty? Have another. Have three more; have a hundred. Have so much you never wake again, why don't you.

Barker doesn't say that last part to him, of course. She tries not to say anything to him, but keeping quiet is not her strong suit.

In the beginning, when Wiley's nighttime visits to the loft started, she veered off into terror, but over time she has trained herself to pull back from that ledge. Fear is no good; it will exhaust a person; fear will not get you free of him. Fighting's useless too; he's strong as a boar and just as ornery. Crying won't help either, not unless Barker's dead mother can be resurrected by sheer force of tears, not unless Sarah McRae can sit upright in her riverside grave and blow her child free, push her offspring into motion, sail her to safety on a sea of hog shit.

Some days, Barker feels her mother's spirit beside her, silently observing all. Other days, she's relieved to find no hint of Sarah McRae anywhere. She does not want her mother to know what has happened to her.

Barker believes in heaven, sort of; God, very much so. She has to believe in Him; otherwise, her father abandoned her for nothing.

He's out there, her father; she's dead sure of it. He used to write to her, though not for a long time now. He's in Hightower, or Ball Ground, or Harnageville, or northeast in the foothills, in the Blue Ridge Mountains. He's witnessing to the miners at Pigeon Roost, or Underwood, or Ligon's Mill; he's with the Cherokee at New Echota, advocating for them, writing petitions alongside their leaders. He's covering mile after mile, preaching as he travels. He finds the unchurched under every rock he turns over; he's panning for heathens. He is everywhere and nowhere; his cause is everything and nothing; he's the finest circuit rider Georgia has ever seen, which means Barker never sees him. And he's very busy, even now, even in his disappearance, so busy she doesn't want to interrupt him.

One time, a bedridden widow Lorenzo visited gave him a gift, the nicest suit Barker and her mother could imagine—fine woolen pants, a satin waistcoat, a warm cloth coat, brimmed hat, new boots. Lorenzo returned everything but the boots, which he accepted because, he said, they would help him cover more ground in his circuit riding. All else went back to the widow to wait for a man unholy enough to accept them.

In her dreams, Barker has mixed her father and God up together; she has shaken and poured them out into a single jar. She has reimagined God as a frontier preacher with a beaver cap, a calfskin vest, and a beaded necklace given to him by the Indians. This itinerant God carries a Bible and warns of coming judgment, and he yields no profit from his preaching. When settlers offer him payment or gifts, like that widow did, he declines; he tells them to give their coins to the slave, to the Cherokee or the Creek, to the orphan. He's a hunter not of pelts but of souls; he has no tolerance for those who harm the vulnerable. And in her heart, Barker believes that if her father had been present the first time her uncle put his hand on her, he would have stopped Wiley Wood straightaway; he would have administered swift justice directly.

In the absence of that incarnation, the beast must be taken out another way.

And now, right now, right this moment—day's end, Maundy Thursday, the day before the day before the day before Resurrection, and not an hour after the lottery messenger has left:

There's blood on the sheets. Blood everywhere and worse, your uncle screaming and retching. Something has happened; several things have happened. Everything swirls and pitches, a disaster on the rough plank floors.

Wipe your hands on the feather mattress. Clean yourself, clean your legs, calves, ankles. Scrub at the spots on your dress.

—Git back here, he rages. And again, seething, boiling: —You bitch!

You can't find your boots; you can't see where he tossed them. Take his instead. Wiley and his dainty feet, his womanish feet, that's what they are, though you never dared say that to him. You never said a lot of things.

Stay here, stay in this moment. Right now is all you have. Think forward, not backward. Don't look back, just move.

His voice fills the room. —Git back here, Barker McRae; git back here so I can kill you!

Coat in hand, stolen boots on your feet. Turn, pause, your hand on the door. The lottery papers! Don't forget them. Those forty acres lit the match; they ignited the argument—then you blew on the flame.

Snatch the papers off the table; tuck them under your arm. You'll think about what to do with them later; you'll figure out everything later. Right now, your task is one thing.

—Goodbye, Uncle, you say, or maybe you just think it. Then you're gone, out the cross-beamed door, into the late gray day, into the blur of sleet and slurry.

Fly is what you'll do. Fly hard, fly fast. Find Birdie and take him with you. Fly north; it's the direction your father once used. Your whole life both behind you and in front of you.

Fly *unconscionably.*

Part One

April 1833

Watkinsville to Goddard's Ford

1

IT BEGINS WITH the messenger: Matthew Higgenbotham. He has five lucky drawers to notify, four once he's done with the farm in front of him. His stops lie scattered across several counties, a week's ride if he doesn't dawdle.

Yes, he can be done in a week if he hurries; he can ride back to Milledgeville, collect his final payment, quit this messengering, and be done with Georgia permanently. If nothing goes wrong, if nothing comes up to delay him. And things tend to go wrong for Matthew Higgenbotham.

He pulls the lottery papers from his satchel and rifles through them, licks his finger to turn the pages, checks that the documents are in order. *The above plat is a representation of the tract of land situated in the 15th District in the plan of said district by the number 96, surveyed on the 11th day of August, 1832.*

The recipient's name follows—*Barker McRae, ORP* (short for *orphan*)—and then comes the name of her guardian, *Wiley Wood, captain, Militia District 221.*

Yes, it's all there: *Forty acres hereby awarded*, et cetera. All the grants say that much, all the gold lot rights, anyway, the plat on the form drawn by surveyors to the scale of ten chains to an inch. They've reduced Cherokee country to a series of ink sketches.

Higgenbotham knows it's Maundy Thursday, but he doesn't care. He's too old for church. He's too old for this job. He has a face he used to recognize but no longer cares to try, a face to make a man avoid mirrors. Wrinkles galore, sorrowful blue eyes, and lately the skin on his neck has lost all decorum, has taken to jiggling and quivering to a beat of its own.

He shivers inside his coat, shifts his sit bones atop his swaybacked mare. The late-afternoon sky promises sleet over Clarke County by nightfall. *Welcome to Watkinsville,* he thinks. Another town with too many trees sawed down, another stop on the map a man would just as soon forget about, even if this one's the county seat.

He pulls out his watch: four o'clock. Not enough time left to fit in another lottery notice after this one. Not enough time left for much of anything. Higgenbotham turned sixty-four this year, and his mare Mandy, lowering her grizzled head to crop at dead grass outside the dogtrot, is about the only thing not too old for him on this journey. She shouldn't be out in this weather either; she has trouble with her balance. On the road, she trips over ruts, stones, memories. When she lifts her head to regard the barn behind the settlers' cabin, Higgenbotham rests a palm on the mare's neck, feels her lagging pulse beneath his gloved hand.

—Soon, he tells her. —We're nearly done. We'll be on to the inn at Athens shortly.

He's been on the road half a year this time. Back at the state capital, the commissioners have been meeting at the courthouse to oversee the disbursal of the lands of the Cherokee Nation. They're giving away Cherokee country farm by farm, stream by stream, apple tree by apple tree. One commissioner will crank a wooden drum filled with tickets holding the names of lottery entrants, while another turns a second drum filled with tickets specifying the lots up for the taking. After they pair a recipient with a lot number, it's Higgenbotham's job to ride out and inform the fortunate drawer. The last he heard, 133,000 Georgians had registered for 35,000 gold lots. Four-to-one odds aren't great, but they aren't terrible either. A lot better odds than the ones being given to the Cherokee.

The door to the dogtrot swings open. It's a board door, strengthened by crossbars on the inside, wartime footing in a county that's seen no Indian skirmishes in some time.

—Wiley Wood? Higgenbotham says.

A bearded man steps through the door and faces the messenger. He wears a patch over his left eye and an alert, suspicious expression in the other.

—What's your business? State it quick.

Higgenbotham notes the rifle leaning against the wall of the covered passageway. —Captain Wood, he says. —I bring you good news from Milledgeville. A member of your household was selected in the lottery. You're to receive forty acres in the Cherokee goldlands.

The man stops short, pauses in the overhang between the cabin's two sides. He shakes his head like his ear has water in it. —Forty acres?

—Yes, Higgenbotham says.

—The lottery, you said?

—Yes, Captain Wood, Higgenbotham says again. He's used to repeating himself on these visits. —The lottery for the distribution of the lands belonging to the Cherokee Nation. Also known as *an act to lay out the gold region in lands at present in the occupancy of the Cherokee Indians, into small lots, and dispose of the same by separate lottery.*

Higgenbotham clears his throat. He always relays the news this way, jabs the cold facts, the full titles, into the conversation. Someone has to remind these lottery drawers of the mess they're stepping into. Giving away land that belongs to someone else is a special talent of Georgia's. That and flooding everyone in rivers of ink and paperwork.

—Well, damnation and two cups of coffee, Wiley says. —Damnation and I'll be damned and glory be. Forgot I entered that.

He steps off the front stoop and breaks into a jig, right there in front of the messenger. He's meaty and potbellied with slightly bowed legs, and as he flings his arms up to the sky and dances, Mandy the mare makes a queer sound in her throat. Higgenbotham pats her on the shoulder. Sawdust flies off Wiley's coat and trousers as he leaps and thumps about, traces of sap and bark coming off him, remnants of the sawmill and the old Georgia forests.

—Gold, he sings out, his breath coming in plumes, rising to follow smoke from the cabin chimney. —Gold! By God, I'm saved!

Higgenbotham glances around. This farm is possibly one acre, a patch of unyielding earth, a few forlorn pine trees behind the barn, a single rotting hog pen. A man could grow corn and squash here and not much else in summer, and in winter, he'd have to cut the dried cornstalks and dead squash vines and burn them for warmth to keep his wife's teeth from chattering. Assuming he had a wife, that is.

—The grant's in the orphan's name, Higgenbotham says. —I'll need to speak with her. Is Barker McRae your ward? The papers say you're her guardian.

Wiley Wood stops dancing. A sudden sour slump in the shoulders. A complication; he wants his name on the rights, his and no one else's.

—Captain Wood?

—Hold on, then, the mill worker growls, and shuffles off toward the barn and pen. Higgenbotham waits.

After a few seconds, he hears the squeal of irritated hogs, and Wiley returns gripping the arm of a bony, half-grown girl who clutches a feed pail to her chest. He has the girl by the elbow, and he leans toward her as they walk, whispering into her ear. She tries to pull her arm away, but he clamps harder, keeps talking to her. Her nose is running, and she wipes it on her sleeve as they approach. When Wiley releases her, she makes her way toward Higgenbotham, still swiping at that nose. She comes to a stop before him and peers up at him doubtfully.

First things first: Higgenbotham produces a handkerchief, offers it to her. She shakes her head, won't take it.

—Barker McRae. Is that your name? he asks.

A savage shrug, followed by a glance over her shoulder at Captain Wood. —I'm the one on your lottery ticket, mister.

—*And you're my ward,* Wiley calls out behind her. —Say it.

The girl scowls. —And he says to tell you I'm his ward.

Higgenbotham suppresses a smile.

She's gangly and thin, her pale pinched face framed by a plain bonnet. She wears a homespun dress the color of butternut and a pinned apron. She has no coat to speak of. The hem of her dress barely covers her shins. Warmth is a luxury reserved for those who don't have pigs to feed. Higgenbotham glances back at her guardian.

—G'on now, Wiley says, coming up behind her; his hand clamps again on his niece's shoulder. —Introduce yourself proper. Did you say *sir?* I told you to call him *sir.*

—It's all right, Higgenbotham says. —I don't require airs.

—Hello, *sir,* Wiley says, ignoring him. —Say it.

The child's eyes find Higgenbotham's. The strings of her bonnet have fallen into her slop pail, whatever swill she's feeding the animals.

—Is your name Barker McRae, miss? Higgenbotham asks again.

She nods fiercely, once.

Identity confirmed; time to give his customary spiel. The list of lottery abbreviations Higgenbotham has had to memorize for this job would be amusing if it weren't so vexing. *FA* for father living but absent. *H of F* for head of family. *I* for idiot. *ORP* for orphan. *OSIW* for orphan of a soldier of the Indian wars. *S* for soldier in the War of 1812. *W* for widow. And so on.

—I bring you good tidings from Milledgeville, Higgenbotham says, and proceeds to read from his papers. —*B. McRae, orphan, guardian Wiley Wood.* He looks up. —You've won the rights to forty acres in newly established Lumpkin County's first section, fifteenth district. Near the confluence of two creeks.

Barker sets down her pail with a clank. —Let me see that.

Higgenbotham hands the papers to her. She scans the first page, whispering under her breath, frowning. She can read, apparently, he'll grant her that. Fast, too, from the look of it.

—This plot's deep in the hemlock forests along those creeks, he says, offering an explanation. —It's a gold lot. There could be prospectors on it. Some men have panned out ten thousand dollars' worth in one day in Lumpkin County. Though I suspect those claims include a bit of braggery.

The girl's eyes lift to his. Her mouth has parted slightly.

—How old are you, Miss McRae?

—Sixteen, she breathes.

—Fourteen, Wiley interjects, stepping forward. —She's fourteen and no older. I'm her uncle. She's been bound out to me since the day I agreed to feed and house her. She's my ward.

—Am not, Barker says, looking at Higgenbotham again, her gaze hard as she hands the papers back to him, her eyes so forcefully green that for a moment, he doesn't know what to think. —I am not that man's charge, mister.

Higgenbotham has no idea how old this girl actually is or whose ward she might or might not be. As long as she's under eighteen and missing a parent, one or both, she's an orphan in the eyes of Georgia. Most likely, her uncle added her name to his own application to give himself an extra chance at winning. People did that sort of thing all the time—added dependents or invented widowhoods or made themselves out to be veterans of one war or another to increase their number of lottery draws permitted. Sometimes friends and neighbors will rat the fibbers out, hoping to receive acreage rights themselves, a reward for informants. Occasionally, Higgenbotham will weigh in on the fray, attempt to sort truth from fiction. Other times, though, times like today, it's late and he's tired and his nightly whiskey is calling him.

—She ain't sixteen, Wiley says again. —She's fourteen and in my care. She was left here after her ma died of a broken heart and her pa abandoned her. I'm her guardian; I tell you, that land's mine.

—Fever, Barker says right back, looking at Higgenbotham when she speaks. —My ma died of fever. And my pa's coming back for me. If that claim's in my name, it's rightly mine.

She picks up the slop pail. An eggy stench rises from it. Behind her, over the barn and the dogtrot, the sky is darkening. Wiley sidles over to Higgenbotham and tips his head, indicating the need to talk privately. He walks the messenger a few paces away from the girl.

—Her pa ain't returning, he whispers confidently, man to man. —He left to preach to the Injuns. He went to martyr hisself, Crazy Lorenzo did. I'm her pa now.

—Are not, Barker calls out; she has followed them and ducks around her uncle's side to peer up at Higgenbotham again. —He ain't my pa, and he knows it.

—Git inside, her uncle barks, shooing her backward so she nearly stumbles. —Go on, now, girl, that's enough. Stop bothering our visitor.

—I ain't bothering him, Barker says. —Am I bothering you, mister?

Again that gaze locks onto his.

Truth is, Higgenbotham doesn't much care who winds up with these forty acres. It's all stolen land no matter which way you slice it. Those lots aren't all they're made out to be either—level farmland it isn't. Chances are the site will prove impassable, overrun by rhododendron and laurel so dense a man has to crawl through them, with grinding slopes and plunging hillsides a horse could topple from if it slips or spies a copperhead.

Chances are as well that this grant will soon pass into the hands of a speculator. Any time the commissioners draw a gold lot out of the drum, the mining companies send their runners out behind Higgenbotham, company men to chase down the lucky drawer and buy or swindle the rights off him. By this time next week, Barker McRae and Wiley Wood likely won't have any acres left to argue over.

—Go back inside, Wiley says to his niece again. —I ain't telling you twice. Go help your aunt with supper.

—You *did* just tell me twice, Barker says, and Higgenbotham suppresses another smile.

No, the fact is, at the end of the day what happens to *B. McRae* and her militiaman uncle isn't his concern. Higgenbotham has other things to worry about, like a nerve up his backside that spasms after long rides and a move back home to Vermont that he's been dreaming about for years but still hasn't managed to pull off. He was hired for this messengering role by a state commissioner who told him it paid well and he would enjoy being on the road again, an elected official who said they needed honest public servants in the saddle. If this land was going to be wrestled away from the Indians, at least Higgenbotham could help make sure the process wasn't a bloodbath; at least he could see that the few protections the Cherokee still possessed would be upheld. So he took the job.

At heart, Matthew Higgenbotham's a realist; he knows there's little any man can do to make life fair or even bearable for the vast majority of suffering people. But pragmatism isn't a recipe for a clear conscience; it isn't a recipe for sleeping through the night.

That's why God invented whiskey.

—Captain Wood, he says after Barker has stalked off and disappeared inside the cabin. —How do you wish to proceed?

The mill worker adjusts his eye patch, tightening the leather strip that knots behind his head. —She hain't been right since she came here, he says. —Her head ain't on straight. She throws tempers.

—She seems sensible enough to me, Higgenbotham says.

But sorting out this land's rightful owner isn't his responsibility. Best to save that business for the lawyers. His only task today is to recite the necessary laws, procedures, and codes and to collect the grant fee.

He tells Wiley that if any Cherokee have built improvements on the land, he'll need to wait for the government to sort out that claim. —Do you understand? he says. —They still have rights.

—Do they? Wiley snorts.

The fee comes next. Wiley smacks his forehead when he hears the amount. —Ten dollars!

—It's an expense, Higgenbotham says, nodding. —And if you all keep the lot, you'll owe property taxes on it as well.

Wiley scowls. —I already paid to register. Ain't paying taxes to nobody.

—Then sell the rights, if you'd rather, Higgenbotham says. —You'll clear a thousand, five thousand dollars off it. All I need is the grant fee on your ward's behalf.

The mill worker shakes his head. —I can't git you ten dollars. I can git you five dollars only.

Higgenbotham tugs the brim of his felted hat; sleet has started pricking his face and neck. North of this man's farm, the inn at Athens is waiting. The inn and the company of Thrasher, tavern keeper, man of few words and generous pours. He glances over at Mandy, whose coat is dusted with ice crystals. He offers her an apple from his bag, but she won't take it. She wants dry hay and a livery stable; apples are bribes and she knows better.

Five dollars will have to suffice. Higgenbotham hands the papers over to him.

—Pay the rest by post, he says, and takes the banknotes Wiley hands him.

In the saddle, he checks the straps on his bags, bends to adjust his stirrups. It's an hour's ride to Athens if they maintain a smart pace. Straightening, he glimpses an angular formation of geese against the sky, their wings beating in unison. This part of the country, it's hard to tell if they're late flying south or early flying north. Being on the move is what matters.

—Safe travels, messenger, says Captain Wood, now placated, now friendly as can be. He pats Higgenbotham's mare on the rump. Her coat twitches. —Thank you for my good news. I needed some good news today.

Higgenbotham adjusts the reins. He always says the same thing to these lottery winners as he's departing, a line he tries to constrain but that comes bursting out of him anyway.

—Be careful what you yearn for, he says as he guides the mare toward the wide dirt road. —You just might get it.

The sky has dissolved into freezing rain. It's going to be a late spring; winter has kept all its teeth. Mandy picks her way forward.

When they pass the cabin, Higgenbotham sees the McRae girl reappear in the window. She peers out at him, her face sharp and wan, her bonnet removed. Her hair, he sees, is flame red.

An oddity, that's what she is. An oddity or trouble coming. He tips his hat to her and rides on.

2

THERE'S MILLIONS IN it, they said five years ago when the madness started. There's gold in the mountains, gold in the creeks, gold in the bear caves and river bottoms, gold in the mud beneath our feet. Veins of it everywhere, deposits of the highest purity. Find a spade or a shovel; carve a trough for rocking. That and a pinch of luck are all you need.

The rush has been on since 1828, but it's only in the past year that they added the goldlands lottery, only in the past couple of years that Higgenbotham has seen politicians taking over the business. They held elections across the state for ninety-six district surveyors. Gold districts in the north, suitable for mining, were divided into lots of forty acres each. Land districts to the south, better for farming, were parceled at a hundred and sixty acres each. The elected surveyors rode into Cherokee country armed with chain carriers, packmen, cooks, horses, rattling wagons. Doggedly they measured and inspected, climbing trees, marking stones, notching fences, dragging their chains and poles like an unwanted conscience behind them.

Indians? What Indians? the politicians said when the Cherokee protested the latest invasion. *We have a charter. See?* Georgia's charter dates to 1732, granted to Oglethorpe by King George II, whom the colonists thanked for his pains by overthrowing his successor. *Don't tell us how long the previous inhabitants preceded us; we don't want to hear it. We're Georgians—we have paperwork. Did you know our great state once extended all the way to the Pacific Ocean? Now get this lottery started or we'll be overtaken by foreign marauders, devils we didn't know existed until the world showed up at our door.*

Though that last part might also be what the Cherokee are saying.

Higgenbotham takes a swig from his flask and recaps it. Sleet has slickened the road, whitening grooves carved by earlier stagecoaches. Ahead, in the dusk, sprawls the west fork of the Oconee, whip-fast and never clear, not his favorite river.

—Watch your step, he says to Mandy.

Brown current rushes by as the mare gingerly crosses. The water reaches just above her knees but no higher. She heaves herself up the far bank, and they continue, following the postal road, which is in terrible shape, but that's the way things are around here; good roads in Georgia are rare. Higgenbotham should know—he used to run mail for the US Post Office Department. He rides now past cotton factories along the river's edge, most shuttered for the night, though he glimpses spinners and weavers departing through a side door, their bodies bent against the weather. They use paid and unpaid labor out here in Clarke County, free and enslaved side by side; they'll take what they can get—industry's exploding. Yarn spinning, cloth weaving, cotton-ginning, cotton pressing, saw- and gristmilling, more. *Any way that makes us money, any way that frees us from the tyrants in Washington City*—that's the Georgia credo.

Higgenbotham pulls his coat tighter. He spent the past three decades as a letter carrier and the past six months as a lottery messenger, his final act before hanging up his boots or his death, whichever comes first, and he's witnessed more strangeness in his present role than in all his years of mail riding put together. Gold will do that to a region. He's seen Cherokee and Creek farmers side by side with Savannah gentlemen and English and Scottish migrants, miners of all races, creeds, languages, panning and shoveling together. He's watched Georgia Guardsmen tear through farm and field, arresting whom they chose, berating whom they would, one day kicking the whites out of Indian country, the next day—or seven—harassing the Indians for panning in their own creeks. He's seen county militiamen, hardscrabble bastards like Barker McRae's uncle, wielding ancient bayonets as they gallop toward whatever rogue mission they're pursuing, some of their weapons so old they likely saw action before the Revolution. He's witnessed Pony Club men, armed bandits on the postal roads, stealing horses and cattle, driving Indians from their homes, running their loot to Kentucky and points north, raucous thieving bands of whites from all counties. Nothing unifies like quick money and the prospect of a fine fast colt.

And that's just for starters.

Mandy trots past a row of newly built homes. They're entering Athens at the south end. Garden plots lie quiet, rimed with frost and frozen rain. This town used to be just a bare-bones trading settlement on the banks of the Oconee. Then the charter for the state's first university came. But at least it's not complete mayhem down here yet, at least it's not the world descending. Up north, everyone who has a pot to piss in is using that pot for gold panning.

Down a side street, a dog barks a question, is answered by another. Needles of sleet dampen Higgenbotham's cheeks and bearded chin. Mandy treads carefully, her coat frosted with ice pellets.

—Go on, now, he says to her. —Hay's a-waitin'.

Higgenbotham lets himself use southern idiom only in private, only when he can be certain no one hears him. He has lived in Georgia so long, most people have forgotten he isn't from here. Once upon a time, he was young and hopeful and from New England. Once upon a time, he had a lovely wife, but tragedy struck them. The road's been home to him, one way or another, ever since. He's been alone, one way or another, ever since also.

Past a town courthouse enveloped in twilight, Mandy stops and sniffs the air, ears flicking backward. Higgenbotham read somewhere that construction costs for that courthouse reached three thousand dollars. The lottery papers he just turned over to Captain Wood could bring in two or three times that much. Land rights are at a premium; the frontier's disappearing. Mandy sniffs the air again as Higgenbotham coaxes her on.

—What is it, girl? he says. —We're nearly home. As much home as Thrasher's can be, anyway.

No other riders or wagons are on the road. The shops of Athens are silent, closed for the night. The jail is closed also. Overhead, the clouds have given themselves over to flurries, the snow and sleet now interchangeable.

—Don't tire on us yet, Higgenbotham says, patting the mare's shoulder; Mandy sighs and pulls forward. —Our bones do ache.

Then he hears it: In the distance, hoofbeats, hammering north, headed in this direction.

Higgenbotham twists around in his saddle. Whenever something or someone shows up on the road behind him after sundown, his first thought is always horse thieves. Has he remembered his knife? He reaches down and probes inside his boot, finds the leather sheath. He doesn't carry a pistol, odd as that might seem. Thirty years as a postal carrier taught him that guns invite more trouble than they resolve. Nice and calm and unobtrusive is the wiser choice for a messenger. Nice and calm and a sharp blade if necessary, if a mischief maker comes too close.

Mandy pulls at the bit—*now* she wants to run. Higgenbotham scans the road. The encroaching dark outlines a distant figure. It's not horse thieves. It's that girl, Barker, from the one-acre farm, riding a big bay colt, a rawboned beast, galloping in this direction. She's driving him hard. He's muscular, sixteen hands if an inch, a ripping strong runner from the looks of him. Barker's bonnet has slid back on her shoulders, her expression hardened with concentration. She urges that colt through the swirling condensate, directing him up the road toward the messenger. Yes, she has Matthew Higgenbotham in her sights; she's headed his way and no other.

Higgenbotham takes a long breath. It's time for Tennessee whiskey; it's not time for an unwanted companion. Never does he miss his evening whiskey. One time, a mudslide wiped out a road he was traveling on near Winn's Ferry, and he had his drink even then, reclining against the trunk of a sturdy oak as turkeys being driven to market stopped to roost near him. He spent that night listening to hundreds of the birds gobbling in the overstory, their drover passed out beneath them, the turkeys roosting so high that as Higgenbotham's whiskey disappeared and his thoughts softened, he could almost mistake them for stars talking.

She's thirty yards away, twenty, ten. The approaching colt snorts, tossing his rust-colored mane. Mandy makes a small, strangulated noise in her throat, the sound of fear or possibly flirtation. Higgenbotham reaches forward to pat the mare's neck, but in the same instant, the colt sidles up beside them, bares his long teeth, and snaps at Higgenbotham's hand.

—Christ, he says, jerking back. —Restrain your horse, miss. What are you doing out here?

The girl's out of breath, and she's bleeding, or blood is on her—that might be the more accurate phrase. Diamonds of sleet are in her hair and on her coat. At least she's wearing a coat; she wasn't earlier. She's wearing men's boots, too, Higgenbotham notices, her uncle's, most likely. Which raises a question: What boots is Captain Wiley Wood presently wearing?

Mandy makes the same embarrassing sound again. The colt whinnies a reply. Higgenbotham starts to repeat his question to the girl, but a welt along Barker's neck stops him short, a laceration and nearby bruises blooming. Dried blood rims her ear. She didn't have those injuries at four o'clock this afternoon.

—Child, he says. —Are you all right?

—I cut him—she starts, hesitates. —I cut him, and it's bad, and he's comin' for me.

The bay colt dances sideways.

—Cut whom? Higgenbotham asks. —Your uncle? What happened to you?

She swivels around, craning her neck to take in the street behind them. Higgenbotham follows her gaze, searching for he knows not what, the air thick with twilit winter, a thousand hisses of frozen precipitation. What he sees up the lane is enough to make his questions stop.

Three horsemen ride side by side, their coats flapping in the wind, pace steady. Straight up the Athens lane they're advancing, half a mile away or less, headed straight toward the girl and Higgenbotham. Three heavily armed members of the Clarke County militia.

Barker wheels her mount around. The colt stamps his feet, pulling, nearly breaks her grip; he's desperate to get away. Higgenbotham blows out a breath. If this big bay colt is scared, that means something. Higgenbotham trusts animals; he does not trust most people. Barker looks up at him again.

—Mister, help us, she says.

He's going to regret this moment. He can see that much already. He's going to rue the day he set foot on Wiley Wood's farm and delivered his good news to that bowlegged militia captain. But this girl—he can't just ride away. Blood oozes from her ear. She's not touching it, not wincing, not tending the bruises around her neck either. Injuries like that and a child doesn't complain, doesn't say anything? It isn't a good sign.

—Come on, then, Higgenbotham says after a pause, roughly. —Follow me. Hurry. And don't let that colt bite me again.

Instantly Barker obeys, tugging at her reins, leading her horse to follow. Higgenbotham directs Mandy across the street, toward a narrow alley he spotted earlier. It's a flimsy hideaway, tucked off the lane between a confectionery and a lawyer's office, barely wide enough for the horses, but it's all they've got. At its end, the alley opens onto an empty lot behind the stores, hidden from the street and exposed to sky.

The horses advance through the alley toward that opening, Mandy in front, the bay colt following. The brick sides of the two shops are so close that Higgenbotham could touch their opposing walls at the same time if he stretched his arms wide, if he had a more impressive wingspan. He doesn't want to stretch his arms wide. His body was not meant for a cross shape. The colt whinnies again.

—Quiet, he whispers. Mandy trembles beneath him, a tremor beneath her coat. He touches the mare's side, and she stills as they pass through the alley and reach the lot behind it. Overhead, sky is visible, flurries falling on them.

—Now we wait, Higgenbotham says quietly. —Now we wait for them to pass by us.

Barker swipes at her nose and stifles a sneeze. When she squeezes out a second one, Higgenbotham finds his handkerchief in the recesses of his coat and thrusts it at her. This time she takes it.

—What's your name? she whispers at him in the darkness, her nose and mouth hidden in the handkerchief as she blows.

—Higgenbotham, he says.

But he doesn't want her to start relying on him, doesn't want this child to start thinking he's the solution to her problem, so he adds, as severely as a whisper allows: I'm just the messenger.

Barker's not frightened. She's agitated but not frightened. She has moved past fear; she's swimming in a different river.

To soothe herself, she begins to hum. Something simple, something from her father's old Watts hymnbook. *O God, our help in ages past / Our hope for years to come—*

If she shifts in her saddle, she can see through the alley into the road, where one of her uncle's riders sits tall and straight-shouldered, the street behind him snowy and glistening. He's young and wears a shabby coat, too shabby for the proud posture he holds. A yellow bandanna circling his neck appears to be the only clean thing on him. He carries a rifle slung over his shoulder, an old muzzle-loading flintlock, the same kind Barker's uncle owns. If this fellow is one of Wiley Wood's militiamen, he's not one of her uncle's favored few; he's not one Barker has seen around the farm.

She hums on, keeping the sound small, as tiny as a worm burrowing in loam. Around these parts, people trust their county militia more than any federal soldiers. Unless you cross one of those county men, in which case watch out, in which case the tables turn.

—He needs a doctor, one of the horsemen, one she can't see, calls out. —We oughta fetch one.

—His wife'll do it, comes a reply. —Not sure a doctor'll get there in time, though.

In the darkness behind the alley, Higgenbotham glances sharply at Barker.

She shrugs helplessly, lowers her volume but keeps humming. Higgenbotham lifts a finger to his lips. She ignores him. A thin little worm she is, a noise that cannot stop itself. She can hear the swish of a riding crop in the street, the squeal of the men's horses, the shush of sleet and snow falling. She glimpses all three riders now, from afar, moving shadows through the snow.

Just last week, some of Uncle Wiley's regiment men visited him at his farm, five or six of them lounging out on the covered passageway in their hats and coats, smoking their pipes, swapping stories. Wiley told them about how he'd kicked one of his sows when she couldn't give sufficient milk for her piglets. He beat that sow with his boot until the blood flowed, and then he told the animal that was the way things would continue if she couldn't produce what she owed. The regiment men found this tale highly amusing—to talk to a sow as if she could understand obligation, labor, the misery of back payments owed!

The youngest horseman here, the one with the yellow kerchief, was not among them as far as Barker recalls. But the other two might have been.

She hums on, but no relief, no happier tale is coming.

With his niece, of course, Wiley tries to be gentler; he repents of any stray bruise he might have inflicted once she apologizes for goading him into doing it. If he's drinking, his behavior is harsher, but he'll sit outside on his rocking chair and squeeze out a guilty tear or two later. Elma will glide in and out of the cooking area while Wiley sits out in the covered passageway and feels sorry for himself. Barker's aunt will whip up treat after treat, prepare his favorites to keep him calm, keep him easy. Honey and preserves on fresh-baked bread will prevent him from metamorphosing.

—Persimmon pudding tonight! Elma will say, too brightly.

Or blueberry pie, preceded by potatoes, possibly roast turkey. Anything to feed Wiley's bottomless need.

And while Elma peers into pots, stirring and scraping, Wiley will summon his niece back to his sitting spot in the passageway. He'll plant a ginny kiss along the hollow of Barker's neck and whisper that he's sorry if he hurt her. *If* being the operative word.

He'll mean it too—his apology, insofar as it reaches. It won't happen again, he'll vow. He's a good man, just dog-weary; no one understands how tired, how exhausted to the bone he is. Every night he returns home from ten hours at the sawmill to a farm that consumes more than it produces and a wife who no longer looks at him. Does Barker understand? Of course she understands, he'll murmur, answering his own question. After all, she's alone too—she's orphaned; being alone is tiring. And to be orphaned by abandonment is the worst kind of separation.

May he brush your hair? He would like to brush your hair; would you let him do that for you?

He calls you his little treasure.

Our shelter from the stormy blast / And our eternal home—

Out on the road, one of the men drops his weapon, and it discharges. Birdie writhes and heaves, jerking at the bit; Barker reaches out with both hands to calm him. She hears a muffled curse, the sound of a rider dismounting. The young horseman is telling another one, the careless one, that he's drunk, that he's useless. —Go back the way you come from, the one she thinks of as Yellow Kerchief tells him.

But as he crouches to retrieve his rifle, the careless horseman catches sight of the alley. He looks directly into it, surveying the darkness, assessing the gap between the confectionery and the law office. He's ten feet from the alley entrance.

—Someone in there? he calls out, weaving slightly.

The other two horsemen aren't paying attention. Barker grips Birdie's reins more tightly. The drunk one grumbles aloud, voices some petulancy; his companions aren't interested in his discovery. He totters over to scrutinize the window of the confectionery. Behind the glass looms a cake with yellow icing, giant-size, two hundred pounds, to be cut and sold for ten cents per slice. He shuffles back over to his companions, mutters a complaint, how expensive everything is these days, how highfalutin people are becoming. He climbs back onto his mount. If someone or something is lurking down that alley, he isn't being paid enough to chase after it. Spurring his horse, he trots off, headed south, abandoning the chase.

After a few seconds, the two remaining men wheel their horses around and take off in a different direction.

Higgenbotham makes Barker wait a full quarter hour before they leave their hiding place. There's an inn a few streets over, he tells her, run by a friend of his who'll put them up for the night. In the meantime, they need to ride like ghosts; ride without a sound. Better to be overcareful than underground.

—Give these Georgia boys time to sort themselves out, Higgenbotham adds. —They need plenty of time and air and space.

Barker knows that already. She knows it better than he does.

At the inn, Higgenbotham heads to the kitchen while an innkeeper with a long silver pigtail takes Barker upstairs to an attic nook so small, he can't stand upright in it. It's the best place she's slept in two years. The man gives her a mug of cider and a hunk of soda bread, points her to a water basin and a cloth for washing. Later, he climbs back up the ladder and hands her a blanket and two pillows. She thanks him; never in her life has she possessed two pillows in one evening. She almost gives one of them back to him but resists the impulse.

Alone, beneath an attic window that leaks cold air, Barker watches snow fall against the pane, erasing her view of the night sky. She's still wearing the dress she put on at the start of the morning, the homespun gown she wore for hog feeding and the messenger's visit and everything that came after. Snatches of Higgenbotham and the innkeeper's conversation make their way up the stairs in the bluish dark.

The two men are catching up, warming themselves by the dining-room hearth; old friends for years, from the sound of things. From above, she hears the faint clink of a glass, the day's miseries noted. *They don't know the day's miseries,* she thinks. They don't know the half of it.

She hears muffled laughter, a door opening. She fights to keep awake, but tiredness has taken over. As she drifts off to sleep, the laughter stops.

3

HIGGENBOTHAM IS ONE and a half glasses into a bottle of Tennessee's finest when two of the same horsemen he and Barker dodged earlier stride into Thrasher's establishment. Behind the bar, Thrasher turns, tossing a cleaning cloth over his shoulder. The innkeeper is past fifty, half Cherokee, wears his long hair tied back with a strip of leather. Higgenbotham is seated by the fireplace. No one else is in the dining room.

—Evenin', one of the horsemen says, approaching the innkeeper. He's young, black-haired, maybe twenty, and wears a yellow neckerchief. —How's about a drink for your poor old nephew, Uncle, how's about it.

The youth doesn't remove his hat and doesn't move to sit. The older man with him is pale and heavy, a bit of a wheezer; both soldiers shiver in their damp uniforms, if they can be called uniforms, if they aren't just rags on a mission.

Thrasher studies the pair. Then he addresses the younger horseman. —What'd you do this time, Johnny?

—Nothin', the young man replies. —I didn't do nothin'.

—That so.

—It is. We're out here on the order of our captain. Girl stole his lottery ticket and his bay colt. Same colt that's in your stables out back right now, Uncle.

—That so, Thrasher says again, and starts polishing shot glasses with his cloth, watching the two horsemen in a brass mirror as he works.

Higgenbotham can see the resemblance between uncle and nephew, the same testy expression, same glossy hair, though Thrasher's is mostly silver and the nephew's is cropped short. Johnny's also leaner and lithe, with the over-built arms of a lumberman. Higgenbotham has seen those tree men sawing down the forest's giants, leaping out of the way when a hundred-footer falls, leaving so many jagged stumps in their wake, like battlefield amputations.

—It's the truth, the older militiaman says. —We're looking for the ward of Captain Wood of the Clarke County company. He sent us to retrieve her and what she stole. We'd appreciate your help, innkeep.

Johnny the nephew nods vigorously. —She's dangerous. If you're harboring her, Uncle, you'll want to hand her over.

—A girl, dangerous? Thrasher snorts. —*Pfft.* I'd like to see it.

—She's an attempted murderess, the older horseman says. —A horse thief *and* a murderess.

—Who'd she try to kill?

—Her uncle, the militiamen reply in unison, and the innkeeper's eyebrows momentarily lift.

From his hearth-side chair, Higgenbotham feigns absorption in the fire. Barker's upstairs in the attic, hopefully asleep. He has told Thrasher what little he knows, how the girl came flying up the road after his visit to Wood's farm, and these riders galloping after her. Thrasher has the final say here, what he will or won't divulge.

The innkeeper sets down a cleaned shot glass and plants his hands on his counter, facing his nephew and the other militiaman. He comes from Scottish and Cherokee stock, emphasis on the Cherokee. —Now, what'd a man go and do to make a little girl try to kill him? he asks. —That's what I'd like to hear.

Thrasher thinks most settlers in this part of Georgia are uncouth and ill-mannered, not up to Indian standards. But he's happy to turn a profit off them if they'll let him. He once told Higgenbotham that people in these parts didn't care what was in his bloodline so long as his prices were fair and his drinks plentiful. He said he charged the preachers twice his usual rate. —Whatever for? Higgenbotham asked. —Because they'll pay it, Thrasher replied with a smile. —Because they shouldn't be drinking anyway.

—I don't appreciate the way you're speaking to us, innkeep, the older horseman says now. —I don't rightly care for it. We're telling you that bay colt was stolen. You're holding thefted property. And the girl, you got her too, ain't you?

—Well, that's a conundrum, Thrasher says. The militiaman frowns, trying to work out *conundrum*. —If I tell you there's no horse thieves or attempted murderesses being given shelter in my establishment, that ought to be the end of it. But y'all aren't the type to take a man's word if you've decided to the contrary. He pauses. —How do I know y'all aren't stealing horses yourselves?

—If we were horse thieves, we wouldn't've come in here asking about the colt, Johnny says, scoffing. —We would've just taken him.

—Not if you were smart horse thieves, Thrasher replies. —Though I must say, Nephew, you are many things these days, and smart is not among them.

The dining room falls silent. Thrasher reaches down to a shelf below the bar, produces a hatchet, rests it on the counter. The head is cast iron and well seasoned, the handle adorned with cardinal feathers. Johnny glances at his traveling companion. Thrasher fought under Andrew Jackson in the Creek wars and can cleave a man's skull at twenty paces. Higgenbotham, warier than he had hoped to be this late in the evening, prepares to rise from his chair.

—You'd not be tricking us, Uncle, would you, now? Johnny says, taking a step back. —You've not seen a girl, redheaded, yay high?

—Underfed girl, the heavier horseman adds. —Mean little thing.

Thrasher studies the cardinal feathers on his hatchet, smoothing the barbs as he speaks. —I've not seen anyone matching that description. You, Matthew?

He angles his head toward Higgenbotham. Johnny and his companion shift their attention to the man near the hearth.

—Haven't seen a child of that description, Higgenbotham manages to say, staying seated.

Thrasher nods. —Now, I've been guilty of numerous sins in my time, but lying to two good men's not on the list. Bar's closed. See yourselves out.

The pair retreats, the older horseman breathing asthmatically, Thrasher's nephew scowling. From the fireplace comes the mellow scent of pinesap and rosemary. The older horseman knocks into a chair on his way out and fumbles to set it right. As the men reach the door, Thrasher calls out: —Oh, and, Johnny, write your mother. She's worried about you.

—All right, Johnny mumbles, head ducked, not looking at his uncle.

Once the men are gone, Thrasher secures the door latch, then checks to make sure it's fast. Turning, he regards Higgenbotham in the firelight.

—They'll be back. And it won't just be my sister's boy next time. It'll be a dozen of them. You need to get her out of here by first light.

The innkeeper walks back to the bar and retrieves a bottle of rum from a shelf. —What in God's name did she do to set a company of militia after her?

He laughs when Higgenbotham tells him that, come morning, he plans to leave Barker McRae behind. —I have four more fortunate drawers to notify, Higgenbotham says. —I have a job to finish.

—Yes, you do, Thrasher replies. —Don't abandon someone who showed up on your doorstep, Matthew.

—She didn't show up on my doorstep. Higgenbotham stabs at the fire's embers with a poker. —I showed up on hers.

The innkeeper shakes his head. —She needs to get out of this county. Out of Georgia'd be better, if her uncle's sending a regiment after her. My nephew's a fool to have joined. He pauses to lift his glass, contemplates the amber contents. —Either way, she can't stay here; it's not safe.

—I'm aware of that, Higgenbotham says.

—So, what, then?

Higgenbotham thinks about the surrounding territory, tries to summon options. The goldlands are no place for children. Near Auraria, the heart of the prospecting region, he's seen squatters setting up shacks in hemlock forests so dark, you could slit a man's throat without him ever knowing his enemy was coming upon him. He's watched Spanish ruffians and New York professors equally out of their minds with drink crouched in the current alongside peddlers and harness makers, all yearning for the same thing: a spark of gold, a flash of their futures in the water. He's seen men trade punches by day and unroll their bed mats next to each other by night, some lying in each other's arms, freely as can be. He's ridden through Knucklesville, Scuffletown, Loudsville, settlements named for the countless brawls taking place in them; he's watched white men firing for sport on Indian dogs trying to swim for home across the Etowah River.

—A home for girls? he suggests; it's all that's coming to him. —Gainesville might have a place. I can take her that far, at least. That far's no hindrance.

Gainesville's the last stop before the goldlands, a town on the edge but still within the bounds of polite society.

—No hindrance for you, Thrasher says. —But what about for the girl? Does she have any kin to take her?

—Her father's a circuit rider. Name of Lorenzo McRae. He disappeared a couple of years ago. Her mother's deceased.

Thrasher leans forward, a thought striking him. —Red-headed preacher? Tall fellow, thin as a stick?

—I have no idea what color his hair is, Higgenbotham says, fighting irritation. —I never heard of him until today. I suppose it's possible, given the child's coloring.

—Then I've seen him, the innkeeper declares, straightening, lifting his glass in an impromptu toast. —I've seen that preacher. He's alive. He's west of the Chestatee, preaching to the Indians and the gold miners.

—You jest, Higgenbotham says.

—I do not. He's out there. They call him Crazy Lorenzo. You could find him.

Thrasher tells Higgenbotham what he knows. On a recent trip for supplies, the innkeeper was traveling near the Etowah River when he spotted a preacher in a long-tailed suitcoat balancing on a raft in the shallows. Crowds had gathered to hear this man deliver a sermon and to gawk at the strange sight, a waterborne missionary shouting out the Gospel to hearers back on dry land, pacing on a floating platform, the raft secured by rope to a nearby tree so it wouldn't float him and his words downriver.

—It was a sight one didn't soon forget, Thrasher says.

This preacher looked as if he hadn't had a decent meal in weeks. He had long red hair and no beard to speak of. He paced and swore up there; he sang and wept also, if Thrasher's memory serves him correctly. He spoke in plain language any ordinary man would understand. At one point, to accentuate his message, he leaped into the river. He then wrestled himself back onto the raft, wet as an otter, wrung out his coat sleeves, squeezed the river from his hair, and kept talking.

—What was his subject? Higgenbotham asks, curious despite himself. Generally, he is no admirer of religion. His late mother, God rest her Presbyterian soul, was devout enough for both of them.

—He said greed was the unpardonable sin, Thrasher says. —He said men who spend their lives chasing personal gain would fail to enter the kingdom of heaven.

—Hard to find fault with that one.

—He cursed the lawyers, the bankers, the mining companies, Thrasher adds, then pauses to sip his drink. —He cursed your lottery commissioners too. Said the gold mines would be in all respects the ruin of this state and nation.

Higgenbotham nods. Another point he would concur with.

—He didn't let up till he had the crowd on its feet. People shouting and whooping, whites and blacks and Indians all in a tumble. I saw a couple women rolling along the riverbank, some sort of holy seizing. Quite a sight, all those petticoats, and all that female shrieking. Thrasher takes another swallow of rum. —That preacher's your girl's father.

—Maybe, Higgenbotham says. —There are a lot of circuit riders out there.

—Not a lot named Lorenzo.

—Maybe, Higgenbotham says again and falls quiet.

Thrasher sets down his glass and stands, reaches for the lantern. It's near midnight. —Well, this one also preached against the Cherokee removal. So he can do no wrong in my book.

—Then you take her to him, Higgenbotham says, and rises to follow. —You like that preacher so much, *you* find him. You can serve him a drink, charge him twice what you charge the rest of us.

Thrasher, chuckling, leads the way to the stairs.

—What that child needs, the innkeeper says as they climb, is someone who can find her pa quiet and quick-like, someone who can deliver her to him without incident. Someone who can pass through gold country unnoticed. He tosses a haughty look over his shoulder. —*I'm* not unnoticeable.

—And I am? Higgenbotham asks.

Thrasher shrugs. —She needs kindness, he says. —She needs someone who knows the roads. And both those traits, my friend, you possess in sufficient quantity.

Higgenbotham leaves his bed early the next morning, before sunrise. He repacks his bag and heads outside, relieves himself in an outhouse.

In the livery behind the inn, he saddles up Mandy, placing the bridle over the mare's head and adjusting the bit; she's not pleased to be back in her traces. He checks on Barker's colt, who *is* pleased, who is raring to go, finds sleep the dullest thing to be endured. The colt's big brown eyes follow Higgenbotham around the stall as he pours oats for both horses. Afterward, Higgenbotham heads back to the inn to rouse Barker.

He finds her curled under a woven blanket, one pillow under her head and another flung to the floor in sleep. For several seconds, he stands there, deliberating, contemplating walking away, inwardly wrestling. Part of him wants nothing more than to leave this child behind, to steal out of here and remain on his own. Thrasher's a decent sort, and good-hearted. The innkeeper will figure some solution out for this girl if he has to, if she has no one else to help her.

But those bruises on her neck—Higgenbotham looks at them again. They're worse now than they were last night, a glaring and angry purple. He doesn't want to check her ear; he doesn't want to know. He assumes Wiley Wood is the cause. Briefly, he hopes she struck her uncle back. He hopes she went after him so hard and fast, she made him squeal like those hogs he raises.

It's not a charitable thought. But it's likely warranted.

He sighs. Leaning over, he gently taps Barker's shoulder.

—It's time. Wake up, miss. Time to be underway.

She snaps into alertness, blinking away sleep. She squints up at him, disoriented, momentarily uncomprehending.

—No, she says. —No, don't take me back there.

—I need you to pack up. We'll talk on the road.

When her expression of alarm deepens, Higgenbotham tries again. —We're not headed south. We're headed north. Toward gold country. Toward what remains of the Cherokee Nation, if you want to be accurate about it.

Barker sits up. She has tried to clean herself, he can tell, noting the water basin beside her cot, the dried blood from her ear mostly washed off, her skirts neater also. He picks up her coat and hands it to her, bumping his head against an attic beam in the process. This nook is so small, he's stooped like a vulture waiting for a meal that hasn't come.

—Your father was seen not long ago, he says. —Preaching along the river Etowah. Chances are, he's still in the territory. If he's not, someone there will likely know of him.

She's wide awake now, fixed on him, her face grave, suddenly older than her fourteen years.

—I can take you so far as the Chestatee River, Higgenbotham says. He speaks slowly, declaring what he can and cannot do, articulating the limits of his charity. —I can get you partway there. But finding your father's going to take more time than I have. I'm a busy man; I'm on a schedule of lottery notifications. You'll be on your own after the Chestatee.

Barker continues looking at him, a determined sizing up, an assessment so stern it crosses over into judgment. Her expression reminds him of his late mother. She reaches for her uncle's boots, shoves her feet into them, and stands.

—Hurry up, then, she says, if you're so busy. Time's wasting, mister.

4

THEIR FIRST THREE days on the road together are a disaster. It snows almost the entire time, softly at first, with flakes as fine as gentlewomen's lace drifting from a silver sky. Snow dusts the fields and meadows and washes the scarecrows white; it mounds along the waysides. When the road freezes, frostbitten mud pushes up from the ruts, forming frozen gargoyles. By midmorning on the first day, Mandy has slipped twice on ice. She recovers her footing but refuses to go any faster than a walk afterward. They cover three miles in an hour. They might as well be traveling backward.

For a while Higgenbotham tries to walk beside the mare, but a nerve in his right gluteal has flared up again, troubling him, forcing a limp; he's little better off than Mandy. He checks and rechecks her leg, her knee; remounts; rides; dismounts again after she slows still more. The weight of a full-grown man on a lame old mare—the unfairness of him! He cajoles, exhorts, apologizes. When Barker asks if they're almost there yet, he tells her they won't be anywhere for a while, longer if she keeps asking him.

She says something under her breath to Birdie, and the big bay trots off. Clumps of frozen earth spray up behind him; a chip of iced mud stings Higgenbotham in the cheek. When the colt spots a great blue heron flying low over a stream, Birdie swerves, rearing, unseating his rider. Barker lands on her hindquarters in the snow.

Higgenbotham guides Mandy over, checks to see if the child's hurt. She's breathing fast but stands quickly, brushing off her sleeves and skirt. She tightens her bonnet, fastens the ties in a double bow, the same kind of knot that Higgenbotham saw on the leather strap at the back of her uncle's head the day before. Captain Wood must have been having his niece tie that eye patch on for him in the mornings.

—Are you hurt? he asks Barker.

—No, sir, she says, still breathing heavily. —I'm all right.

—Are you, now, he says, appraising her. —Looks to me like you need to rest a minute.

—No, sir, she says again. —We got to get going. We're on the run, remember?

—*You're* on the run, he reminds her. —I'm merely accompanying you.

—If I'm on the run, you are too, she says. —You're in it now as much as I am.

She hauls herself back onto the colt before Higgenbotham can think of a suitable reply. She rides ahead, Birdie tossing his mane, none the worse for wear; the colt has energy enough for all of them.

To find routes off the main road, Higgenbotham consults his compass and his old postal map, faithful standbys of his former profession. He needs side trails, old hunting paths that can bring them to the Chestatee River without their being spotted. They'll travel through Gainesville on the way; he'll inquire about Lorenzo McRae there. Gainesville's close enough to gold country that people might have seen or heard of a traveling preacher matching his description in mining territory.

Higgenbotham reaches for his good flask, the non-water one, manages to restrict himself to two miserly sips. He is resigned, pensive, mildly hungover. The needle on his compass has developed a tremor—either that or the hand holding it has. He does not love this goodwill mission, this delay of his final lottery notifications, this chore pressed upon him by duty and Thrasher's admonition.

—When did you last have a letter from your father? he asks her.

Barker bites her lip before she answers. —A couple months ago.

—Are you sure? he says.

She looks away, out at fields covered in drifts of swept white. Her plaited hair has partly escaped her bonnet. It's as deep ginger a hue as he's seen.

—Maybe a little longer, she says.

When they stop at noon that first day, snow falls in clumps from the trees onto the horses' backs. Higgenbotham rummages in his bag, produces two apples and a hunk of yellow cheese. Flecks of ice glint in his beard as he pares the apples and cuts them into sections. He has enough goodwill to escort Barker McRae into gold country but not enough to carry out that task cheerfully.

—Your uncle, he says as he offers Barker a slice. —He's a regiment captain?

—Yes, sir, she says, taking the apple piece and biting into it.

—And his friends? They're militia too?

She shrugs. —Ain't everybody?

Higgenbotham feels his stomach tightening.

It snows so much that first day, the sight rivals anything Barker has seen since the time she traveled with her parents through the mountains between Tennessee and North Carolina, back when her mother was still living. She remembers that trip, how she woke early one morning and left the tent to find her mother standing alone, a blanket draped over her shoulders, watching scarlet dawn rise over layers of snow-covered mountains.

As she took in the sight of Sarah McRae's small form against a first light of endless mountain ridges and valleys, something came over Barker—some new sense or awakening, an awareness both wondrous and frightening. Time was in the mix, too, time and the sound of a voice whispering.

She didn't tell her mother about the voice, but she did seek out her father later that morning. Lorenzo was still asleep, cocooned in his tent; twelve hours of preaching the day before would do that to him. Barker remembers tapping him on the arm, and his eyes opening, alert and attentive. She told him that the Holy Spirit appeared to be pressing Himself upon her, that the Holy Spirit was trying to deliver a message to her.

Lorenzo sat up from his bedroll, his hair tousled from sleep. He reached for his spectacles, which he wore when no crowds were around to notice his nearsightedness. He asked her what the Holy Spirit's message might be.

Chewing on the end of her braid, as she was wont to do back then, Barker replied: —I don't know, but He's sure trying to tell me something.

Her father didn't laugh at her. He didn't tell her to stop her silliness, to leave his tent and let him sleep. Normally, Lorenzo would send Barker away if she interrupted his resting, his thinking, or his praying, three activities that occupied the lion's share of his non-preaching time. Once, he told her that she spoke poorly—he said she conversed with surprising ineptitude for such a bright girl, for the daughter of a preacher who loved the spoken word. Granted, he was in a bad mood that day, so he might not have meant it fully. But Barker never forgot what he said.

On this occasion, he said no such critical thing. He took Barker's hands in his and gripped them firmly. He looked into her eyes, regarding her with warmth and concern—and something else, she noticed, some new element. Something like expectation.

—Then we will pray together, he said. —Just like this. And together, we'll ask the Lord's direction and leading for you.

He took her seriously that day. He didn't tell her she thought cleverly but spoke poorly. He believed his child had something worth saying.

And it's been almost two years now since he's written to her.

Late that first day, a troop of horses thunders up the road behind them, the worse for wear but still fast, the identity of the riders impossible to make out from a distance. Higgenbotham dismounts hurriedly so he can lead Mandy and Birdie into the woods. Light snow falls around them.

—Off the road, he urges Birdie, tugging at his reins, careful to avoid potential nipping. —Off now. Hurry!

From their hiding place, Higgenbotham and Barker watch the militiamen, their clothing ragged and worn, not a matched uniform among them. Several have tied the soles of their boots with twine. Four of the soldiers carry muskets and the remainder anything that could pass for a weapon—

an umbrella, a bayonet, a wagoner's whip; one holds a plank of wood. The rider in front is lean and youthful and wears a yellow neckerchief. He sits steady and straight on his palomino pony, too poised for his surrounding company. Higgenbotham directs a grim gaze toward Barker.

—Those are the same ones that came after you, he says in a hushed tone. —Only now there's not three but ten of them.

Barker doesn't reply, but she also doesn't take her eyes off the riders.

—Did you kill him? he whispers at her. —Did you kill your uncle Wiley?

—I never killed nobody, she whispers back hotly.

Higgenbotham surveys the regiment men again. There are twelve, not ten; he miscounted. —Are you sure about that? he says.

She turns to stare at him. His late mother shows up again in her sharp little face, unsparing in its righteous ferocity. —Well, he weren't dead when I left him, she says. —But he'll not travel again, or not without help, anyway.

—If twelve men aren't help, I don't know what is, Higgenbotham tosses back. —And others could be with him.

The horses and riders trudge by, the animals' heads bowed against the weather. Barker hunches low in her saddle, watching them from their hiding place, framed by a patch of unruly holly. Higgenbotham starts to say more, to ask questions, but thinks better of it, reaches for his flask instead. It's nearly empty; replenishment will be needed.

Although the soldiers pass by without incident, Higgenbotham stays jumpy afterward; he snaps at Barker twice.

He finds an obscure trading path along a low ridge paralleling the main road. They take it, but he loses his way in the snow, forcing them to circle back and retrace their steps. He utters a few choice words before they find the trail again; Barker gives him another look.

—Enough, he says to her. —Enough of that face, will you.

When he was younger, in his prime, a snowfall like this one wouldn't have bothered Higgenbotham one whit, wouldn't have blown him off course. But those days were longer ago than he cares to admit.

Their route ascends through stands of chestnuts and maples. The horses sidestep small holes dug in the snow by some industrious mammal. Higgenbotham spies a fox slinking along the edge of a meadow, its russet fur brilliant against white. He steals a nip from his flask. Another half mile goes by before he takes a second nip, with Barker watching. Then his flask is empty and his mood churning.

Near the town of Jefferson, he tells her that since he has assumed the burden of escorting her to the Chestatee crossing, the least she can do is explain to him the true nature of the risk he's shouldering. Three of her uncle's friends poking around Athens as part of a single night's carousing is one thing; a company of rogue militia in full pursuit of a child across the goldlands is another.

Barker takes in the sight ahead. Jefferson has a brick courthouse and a brick jail and a dubious-looking travelers' rest with paper covering the windows, a way station Higgenbotham won't let them stay at. He says it's the kind of stop Clarke County militiamen might find hospitable.

—I'm not the one that started it, she says.

—Those men don't care who started it, Higgenbotham replies. —What in the world did you do to him?

They spend that night on the floor of a blacksmith's workshop just outside Jefferson. The smith tells Higgenbotham he'll reshoe Birdie and Mandy in the morning; both horses need tending. The smith applies a salve and a wrap to the mare's knee to ease her lameness, and he takes pity on the humans too, offering Higgenbotham and Barker a place to wait out the waning storm.

After a late meal the blacksmith's wife serves, Barker rolls her sleeping pallet onto the workshop floor and lies down on it. She listens to the fire whistling in the smith's furnace as she huddles under a borrowed wool blanket, grateful for the change of clothing the smith's wife brought her. It's a gingham shift, long in the hem and too large up top, but it's clean and dry; it'll do. Barker's stomach is full of ham and buttered bread, onion soup, hot cocoa. As she rests, the heat from the furnace evaporates the damp from her other dress, which she has draped over a stool. It steams dry the saddlebags, too, and her bonnet, and Higgenbotham's felt hat, which he removes only for sleeping. All the damp things around the blacksmith's smoke-filled shop are singing their way into steam.

Barker thinks of her father, his ceaseless preaching, the many years she and her mother traveled through Georgia and Alabama and beyond with him. She thinks about the last time she saw him and about how much God must need him now, how important Lorenzo McRae must be for God to keep a father from his daughter so long.

She deliberately does *not* think of her uncle. But the image of Elma Wood squeezes in, unwanted. Aunt Elma with her ceaseless cooking, her willowy grace, her silence in the presence of Uncle Wiley. Elma and the hogs and the vegetable patch all back there, waiting for her.

Higgenbotham has set up his bedroll near the shop door. He sits now with his back against the wall and smokes his pipe in the flickering dark. After a while, he begins talking to Barker. She doesn't mind. She would rather listen to tales of this old messenger's life than think about what she left behind.

He tells her he used to pass through these regions on horseback long ago, in the years before mail delivery was contracted out to stagecoach lines. He used to carry mail in his two saddlebags for a dozen post offices at a time, which left him room for nothing of his own but a change of clothes and an umbrella. Then he says that the town of Jefferson used to be called Thomocoggan and was beloved by the Indians for its abundant forests, creeks, and springs. Whenever a white man sets out to build a settlement in Georgia, Higgenbotham says, the first thing he does is saw down everything that could provide him with shade come summertime.

He shakes his head disapprovingly.

Barker asks him why he's speaking about white men like he isn't one of them.

—Fair point, Higgenbotham says, and keeps talking.

He finishes what's in his pipe and starts on another, pulling cured tobacco from a small pouch. He tells Barker that he's four lottery visits away from finishing his messenger role and leaving Georgia for good. His old childhood home isn't much, but it's better than nothing. It's all he can think about nowadays, he confesses. It's a saltbox house with a sloped roof and five acres near Rattlesnake Mountain. His mother, a Revolutionary widow, died years ago, but her house has remained, waiting for him.

—I remember the smells, Higgenbotham says as he lights the pipe, taking a long pull. —Of that house. The dried thyme and basil, the garlic she used to hang in nets in the kitchen.

—Where is it? Barker asks, her head lifting, interest renewed. She would like to live in a home that smelled of thyme and basil. —Where's that saltbox house?

—Brattleborough, Higgenbotham replies huskily. —God's country.

—That North Carolina? she asks.

He sighs, corrects her mistake, draws on the pipe again. Barker struggles to keep her eyes open. Fatigue and the warmth of the smith's shop have taken hold.

Higgenbotham tells her that as soon as a man declares, *I'm four lottery visits away from my Vermont departure,* something will come along and doom either him or his yearned-for escape. Pipe smoke drifts upward as he speaks. —A man can choose what waistcoat he puts on in the morning, he says. —He can choose how he speaks to other people. But beyond that, most things lie out of his control.

—Try being a girl, Barker says, rousing herself enough to reply. Something about this statement vexes her. —Try being born to wear skirts. Or, worse, being born to live in chains and servitude. You got more say than you think.

Higgenbotham looks over at her. He's tired; his own loquaciousness has sapped him. Too much drink has been consumed.

—Fair enough, he says. —Fair enough and well stated.

He extinguishes his pipe, taking care to return the unused tobacco to his pouch. He rolls onto his side, wishes her good night.

—Good night, Barker replies.

She lies on her stomach, chin in hands, facing the furnace. Her thoughts fly like sparks from the smith's forge. She should pray for her aunt Elma, but to pray for her, she must first *think* about her, and to think about Elma Wood is to think about Wiley also; she cannot separate them. And she would rather not do that; she would rather not spend a second longer on that foul lout than necessary.

On the second day the snow stops, and from a low ridge Higgenbotham and Barker spy federal troops on the road to Gainesville. It's a substantial company, forty or fifty men, many on foot, milling around the banks of the Middle Oconee, sizing up what used to be a bridge. The water has started to recede from the storm, but it still flows fast, as brown as the cocoa the blacksmith's wife made the previous evening. Part of a wooden fence floats by in the current.

—Wait here, Higgenbotham says, and hands Barker the mare's reins. He walks down to the road and strikes up a conversation with the company commander. Barker hasn't seen federal troops in person before, but she knows about them; she knows they come and go out here. Her uncle often complained about them, said they had no business down in Georgia, said that how Georgia handled its Indian problem was no one's business but its own. The federals were only here to make a show of themselves and then turn tail for home. —They're afraid of us, Wiley used to tell her.

While the two men talk, Barker watches troops wading into the river, US soldiers lifting their knapsacks and rifles as they cross the swollen water. The river reaches their calves, then their knees. One soldier takes a faulty step and tumbles, and the current sweeps him downstream. He rights himself, sputtering, a hundred or more yards from where he started. He makes it up the bank, soaked and shivering, pulls off his boots, pours water out of them. His companions call out to him, checking to see if he's all right. He waves them off, drenched and embarrassed but unhurt.

Higgenbotham, making his way back to Barker, must raise his voice to be heard over the water. —The ferry's operating, he says. —We'll cross there. Half a mile up. Twenty-five cents for ferriage.

—We can cross here. Barker points at the wading soldiers. —Birdie wants to cross. I've been riding him since he was one year old. That water ain't deep.

—For rivers, deadly's measured in speed, Higgenbotham says. —We'll take the ferry.

—I can do it, Barker insists. —That soldier who fell, he weren't watching his footing.

But Higgenbotham's not listening to her; no one is listening to her; no man has ever listened to any woman that she has known.

At the ferry, the operator hauls his raft hand over hand using a rope of twisted hide lashed to trees on the opposite bank of the river. The horses swim behind, relieved not to be swaying with the passengers on the thick planks; they don't trust movement beneath their feet. The ferryman studies Barker with so much interest that Higgenbotham steps into the space between them, blocking the man from looking at her. There are few females in these parts, fewer still redheaded girls on the cusp of womanhood.

—Button your coat, Higgenbotham says to her.

Barker eyes him; she's buttoned to the throat already.

He tells her what else he learned from the federal commander. Those US soldiers came across a group of county militiamen a little while ago, hunting for a white girl.

—Not two hours before, Higgenbotham says. —The militiamen passed the federals on the road. They're out in front of us. The commander said he counted thirteen men and a wagon.

Wiley's men tried to pass themselves off as members of the Georgia Guard, he adds, a more reputable force, but the federals didn't buy that claim. They sent the group on its way without assistance.

—That's all right, then, Barker says. —Right? They've lost our trail.

—It's not all right, Higgenbotham says. Noticing the ferryman listening to their conversation, he lowers his voice. —It's not all right, he repeats with soft ferocity. —They're still on the road; they haven't turned back, and their numbers are growing.

Barker sets her mouth and looks away from him.

They reach the other side of the river just as the sun crawls out from a bank of clouds. The horses, completing their swim, haul themselves onto the slushy bank behind them. The ferryman glances up as he secures the raft, welcoming the sunshine. When he speaks, he reveals himself to be from parts foreign.

—*¡Miren!* he calls out, gesturing at the expanse of water and sunlight. The river dances with a thousand reflected orbs. —*¡Miren esta hermosa tierra!*

Look at this beautiful land!

He steps around Higgenbotham and blows a farewell kiss at Barker.

They spend that night in a stone springhouse over a creek on an abandoned farm a few miles south of Gainesville. Past midnight, a final round of winter returns. Ice strikes the shingles, waking Barker from a dream. She rockets upright from her blanket.

What was the dream? She had left her uncle, but her feet had caught under the floorboards of the dogtrot, trapping her by the ankles. She couldn't escape without sawing off her feet, but if she sawed off her feet, she wouldn't be able to leave him; she would never run again. She was caught both ways.

She rises now and makes her way over to a lightly snoring Higgenbotham. The creek runs directly below this springhouse, and someone has carved a hole in one of the floorboards and hung a ladle on the wall for drinking. The rushing water below leaves the springhouse even colder than the air outside would make it.

Hugging herself against the chill, Barker studies Higgenbotham's face, his prominent forehead, those wrinkles and furrows. She crouches down and pokes him in the shoulder. He grunts. She pokes again, harder, and his mild blue eyes flutter open.

—Can't sleep? she says. —Me neither.

She settles in for a chat beside him. Groaning, he rises up on one elbow, pats around for his pipe and tinderbox. Soon the stone walls glow with pipe light. Earlier, they helped themselves to a jar of blackberry preserves from the springhouse shelves, though Higgenbotham will leave behind a couple of coins in case the owner returns. He carries spare coins and scrip from multiple countries in his pouch—guineas, livres, ducats, doubloons, more. Not because he's traveled the world but because the world has traveled to Georgia.

Barker wraps her arms around her knees. She has not removed her coat. Higgenbotham sits up and takes another draw from his pipe.

—You know what the Bloody Bill is? he asks her after a while.

She shakes her head.

He tells her that the Bloody Bill allows the president of the United States to call out the army and navy to enforce the laws of Congress.

—And that doesn't sit well in this part of the country, he says. —Georgians do not want federals inserting themselves into their private affairs. So the local fellows play at forming their own armies. He coughs. —Men like your uncle Wiley.

—He ain't playing, Barker says.

Higgenbotham lowers his pipe. —A question, he says. —What happened to the lottery papers I gave to him?

A ham roll wrapped in waxed paper is visible in his opened saddlebag, leftovers from the blacksmith's supper. Barker reaches for the roll, unwraps it, and tears off a piece for herself.

—Did you leave those papers with Captain Wood? Higgenbotham asks her.

She takes a bite and chews steadily, meeting his gaze, saying not a word.

—Tell me you left them with your uncle. Tell me you weren't foolish enough to bring them with you.

A hint of a smile escapes her.

—Barker McRae, he says. —You did not.

She tears off another piece of roll and pops it in her mouth, then reaches for one of her uncle's boots. She proceeds to pull out a paper scroll, dented and flattened but intact, the same claim documents Higgenbotham gave Wiley Wood not three days ago.

Lot 96, forty acres hereby awarded to B. McRae, ORP, guardian Wiley Wood.

—Goddamn it, Higgenbotham says, smacking his palm on the floorboards when he glimpses the grant. —Goddamn it all to hell.

—Don't take the Lord's name in vain, she says.

—I'll take whatever name I want to take. Let me see that.

He reaches for the papers, but she snatches them away, rolls them back up, and slides them into the boot, eyeing him defiantly. Outside, freezing rain plinks against the springhouse roof.

—Child, he says. —You take forty acres in the goldlands from a man like your uncle Wood, captain of whatever yokel troop he thinks he's commanding, and you're in for a world of harm, more than you were already.

—It weren't his, she says right back, as straight and unyielding as he is. —It weren't his to take.

She regards him calmly. Her face is austere, so resolute and pale that looking at her gives Higgenbotham a headache. —You yourself said it. I heard you say it to him, she says. —You said the grant was in my name.

He taps out the embers in his pipe, extinguishes them with the bottom of the bowl. He takes down the ladle and forces himself to take a drink from the frigid creek. They'll reach Gainesville in the morning. After that, they'll cross the Chattahoochee. One river after that, Barker will be on her own.

—I wish you'd left those papers with him, he says. —He would've given up chasing you. He would've had his men turn back at the Chattahoochee or at the Chestatee, if nothing else. But not now. Not with forty acres at stake.

Resignation has etched deep lines in Higgenbotham's forehead.

—He will not stop hunting you, he says.

5

HE GETS THEM old, his newspapers; he exchanges them with his friends at the sawmill. One of them knows the Clarke County postmaster, and through that contact they acquire and pass around copies. Reading in the round, they call it. News three months old is still news in Georgia.

Those who can read take the papers home first; those who can't wait their turn. When a nonreader brings the prize home, someone in the household who possesses sufficient letters—a spinster sister, grandfather, eldest son—will read the updates aloud, deliver news on town and world.

You are that reader for Wiley Wood.

His favorite is the *Cherokee Intelligencer*, no friend to those for whom it's named. But he'll take the *Southern Banner* in a pinch—he likes the illustrations and advertisements. Wiley will push the pages flat as you're reading so he can study the drawings. He dreams of carriages, barouches, gigs, sulkies made to order. If he's feeling domestic, he might contemplate perfumery at Shaw's for Elma or a waffle iron for his upcoming birthday.

That latter item he did buy, brought it home from the store with a ribbon tied around the iron plate. He walked into the dogtrot announcing that you would now cook him waffles in the morning. As if making him waffles was a privilege, a dispensation you'd been praying heaven might grant!

Another time, one of Wiley's regiment men showed up with the inaugural issue of the *Western Herald*, printed in the heart of the goldlands. You devoured that newspaper late at night, in private, by tallow candlelight, while Wiley slept the sleep of the underpaid mill worker. Never had you encountered such vivid accounts—madcap chases through stream and hollow, fistfights between whites and Indians, Cherokee children finding gold nuggets the size of duck eggs, runaway slaves fleeing into the region, runaway horses and oxen fleeing out of the same.

From those pages you also learned that all gold is not created equal. Its value changes depending on how pure it is; in this regard, gold is not unlike a woman. How it's refined and appraised also comes into play, what kind of trials it has endured. You read of gold ore sunning itself on Crown Mountain, gold nuggets showing off in Duke's Creek, gold flakes plucked from the mud or lurking in granite, hiding, trying to remain unseen. There is spun gold, wire gold, gold crystals suspended in white quartz, gold dust fine enough a person could snort it. Some streams come so laden with gold that the newspaper says the water runs yellow, though you're not sure you believe that last claim; you would have to see it.

And the speeches! These parts of the newspaper you skim quickly. Do states have the right to resist the decrees of the US government? Yes, say some—those decrees are the stuff of idiots. No, say others. Or maybe. Or yes for Georgia but no for South Carolina, or yes for South Carolina but no for Georgia, or yes in the case of tariffs and Indians but no for other causes. Over and over, page after page, you encounter proclamations, hues and cries, fists shaken. Let the gingerbread-bodied Northerners mind the log in their own eye before they pluck the speck of dust from Georgia's. Let Jackson carry out his promises to us. Let Wilson Lumpkin stand up and be a man for once, time for our governor to be a leader and not an opossum. Give us our land; we've been waiting for it; it's ours if we say so, if we improve it. *Vacuum domicilium!* What good is land that doesn't earn anything? It's ours if we want it badly enough.

You fall asleep dreaming of rivers of gold.

An Indian boy found a piece of gold last week at the Altuna Mines that weighed upwards of thirty pennyweights. Another piece was found about the same time and place by an Indian girl, the object said to be as large as a hen's egg. So anxious was the girl to secure her prize that she ran home with it instantly and would not permit any person to weigh it.

Your uncle Wiley will sit in his porch chair with these newspapers, enthralled by such tales, while you and your aunt prepare the nightly meal. Wiley can read, but only just, only with effort. He'll rehearse the same paragraph multiple times, and when he tries to read aloud, he tends to flip words, so the sentences come out jumbled. Frequently he calls you over to clarify a sentence for him, usually when you're punching down dough for bread or chopping carrots. Or making waffles, once he bought that birthday iron.

Wiping your hands on your apron, you'll stop preparing whatever you're cooking, head out to the covered passageway, and tutor him.

One time you made the mistake of laughing during his tutorial. You weren't meaning to mock him; what your uncle said just struck you as amusing. He had meant to say, *The awful crisis which now stares us in the face*—he was reading another speech about the Indian problem—but instead, he read, *The awful face which now stares us in the crisis.* When you giggled, Wiley's big head jerked up. His one good eye found yours.

—What was that? he said. —What?

Immediately you stopped laughing.

He wouldn't drop it. He insisted that you had made fun of him. But you hadn't, not intentionally. Your heart began pounding. —Never mind, you said.

—Never mind *what*? he demanded. —You disrespecting me again?

A cold wind blew through the covered passageway, a chill you could feel and almost see. Birdie in the barn must have felt it too, because out of the blue, he whinnied loudly.

—I didn't laugh, you said to your uncle hurriedly. —It was a sneeze.

Wiley wasn't buying it. —What kind of sneeze is that? he said. —How do you expect me to believe that?

You backtracked. Twisting your apron, you looked longingly over your shoulder at the kitchen door. *Aunt Elma!* you thought. *Help me!*

Yes, you had laughed a little, you said. But it was only because you were so happy to be out there in that dogtrot reading with him, only because you enjoyed these times with your uncle Wiley so much.

This claim irked him more. Your uncle does have an ear for inconsistent reasoning, you'll grant him that. —First you say it's a sneeze, and then it's a laugh, but not a laugh at my expense, he said. —If not that, what? His voice was a hammer. —What kind of laugh's a laugh like that? Why say it was a sneeze at all?

You said, floundering: —It was a laugh for joy.

—For joy? If for joy, why ain't I seen you smile once today? Why do I have to call you over every time I need something? He was on a tirade now, not to be interrupted. —Why don't you come to me on your own, come sit with your uncle Wiley? Take some initiative, ask if you can do something. Be *helpful,* why don't you?

—I am helpful, you said (you made the mistake of saying). —I'm doing all this cooking.

—*All this* cooking? Then what's my poor wife up to in there? You saying Elma's neglecting her duty?

—No, you said desperately. —I only meant—

A lecture from him followed, a defiant haranguing. You've since forgotten the contents; your memory generally tries to scrub away these moments as quickly as possible.

Whatever he said, it likely went on for a while.

—All right, you ventured when he finally stopped. You would surrender; you would find a way to soothe him. Elma had not appeared. —Maybe I don't smile as much as I should, but I don't mean nothin' by it. I just forget to think about what my face is doing.

Wiley shut his *Western Herald* with a clap. He was ready. —Well, how am I supposed to respond when you give me a sour face every time you pass by? And I the one who feeds and clothes you, I the one who took you in when no one else would have you?

He rocked back in his chair. —I would think you could give me a word of thanks once in a while. I would hope you could set aside your sulks long enough to do that for your old uncle Wiley.

And you said, foolishly, stupidly: —But I do say thank you; I say it all the time.

For you do; you say it so much the little orange tabby that sleeps out in the barn with Birdie has decided it's his name, thinks *Thank You* is his signal to come running. But on this occasion Wiley wasn't having any more objections. Your aunt had left him to slaughter you without interference. Elma had slunk out the back door as the quarrel started, escaped to the storehouse with its shelves of cured ham, dried beans, Wiley's prized stash of Havana cigars wrapped in oilcloth, so dear he never allows himself to smoke any. You weren't surprised by her absence. You hated her for it, but you weren't surprised by it.

Your aunt will never defend you on these occasions, because defending you only angers him more, leads to him threatening to harm one or both of you or promising to pour a kettle of boiling water on the cat, which one drunken time he did try to do, but Elma snatched the poor thing up from the floor, receiving a peripheral scalding herself as Thank You darted, his terrified tail high, out the door.

—You don't mean *Thank you* the times you say it any more than you mean *Sorry* the times you say that, Wiley said next. —I know you, Barker McRae.

The injustice of this claim made your face grow hot. You tried to swallow the unfairness, but it got stuck on the way down. It lodged in your craw. So you waded back in once more.

You reminded him that the times you *do* say you're sorry, he'll tell you not to apologize. Your uncle wants honesty, or so he has claimed; he's an honest chap, simple, true, forthright, if imperfect. That's how he likes to put it.

—Yes, indeed, Wiley replied. —I let my *yes* be *yes* and my *no* be *no*. He nodded with that hoary head of his. —That's all I ask of you too.

—But—

—*Enough*, he said, and you could tell he meant it.

His head is very large. His head reminds you of a bison's, even though you've never seen one in person. The bison are long gone from Georgia. Drawings and imagination are all you've had to go on.

In the morning begins the long hard slog of appeasing him, of righting this capsized vessel. Sunrise after sunrise you've faced this situation. Your aunt will reappear for these endeavors. This side of the argument, this side of her husband, she can handle. Does he want maple syrup with his waffles? Extra sausage? How about apple butter? Elma will make some coffee. —Would you like coffee, Husband?

Wiley will shuffle into the kitchen, half dressed, his shirt untucked. His braces have fallen past his knees; he has been in the privy, doing his morning business. He's clutching his beloved newspaper again, still awaiting your input, your tutelage.

He doesn't see any reason not to; he's forgotten whatever happened yesterday. He's forgotten other things too. Every day he starts afresh; every day he is washed clean by his own aversion to the truth.

The Cherokee question's on his mind again this particular morning. He fancies himself an expert. To the best of your knowledge, your uncle hasn't talked to a real live Indian in ages. They're mostly gone from Watkinsville. Clarke County settlers moved the Indian boundary from fifteen to fifty miles away years before you moved here, elbowing out almost all the Indians except mixed-blood planters and itinerant traders.

Wiley settles in at his table. He reads aloud, slowly, his finger tracing each sentence, his finger sliding ahead of each word like a lookout.

Are we now to be dispossessed of our premises? Are we to be interrupted in the enjoyment of our property?

Are we, with our grants in our pockets, to be thrown out of doors and ordered to depart from our own houses?

No, the slightest touch of this sort will be considered an assault, which under our laws will justify a battery.

—Amen, he will say, his fist thumping the table, rattling the cutlery. These readings take place shortly before he enters your names in the Cherokee land lottery. —The Supreme Court of the United States is assaulting us!

These are not battles you can win. If the federals can't win arguments with a man like Wiley Wood, what makes you think you can? So wave the white flag, make peace, serve him his waffles and his dead fried pig, plaster a smile on for him. When Elma finishes washing pots and ducks out of the kitchen, you throw her retreating form a disgusted look.

She won't meet your eyes. Inert, that's what your aunt is, inert and smart simultaneously, like the rat you once found pinned between split logs in the woodshed, its tail crushed, its body unmoving. As soon as you lifted one of the logs, the rat scampered away, reborn.

Lifting the log off Aunt Elma is going to take a good deal more ingenuity.

So—yes. Give Wiley Wood what he wants; give him bright and pink and cheerful. Don't tell him what's in your heart, where you've begun to grow fangs, the jaws of a viper. In your heart, you've called out your uncle's lies and misstatements; you've shouted out his sins, which are numerous, which are legion. In your heart, you've begun to imagine yourself standing before a vast crowd, pacing on a platform before an audience of a thousand. A valley of faces turns toward you in this fantasy. It's a revival, a religious awakening, and you're the preacher; at long last, you are permitted—no, *expected*—to speak!

None of these things do you say at breakfast to him.

For his part, Wiley Wood has always stopped and started with his words; he's always had trouble finding the right phrasing. Especially when he's tired, which for a mill-working farmer occurs with some regularity.

Elma hasn't helped things. He never expected his wife to take the turn she did. He thought she would go on smiling like a bride at him forever, *ticktock*, *ticktock*, like a clock that never needs winding, never needs repair, not even after the man of the house sweeps it off the mantel in a momentary fury. He never thought she would transform over ten years of marriage into a fretful shadow. He's thirty-nine years old, Captain Wood, and he has yet to learn that actions have consequences.

In the early days, he tried to complain, to make his needs known to her, but over time Elma stopped speaking to him unless she absolutely couldn't avoid it; she stopped looking at him too and quit addressing him by name; she never called him anything other than *Husband*, a term she did not deploy with sufficient cheer. She barely acknowledged his existence, truth be told, except insofar as she cooked for him, foisted plate after plate upon him. Was she fattening him to make him soft, to weaken him somehow? The times he took after her to teach her a lesson, she absented herself even more from him afterward.

Then—miracle of miracles—Barker McRae appeared.

And, yes, he's an inept reader, let alone orator; Wiley struggles with his sentences, despite captaining a county regiment and leading a team at the mill. He knows his limits. His niece is more articulate than he is. She's also fiery.

Barker, at least, will stay in the room to argue with him.

Wiley went to a Methodist camp meeting shortly after Barker arrived at the farm. He went and stood at the edge of the crowd; it was one of those unending, sweltering four-day affairs, a revival a day's ride south of Watkinsville. He went to listen to Lorenzo McRae; he wanted to learn what this preacher who had turned his child over to him was all about. He didn't bring Barker on the trip.

Lorenzo delivered a sermon that day Wiley will never forget, a speech that made the settlers in the audience see double, enraged by every inflammatory word. He preached about equality, about how all men are equal in the eyes of Jesus Christ, and the women also. He didn't hold back. He pressed forward, wheeling and indicting as a preacher will, trumpeting home his point, his shirtsleeves rolled past his forearms, ready to do God's dirty work. *In Christ there is neither Jew nor Greek, male nor female, slave nor free nor Indian.*

Really? Not so in Georgia, Wiley wanted to tell him.

One man in the audience pelted Lorenzo with rotten vegetables. He kept preaching. Another flung a gourd.

Lorenzo laughed. Nothing stopped him. He spoke on and on. Gradually, he won that crowd over. Gradually, he persuaded them that if all human beings are created equal, that meant anyone in that audience could be the son or daughter of a king; that meant anything was possible in the span of a single lifetime, thanks to the Holy Spirit's leading.

When he called for sinners seeking salvation to step forward, many in the audience wept. Fifteen people came up the sawdust trail that day, marched to the altar rail when Lorenzo summoned them.

Wiley surprised himself by nearly trotting up there and joining the converts. The urge to join that altar call was spontaneous, physical, perspiratory. The desire to make a man like that notice you! To make Preacher Lorenzo turn his head and regard you with approval, smile at you and call you the equal of kings!

When he returned home, barely escaping Lorenzo's thrall, Wiley didn't tell Barker what he'd witnessed. When he was away from the crowds, away from the spectacle, his usual disposition reasserted itself. His cynicism and love of hierarchy returned, thank goodness.

Lorenzo McRae's confidence, his persuasive powers, his supposed *righteousness* now aggravated Wiley. He would not seek him out again. But the man could speak like an angel.

On bad days, Wiley can articulate just a phrase or two at a time before he must pause, consider his thought, circle back, and lasso it. He will grow enraged if anyone interrupts him or if someone attempts to supply the missing word. One does not supply missing words to Wiley Wood. For then his struggle will be out there on display, and he will drop not only the original phrase but also his ability to pivot and recover, and he will be doubly lost.

Now he's on the move; now, despite warnings from the doctor, whom Elma did summon, whom she walked a mile into town on Maundy Thursday to find, Wiley has prodded himself into motion, injury notwithstanding. He has borrowed his neighbor's mules and wagon, his neighbor's son for the drive. His wound still seeps through its stitches; nonetheless, he is on a mission.

Find Barker. Find the one who did this to you.

Wiley's regiment men have ridden a day ahead, the loyal few willing to take up his errand. He has promised them robust payment for their services. He must catch up with them soon, assume his place at their head.

The doctor does not like this plan. Less than two days recuperating, he argues, is not enough time to mend.

—You are not to travel, the physician says, peering over thick spectacles at his patient. —Your stitches are new. Infection could set in. You must lie still; you must lie on your back for a month.

Wiley has a good laugh at that one. He chortles until his face contorts and his stitches stretch painfully. —Show me a man who stays on his back that long, he says, and I'll show you the coffin he lays in.

The neighbor's son, a brooding, long-legged youth known as Scissors, is of mixed race, born of the neighbor man and his enslaved house servant. Wiley will borrow Scissors for the week, bring him along as wagon driver.

—I'll have him back in seven days, he pledges to the neighbor. —Ten if the roads cause trouble. He has always been slightly jealous of this man living one farm over. Wiley does not have the money to buy his own house servant. —You won't even know he was gone.

Then there are the wolfdogs. Wiley has a friend at the mill, an alligator hunter from coastal Florida who moved to Georgia on a wagon filled with hides and gator oil after he grew tired of being shot at by Seminole warriors. This friend still hunts, though not gators and though he's started to complain because hardly any bears remain in Georgia. Deer are too easy; he'd rather hunt beavers for their pelts, or bobcats—one glorious day this gator hunter killed a panther. He started breeding wolfdogs for sport and out of boredom, and he offers Wiley three of his latest litter to take with him on the journey.

—For hunting, the gator hunter says. —For finding the one who did this to you.

Wiley is grateful, bordering on obsequious. Watching him bow and scrape, the Florida man momentarily regrets his generosity. An overly grateful man must harbor some weakness, some defect unacknowledged. So he lends Wiley the worst of the litter instead of the best, his three wildest and hungriest one-year-olds, juvenile half-wolves with nothing to lose and little training to speak of.

—Keep an eye on 'em lest they bolt, the gator hunter tells Wiley, then realizes what he has said. He steals a glance at the captain's ruined face and apologizes.

Wiley tells Elma he'll be back in a week, two at the most, well before the corn needs planting. If he's delayed and she must go about it herself, she should watch out for the cutworms. He tells her to keep watch over the hogs and hens and not to shoot any strangers without cause.

Hitched in their traces, the neighbor's mules await instruction. They're walleyed and twitchy as the three wolf-dogs bark and pace in the melting snow around them.

—Saw it off. Hush, Wiley says when he hears them.

He summons Elma over to the wagon to bid him farewell. Seated up on the driver's bench, he grips the seat beneath him. The fluid slowly oozing from his stitches is milky; he has to wipe the wound with a cloth every few minutes. Beside him sits his borrowed driver, the youth's long legs extending past the wagon footrest, his wide-brimmed hat pulled so low, it's a wonder he can see the road. Scissors doesn't look over at Wiley, doesn't acknowledge the other man's existence. Scissors will do what his father instructed him and no more: Drive this man north to find a stray niece who has escaped him.

Elma walks over to the wagon. Wiley feels his wife take his hand in hers, feels her cold lips brush his palm. He would rather she reached up and kissed him on the mouth, performed some bold gesture, anything to demonstrate her care, her need for him. But he will not ask her to kiss him on the mouth; he would never put himself in the position of a supplicant. He will never lower himself to needing a woman more than she needs him.

That might be part of his problem also.

When she speaks, Elma addresses Scissors. —Take the bridge, she says. —Don't try to ford the river, not with him in his condition.

Scissors sniffs. —Didn't plan on fordin'.

—His wound's in a bad way, Elma says. —It needs to be kept clean. Needs to be washed twice a day. He won't do it himself. You'll have to do it.

—Ma'am, Scissors replies noncommittally.

—I'm right here, Wiley says, bristling. —I haven't gone deaf, woman. Speak to me if you got something to say.

—All right, Elma says, then turns and walks back to the dogtrot, vanishing, shutting the door behind her. When he hears her disappearing footsteps, Wiley stiffens.

Scissors lays his crop on the mules, and they pull forward in unison. They aren't fast, but with the wolfdogs scampering around the wagon, they're not slow either. How long until they catch up with Wiley's company? —Two days? Wiley asks Scissors. Hope is in his question.

Round about that is all the youth will give him.

6

HIGGENBOTHAM IS BOILING grounds for his morning coffee when he hears singing. He leaves the campfire and finds Barker behind the springhouse, her back to him, facing the creek. Her melody, first tentative, soon swells in volume.

Rock of Ages, cleft for me / Let me hide myself in thee—

—What are you doing? he asks her, interrupting. Pale dawn illuminates the field around them, a patchwork of snow and thawing earth.

Barker looks over her shoulder at him. She's unbonneted, her plaited hair aglow in the morning light. —It's Easter, she says.

—And?

He forgot it was Easter. Holy days are for people who have people.

—There's no traveling on Easter, she says.

Higgenbotham rubs his arms against the cold. Behind him, the campfire whistles and snaps with burning sap. —You'd better believe we're traveling. Your uncle's men don't care what day it is.

She squints at him. —Then no traveling till after the service.

—What service? There's no service. We're in the middle of nowhere.

—The service I am giving, Barker replies, then lifts her head and sings again.

Let the water and the blood
From Thy wounded side which flowed

Be of sin the double cure
Save from wrath and make me pure

Higgenbotham returns to boiling coffee. He plunks himself down on a stump beside the fire and pokes at the wood with a stick. Barker is a portrait of concentration. She belts out three hymns in a row, her voice so robust and youthful that his own lungs begin to ache. He has left Mandy and Birdie by the creek for watering, and they raise their heads, listening to her song. He pours his coffee into a tin cup and blows on the hot liquid. He hasn't regularly attended church since his wife left him. These past thirty years, the road has been church for him.

When Barker moves on to reciting scripture, Higgenbotham calls out, tells her to hurry; they've got no time for sermonizing. She replies that if they're going to be captured on account of honoring Easter, so be it; she would rather be caught than heathen.

—Don't be a fool, he says to her.

He finishes his coffee and starts packing their gear. He uses a pine branch, thick with needles, to dust off the saddles. While he works, Barker recites Mark's account of the crucifixion and the empty tomb, then switches to Luke's account for the Resurrection. Higgenbotham takes note of her change in apostolic source material. He remembers his old Sunday-school days, long-ago lessons in somber Calvinism. In Mark's Gospel, there is no Resurrection, only the sighting of Jesus's tomb, raided and open, the women fleeing in dread from a rolled-away stone. Even the dead can be taken from us; even those we have lost, we can lose again—that's how Mark's Gospel ends. Methodists like Barker prefer Luke's sunnier version.

—Wrap things up, he says. —Or you'll be preaching to the militia.

Barker places her palms together. —Close your eyes, she instructs him.

Higgenbotham lowers his head, the movement reluctant but instinctual. He comes from a long line of devout New England Presbyterians, sturdy folk who regarded their God the same way they regarded their winters: as inexorable realities to be endured without complaint, always keeping in mind the potential for annihilation. He heeds Barker when she asks for silence; the moral authority of a child is not to be questioned. But he keeps his eyes on the horizon while she prays. At his age, he will not close his eyes for anything but sleep or death.

When he asks if they're finished, she shushes him. —Keep prayin', she says. —We ain't done yet.

The sun crawls over the long horizon behind her. Today will break warmer; Higgenbotham can feel it. The snow will start melting in earnest, and the roads will thaw into mud. Wiley's men won't be daunted; across Georgia, impassable thoroughfares are an everyday occurrence. *How many militiamen belong to a county district?* he asks himself. Minimum sixty-three, maximum all able-bodied male residents between the ages of eighteen and forty-five excepting circuit riders and those who make a living on the road. Those like himself, the transients.

There's no way sixty-three Clarke County men have joined the chase for Barker. But some will. And the question is how long they'll keep at it. The question is what Wood's offering as an incentive.

Barker finishes her prayer, and together they saddle up Birdie. As he fastens the colt's straps, Higgenbotham asks her what she plans to do once they reach the river Chestatee.

Ideally, of course, he needs to turn her over to someone who can provide safe lodging, some elderly couple or clean-living widow who can house her until—or unless—her father can be found. Ideally, he needs a person of good character. But those are in short supply in frontier Georgia.

—You could take a stagecoach if we learn where your pa is at, he says. —You might reach him that way. I can give you some money.

Higgenbotham pauses. He's trying to remind her he's not going to be with her much longer; he's trying to reemphasize his limited availability. —Though the stage routes are in flux and the roads are likely washed out, he adds. —And if you take a coach, there's the risk of being seen by one of your uncle's men.

Barker wraps twine around her bedroll. She lowers her head and bites down on the threads to tie the knot tighter. —I guess what I do after the Chestatee ain't your concern, she says through her teeth. —Seein' as how you won't be with me.

—I need you to tell me your plan, Higgenbotham says firmly, trying to inject a note of authority. This tone worked when he encountered Pony Club men, thieves who greedily eyed his horse and mailbags; why won't it succeed with a fourteen-year-old girl? —I need to make sure you're not in harm's way. If you don't have a plan after we reach the Chestatee, I'll have to find you a home for abandoned children.

—No, sir, she says. —No, I don't need that. I ain't abandoned.

But her mouth stays pinched for some minutes afterward.

The postmaster at Gainesville sees and hears all, presides over his fiefdom like a feudal lord. If anyone has heard of Lorenzo McRae or knows his possible whereabouts in the goldlands, that person will be Eaton Harben.

But the postmaster's store has closed for Easter. They'll have to wait and try again in the morning.

Higgenbotham wants an inn and a bed. He needs a bath, and the nerve in his upper buttock is twanging like the string on a plucked fiddle. He counts three taverns, three churches, a cobbler's shop, a tobacco factory, and a building with a sign for a male academy, but he can't find an inn that looks suitable. Gainesville's a center of trade, a gateway to the gold region, built fast on the dividing ridge between the Oconee and Chattahoochee Rivers. The town's getting rich quick, thanks to the lawyers and mine-company owners who've flocked here, not to mention the rushers arriving with gold nuggets and gold dust knotted into their handkerchiefs, ready to spend, eager to blow their earnings.

He finds them a hotel near Gainesville's eastern end off a road with a sign marking the way to sulfur and limestone springs. Higgenbotham would ride on and dip into one of those springs if time allowed him; the water might help his aching backside. But this isn't a pleasure trip; he's not here for his health.

Inside the establishment, well-heeled guests, the women wearing fine coats and silk gowns, the men sporting high top hats and brass-tipped walking sticks, mill about a spacious lobby. These are tourists, or so he gathers, here for the hot springs. One or two turn up their noses as Higgenbotham limps past. At the front desk, a clerk looks him and Barker up and down before informing them that there's only one room available, a converted pantry, the fee the same as for a regular room. Higgenbotham tries to bargain him down, is unsuccessful, winds up paying it. More guests are in the sitting area as they walk through, the wallpapered room thick with perfume, cigar smoke, the scent of leather.

Clutching her saddlebag, Barker goggles at a grand staircase leading to the upper-floor guest rooms. They're not headed up those stairs; they're headed to the service rooms behind the kitchen.

—This place's too rich for me, she says.

Higgenbotham nods. —If it's too rich for you, it's too rich for your uncle, he says. —So we have a night's reprieve.

In the morning, after a breakfast of blueberry oat cakes topped with powdered sugar—a delicacy—and sausages, they return to the post office, making their way to the rear of Gainesville's general store and toward a counter so crowded with mailbags that Higgenbotham's shoulders hurt when he looks at them. The front part of this store sells everything a body might need before traipsing into wilderness: ax heads, pistols, wool blankets, laudanum, and foodstuffs galore. One shelf is filled with blank books to keep track of a person's adventures, to record purchases made or income generated, hot springs visited, Indians removed and relocated.

Postmaster Eaton Harben, bald and mustachioed and wearing a black silk waistcoat and an impeccably tied cravat, raises a hand in greeting when he sees them. Higgenbotham has known Eaton for years, doesn't think much of him. He's a wheeler-dealer, a politician. He hoards information and dispenses it selectively, like the candies he doles out to customers from a jar on the counter.

Higgenbotham introduces Barker and explains that they're searching for her father. —Lorenzo McRae's his name, he says. —Methodist circuit rider, tall fellow, a ginger. Seen last month at a camp meeting along the Etowah.

—Interesting, Eaton says, and fishes a lemon drop from the jar. He offers it to Barker, and she shakes her head, declining. He thrusts it toward her. —I insist, he says.

She takes it but doesn't put the candy in her mouth.

The postmaster leans forward, rests his elbows on the counter. A sign on the wall behind him states his charge as postmaster: THE CONVEYANCE OF LETTERS AND INTELLIGENCE ESSENTIAL TO THE CAUSE OF LIBERTY.

—Do you know how the gold hunters pay for their purchases when they come in here? he asks Barker. She shrugs. —They bring me quills filled with gold dust, Eaton says, wiggling his eyebrows, trying to win a smile from her. —They pay me in golden turkey feathers. Now, what do you think of that?

Her gaze darts to Higgenbotham. *Must I?*

Eaton turns to Higgenbotham also. —What's the matter with her? She shy? She have an earache?

—Her ear does hurt, Higgenbotham replies, remembering Barker's injury. —But I think she also chooses what questions to respond to.

Beside him, Barker smiles.

Eaton doesn't know Lorenzo McRae, but he does know something that might help them more. The Methodists in Gainesville are collecting donations for an evangelistic meeting, the first revival of spring, in mid-April. A weeklong gathering, he says, west of the Etowah River, assuming they can round up enough preachers to go after all the unsaved and backslidden. Freewill Baptist and Christian Connection ministers will be joining the affair also.

He folds his plump hands and rests them on his counter. —Every man of the cloth with means to travel will be at Mary Franklin's mine for it, he says. —If your man's still preaching, he'll be there.

—That's useful, Higgenbotham says. —That just might help her find him.

The postmaster coughs delicately. —But leave the girl behind if you head that direction, he says. —The goldlands are a godless place. They're no better than Sodom before the arrival of the destroying angels!

Barker, who has fled this conversation for the fabric aisle, is inspecting the chintz shawls, running her hand over bolts of calico and gingham, perusing the London duffel blankets. Eaton glances over at her.

—Girl that age, at the edge of womanhood, he continues in a near whisper. —Leave her in Gainesville, I say.

—There's no one to take her, Higgenbotham replies, and regrets his statement as Eaton immediately pounces.

—She could stay with Mrs. Harben and myself! We could keep her while you ride to Franklin for her father.

—I'm not going that far, Higgenbotham says, but Eaton's still talking.

—She could attend the brand-new school for girls here. Nice little place; they teach them to make wax flowers.

—I don't think she'll want to—

The postmaster steps out from behind the counter. —Come over here, little girl, he says. When she doesn't appear, he whistles for Barker like he's calling a sheepdog. —Do you want a new dress? You like those calicos, don't you? That what you've got your sights on, isn't it?

Barker shuffles over, visibly reluctant to join him.

—My daughters were the same when they were your age, Eaton says. He points at her boots. —You'll need new shoes too. And a bonnet, of course, a pretty one, decked in ribbons. How about a new dress? We'll have to measure you. Height and arm length and waist.

He walks over and places his hand on her waist as if beginning a tailor's calculations. Barker goes stock-still, her gaze darting to Higgenbotham again.

—Harben, Higgenbotham says, stepping forward. He briskly plucks the postmaster's hand from Barker's waist so that the hand returns to his side, where it belongs. The postmaster's expression cools. —Your offer's generous, Higgenbotham says. —But she wouldn't stay put, she wouldn't stay in Gainesville if I left her. She's determined to find her father, with or without me.

He pauses, taking note of the other man's doubtful face. —Also, he adds, I promised I wouldn't leave her.

Did he? Well, he has now.

The corners of Eaton's mouth tug downward. —I think that's unwise, Matthew, letting her do as she pleases. She's a child. It's not her decision.

—Maybe not, Higgenbotham replies. —But it's not yours either.

Beside him, Barker smiles a second time.

Their horses make slow progress between Gainesville and the Chattahoochee River, picking their way over sandstone fragments and thawing mud, crossing wagon ruts deep enough that Mandy loses a couple inches in height every time she steps in them. By the time they reach Goddard's Ford that afternoon, Higgenbotham has decided to board his mare and leave her behind for the remainder of the journey. Her limp has returned, and she's noticeably hurting.

He trades her in at a livery yard for a barrel-chested black-and-white pony, as short and sturdy as they come. Mandy will receive shelter and board there until he can reclaim her, courtesy of Higgenbotham's multi-country coin purse.

—I'll come back for you, he says to the mare. Briefly, he rests his forehead against hers. —It's only for a few days. You'll have a little rest here, I promise.

Mandy's grizzled head droops lower.

—No, you haven't let me down, he tells her, whispering so Barker doesn't overhear. —Quite the opposite. I've let you down, as a matter of fact; I haven't kept you out of injury's way.

Near dusk, they cross the Chattahoochee on a ferryboat shared with four prospectors who speak Portuguese, Spanish, and French but not a sentence of English among them. The ferryman is Cherokee and doesn't speak to them in English or any other language, though his silence likely stems from disdain rather than lack of proficiency. The far bank marks the start of the goldlands, albeit barely—the eastern boundary of gold territory. As they approach, Higgenbotham glimpses mounds of earth along the water's edge, trenches dug out of the riverbank, hastily shoveled ditches filled with silt and discarded tools, a wheelbarrow missing its wheel. A few stray panners crouch in the shallows, tins in hand, bending and dipping in the gloaming, glancing up briefly to note the ferry.

Barker is slow to move after the ferryman secures his vessel and ushers them off. She looks around, craning her neck, searching left to right, from bank to river to forest. She's looking for her father. Higgenbotham can sense that much, can feel her sudden swell of hope. He tells her to keep moving.

—Nothing to see yet, he says. —We'll be in it soon enough.

They spend that night at a boardinghouse near the river's western bank. The proprietor's wife, stout and red-faced, barely glances up when Higgenbotham and Barker walk in; she doesn't care who her patrons are so long as they pay in coins. No one wants the shinplasters Georgia banks have started printing. Higgenbotham himself has over fifty dollars in scrip from the Farmers Bank of Chattahoochee that he'll never be able to use.

He sends Barker to their room while he pays. Before heading upstairs, he orders whiskey from the dining room. While he waits for the barkeeper, he peruses the printed handbills tacked to the dining room wall.

WANTED: ONE MULATTO MAN NAMED NEEDHAM, SUSPECTED TO HAVE FLED TO GOLD COUNTRY. HAS LEFT A FREE

WIFE IN NORTH CAROLINA. REWARD ONE HUNDRED DOLLARS.

MISSING: GRAY-SPECKLED FILLY, FIFTEEN HANDS, V. LONG TEETH, NO MANNERS. SUSPECTED TO HAVE FLED INDEPENDENTLY. REWARD FOR SAFE RETURN.

Higher on the wall, one poster has crisp paper and sharp black lettering, no wear and tear from weeks of hanging in a smoky room. It's a brand-new addition.

REWARD FOR INFORMATION LEADING TO CAPTURE OF *GIRL GOUGER!*

Higgenbotham stops short. He reads what follows the heading. Then he reads the handbill again.

REWARD FOR INFORMATION LEADING TO CAPTURE OF *GIRL GOUGER!* LAST SEEN CLARKE COUNTY, APPROX. 14 Y.O., RED HAIR, PRESUMED DANGEROUS. IF FOUND RETURN TO MILITIA DISTRICT 221 (CAPT. W. WOOD), WATKINSVILLE. ALSO REWARD FOR RETURN OF BAY COLT, HEIGHT SIXTEEN HANDS, WHITE STAR, PERSONABLE.

The bartender approaches with bottle and glass and hands them over to him. Whiskey's cheap in gold country, a small recompense for the inconvenience and danger of the region. Higgenbotham has seen miners pay for their drinks by dipping the ends of their knives into their handkerchiefs, coming away with gold dust on the blade tip—a threat and payment simultaneously.

After the bartender walks away, Higgenbotham surreptitiously untacks the handbill from the wall, folds it, and tucks it in his coat. Then he heads for the stairs, bottle and glass in hand.

Wiley Wood isn't chasing Barker in secret. He's announcing her disappearance across the goldlands. His men are fanning out into the foothills and points north, declaring her misdeed, anticipating people's interest. And now there's the crime itself, clearly delineated. It's worse than he had imagined.

Instinctively, Higgenbotham's hand goes to his own eye. He cups it, feels the pulpy roundness beneath the lid.

And Wood had only the one to begin with.

Upstairs, in a windowless room decorated by a lone painting of geese in flight, Higgenbotham finds Barker reading her Bible on a cot by candlelight.

He pours himself a whiskey. He sits across from her on a cot of his own and cradles his glass. Once he finishes it, he pours himself a second round. He asks her what she's reading. She flips the page, seemingly absorbed, choosing not to answer. She's reading the Bible's final pronouncements, Higgenbotham sees, the Book of Revelation, where the world dissolves into apocalypse. He sips his drink. He wants to ask her about the gouging, about what she did to her uncle Wiley.

Before he can get his question out, Barker glances up at him. She has braided her hair into two tight plaits, and her face is freshly scrubbed and rosy. She is impossibly youthful—and primed to judge him.

She points to what he's holding. —You know whiskey's the devil's potion.

Higgenbotham's grip on his glass tightens. —Excuse me? he says.

—You heard me, she says. —You're under the spell of liquor.

—And? he replies, suddenly vexed, suddenly weary. —What of it?

Barker straightens, perching tall on her cot, those green eyes without an ounce of softness in them. —You're about to be drunk, she says. —And that's a sin, mister.

—What did you do to your uncle? Higgenbotham demands, determined to change the subject. —What are you not telling me about your situation?

—I won't talk to a drunkard, she says. —I won't. I've had enough of 'em.

They wade into an argument. Even though he knows he shouldn't, even though it's ridiculous to quarrel with someone fifty years his junior. Barker's hair glows blood red in the candlelight. Higgenbotham has not had much experience with children, with the immense vexations they can generate. He was a father for only one day.

Years ago, decades ago, his wife, Ruth, gave birth to triplets, but the infant girls all died within minutes of their arrival. Their cords had tangled during the delivery, like vines creeping unnoticed around saplings. He buried the infants in a single coffin, together, so they wouldn't be alone. All they had known in this life was each other. His Ruth was not the same afterward. Neither was Higgenbotham, but his wife had the worser run of it.

At one point, he remembers, she told him she would give anything for little wax dolls representing her lost children, figurines that she could look at and touch when she despaired of this world and her place in it. But when he offered to carve such figures for her, she said she didn't want anything more coming from his hands.

Barker crosses her arms now, veers dictatorial. She tells Higgenbotham that Christ told His followers to be not drunk with wine.

He cuts her off with a raised hand. —Sermonizing, he says, is the one thing guaranteed to make a drunk drink more. Not that I am one. You misread things.

He reaches for the bottle and pours himself yet another glass, this time only half full. —See? he says. —Most men would pour more.

—I've seen enough intemperance to know what it is and what it isn't, she says.

—Well, I've seen enough preaching to know what it is and what it isn't, Higgenbotham replies. —Next time you foist an Easter sermon on someone, you might check your sources.

Barker's eyes widen. Higgenbotham should stop talking, but he can't restrain himself. —You swapped out the end of Saint Mark for the end of Saint Luke, he says. —You spoke about the Resurrection, but Mark never mentions that event. You played fast and loose with the Gospels.

She blinks; he's treading into her territory. —Don't be so quick to judge, he says. —My mother was quite the Calvinist. You Methodists are always so worried about God forgetting you, about God not paying you enough attention. He pauses for another swallow of whiskey. —Whereas we

Calvinists are worried that God *won't* forget us, that He won't leave us alone.

He sets down his glass. —The God I grew up with isn't one you'd want breathing down your neck, he says.

Barker is quiet. Then she says that if Higgenbotham intends to do what he promised, namely, help her find her father, he had best steer clear of strong spirits going forward; she won't stand for it in the man assigned to travel with her.

—I wasn't assigned to you, he says. —I did it out of goodwill. I took you out of harm's way because no one else was available.

—You *were* assigned, she replies, twin spots of color flaring in her cheeks. —God assigned you to me. Otherwise you wouldn't be here now, mister.

The air in the guest room is stale. Higgenbotham can smell it all at once, mildew and ancient urine, vinegar from attempted cleanings. Barker starts to say more, but he stops her. —Enough, he says, and she flinches.

He tries again, in a kinder tone. —Miss McRae. Barker. You might want to consider extending your travel companion some grace. If you fancy speaking in public meetings, as I suspect you do, given your Easter display, if you fancy becoming a lady preacher someday, you'd do well to start with grace. Not condemning people. Not telling your audience everything they've done wrong. Save those parts for later.

He takes another sip, coughs when the liquid goes down too quickly. —We already know what we've done wrong, he says. —We are likely drowning in it. We don't need a reminder.

A resigned sigh proceeds from her.

Higgenbotham casts his gaze around the room. It's close quarters, and he's feeling claustrophobic. There's not a single window, not even a smoke hole in the roof. If there'd been a window, he could have at least spent the night listening to the mighty Chattahoochee, its ceaseless rushing.

—Let's make a deal, all right? he says and leans forward, still seated on his cot. —You agree not to sermonize, and I agree not to send you to the closest county sheriff for the crime you committed against your uncle. How does that sound?

She blinks. A pall descends over the room. Higgenbotham wants to see what she'll say, what she'll admit to doing. He wants to know why she did it. But then her hands cover her face, and her shoulders begin shaking. He has pushed too far. He has overshot his target.

He rises from his cot and steps over to hers. He squats down beside her. The position causes his bad nerve to radiate, but he holds it.

—I was exaggerating, he says. —I wouldn't summon the sheriff. Surely you understand that. It's clear your uncle is nothing but bad news in all directions.

Barker won't look at him. Her hands hide her face.

—I spoke out of turn, Higgenbotham says, trying again. —We New Englanders sometimes speak so bluntly, we lose any goodwill we might have earned.

For reply, she flops over and lies on her side, facing away from him. He watches the wall of her shoulder. His mind is a blank. Should he pull the blanket over her? Apologize? Leave her be? Not being a father means not knowing how to manage such moments. But maybe even fathers don't know how to manage such moments.

He returns to his side of the room. He retrieves the handbill from his coat and reads it again. A million unhappy thoughts visit him. He blows out the candle. Barker's breathing deepens. He hears scuttling in the corner near the door, some nocturnality starting up in the dark. The sound stops, then resumes—scratching, nesting, foraging, all the tasks that any given mouse in any given inn must undertake for its nightly survival. *Small creatures, large lives,* he thinks.

He lies on his back, pulls the blanket up to his chin. When he sleeps, he dreams of leaving Georgia.

Part Two

Leather's Ford to Dahlonega

7

THIS IS WHAT it is to be the circuit rider's daughter:

Rise at dawn, rekindle the fire, boil the porridge. Home is a blur, home is the road, winter mist on Black Mountain unfurling. Home is stands of great white oak, preening silver bells, humble hornbeams. Home is strange-smelling houses and unfamiliar adults; it is other people's dinner tables, a spare room or prophet's chamber in homes large enough to offer one. Home is a bend in the road, a canoe on the Chattahoochee, stalks of cane for the horses, wagon grooves so deep you could lie down in the hollows.

Home is a route, the circuit your father travels. Home is not a place; it is a direction. It is momentum.

Your best friends growing up are your mother and father and your Bible. They're also your only friends, if you don't count Dilworth's blue-backed spelling books or *Pilgrim's Progress*, whose pages you tear through at night, whose tales you read over and over. You play Christian and Evangelist with your rag dolls in the wagon, and at night, after finishing your chores—watering the horses, brushing their coats, checking their hooves for cracks and sores—you read more. You dread the times you must forgo your nightly reading and journey to the houses of other Methodists for supper. There you will sit, stuffed into your good dress whose sleeves are no longer long enough, as the men around the table drone on. They talk about elders and deacons, the latest news from the

Christian Advocate and Journal; they ask your father why he doesn't preach more prudently, why he doesn't avoid coarse language; they declare the need for systems, consistency, uniformity.

They talk about the circuit rider's stipend too—*Such as it is*, they will say apologetically, smiling sorrowfully at the three McRaes seated across the table. Meanwhile, your mother will dab her mouth too many times with her napkin, and your father will pick at his roasted chicken, listening to his hosts, wearing a slightly mystified expression. Stipends do not interest your father, though your mother wishes they would. What interests Lorenzo McRae are human souls, the lost and the oppressed, the unchurched, the lowly, the humble. What sets him on fire, and therefore what sets you on fire, are lives in the balance, salvation at stake, the souls he encounters along the highways and byways of Georgia, Alabama, Tennessee, more.

And every hour he must spend at this table discussing administrative matters is an hour *not* spent fanning those flames, *not* counting all things but loss for the excellency of the knowledge of Christ. He will stifle a yawn during these discussions, hide his weariness behind his hand. You love him fiercely in those moments.

Home is also the horses, though they're always being changed out, so you can't grow too fond of any one animal or you'll wind up repenting of your attachment later. Home is watching your father drive his team forward, racing to beat an impending storm, as you ride inside the swaying covered wagon and witness rain dance through the canvas opening, trees bowing and swaying, lightning limning the overstory. Home is nights spent camped outdoors, on the road, looking up at the wide arc of heaven, the sky studded with stars, no cloud cover. And home is watching Lorenzo the day he received a letter announcing that he was *not* being invited to take his ordination examination, that all those hours he'd spent studying Fletcher's *An Appeal to Matter of Fact and Common Sense* and Wesley's sermons were for naught; the Methodists were casting him off, disowning him before he could cause further trouble, before he could become a true headache to them.

Your father stiffened when he read his bad news, but he recovered faster than you thought he would. He said it was up to him and the Holy Spirit now; he said that when man shuts off a faucet, God sends a river. He didn't say who or what the river was.

—At least they won't interfere anymore, he added, and you agreed with him, consoled him; you patted him on the back, even though your mother had said to leave him alone. Your calling is to support your father's calling. Either that or your calling *is* his calling. Somewhere along the way, your duties and his have merged.

What else? Home is wild geese stabbing through rain clouds in spring. It's your father preaching in that same rain, coatless, his white shirt soaked through, beseeching his listeners, who stand transfixed, unable to step away, because of his message or their own reluctance to abandon the preacher in his vulnerable state. Your father has that effect on people.

And he'll speak anyplace that will have him; he'll preach standing on a tree stump in a cleared wood or on a barrel outside a saloon or in a schoolhouse, if it's available. He'll ask for the windows to be opened or removed so the crowd outside can hear what he's saying. There is always a crowd outside the schoolhouse when Lorenzo is within.

One time, he rented out a ballroom for a dollar and a half; the proprietor thought he was a performer, a dramatist offering theatrical entertainment. Maybe he was. Lorenzo preached one of his longest sermons in that ballroom, three hours without pause or hesitation. The crowd stayed silent, rapt and waiting. He capped off his message by reciting Job 21:3: *And after that I have spoken, mock on.* Then he bowed his head, turned, and strode out.

You never want him to face a mocking audience. Or, worse, no audience at all; you cannot bear for your father to suffer people's uninterest, indifference, rejection. You worry when they call him names—*Indianite* one week, *Negrophile* the next. But your father welcomes these accusations; he says Christ would have been called the same thing. One Sunday, a man walked up to the front of the chapel where Lorenzo was preaching and struck him with a whip for saying something with which he disagreed. Another time, a mob pelted him with fruits and vegetables. He had spoken about the Indian problem; he had advocated the Cherokee position too vigorously. Your father didn't mind these insults; he seemed to welcome them. He ducked to miss a flying cucumber, then straightened and caught a flung tomato. He bit into it, to his hecklers' surprise, and preached on. Five people came to Christ that morning.

He dances as he preaches if he has the desire to do so; he weeps up there too; he also curses. He carries a box of Bibles and lets you give them to people. Originally, his circuit covered two hundred fifty miles, but this was not enough territory for the Holy Spirit to make sufficient use of him, so he expanded his route on his own. Before he became a circuit rider, Lorenzo earned a living as a cabinetmaker, so he understands the lives of ordinary people; he knows what it's like to toil with one's hands. He speaks the language of the peddler, the tinker, the sheep shearer, the farmer, the butcher, the gristmiller. He calls out blessings on all who come to hear him, churched or not, redeemed or not; he is no respecter of race or creed or country. When the Methodists cut him loose, he tells your mother he's relieved to be free of them, though your mother does not appear quite as ready to cast off denominational shackles as he is.

She asks your father about money quite often; your mother has developed lines between her eyebrows from thinking so much about it. She asks how he will feed his child without a stipend. Lorenzo replies that they must trust God to provide, that the only way the Lord will *not* provide is if they fail to believe that He will.

This explanation does not make your mother's brow any smoother.

On these and other matters, you align with your father. When you were ten years old, he sold his watch to build a roof for a school in Cherokee country after the missionaries living there told him they couldn't afford anything beyond nails and shingles. Your mother didn't speak to him for a full day afterward. That watch had been her wedding gift to him. You spoke to him a lot that day to make up for Sarah's silence, to help him feel less abandoned.

When your father lays hands on the lame, the diseased, the gangrenous, you yearn to do the same. When he weeps with the widows, you weep along with him. When he baptizes the new believers, you stand at the edge of the crowd and imagine what it must be like to dip them in a rushing creek, cause them to die to their old Adams, their sinful selves, and be reborn. The only people your father does not care to baptize are the wealthy ones; he says it's easier for a camel to go through a needle's eye than for a rich man to enter the kingdom of heaven—that means they're on their own.

In you, he instills a lifelong love of the road, a lifelong yearning to be unfettered, to speak the truth and have it count, to *say* something.

He quotes the Apostle Peter to your mother when she frets about providing for you, her beloved and growing girl, when she shows him how your dress sleeves are too short, leaving your wrists and an inch above exposed. He bends down and kisses your mother on the forehead, on that anxious brow. *Casting all your care upon Him; for He careth for you*, he will say to her.

But he stops quoting that verse after Sarah passes.

West of the Chattahoochee, the country explodes with dreams of gold, the streams and tributaries choked with hope; men wade into the rivers and streams, some of them barefoot, some booted, miners from fifteen to seventy-five, bending as they scoop and shovel, as they pour mud and silt into buckets. They're shouting, always shouting, in multiple languages and accents indecipherable.

There are black men and white men and Indians and mixed-bloods out here, rushers with their tin pans, provisioners selling spades, pickaxes, shovels. There are men with

Long Toms and men balancing on flatboats, and everywhere Barker looks, she sees torn-up creek banks lined with cradle rockers, which separate water from silt and gravel. The miners rock these wooden troughs like mothers soothing babies they never had but always wanted or never wanted but always had, all while praying for gold, that telltale glint, and that catch in their throats as they scrape away layers of mud, their destinies hidden underneath. Everyone wants a new start; everyone wants to wipe his life clean. Who wouldn't, given the opportunity?

Higgenbotham tells Barker to keep close. Don't speak to anyone, don't make eyes at anyone; don't hop off the colt. Keep your head down, your bonnet tied. Make sure your hair stays tucked under it. Keep damn Birdie quiet; don't let him show off, start nickering and socializing. Can the two of you be invisible? That would be preferable; that would be easier.

—And whatever you do, don't preach, he adds. —Men out here don't take kindly to being preached at. By anyone, let alone a skirt-wearer.

—I know that, Barker tells him.

Higgenbotham is having a hard time with his new pony. His long legs drape too far down the animal's sides, so as they ride into gold country, he resembles a caricature of a lottery messenger, a mockery of his current role and not the real thing. Barker offers to let him ride Birdie, but the big colt snaps at him whenever he approaches. He will stick with the pony, who is harmless, at least, diminutive but mighty, albeit prone to excessive communicating. The pony will come to a complete halt in the middle of the road if he disagrees with Higgenbotham's chosen route, his long tail defiantly switching, and no small amount of persuading will be required to prompt him to move on.

At Leather's Ford, also called New Bridge, the crossing for the Chestatee, Higgenbotham stops at a cloudy-looking stream to refill his canteen while Barker takes in her first unfettered view of the goldlands, marveling at the busyness of this outpost, even at dusk, this festering hubbub, this riverine disaster. The river here is wide, more than a hundred feet across, the banks lit with torches. The air hangs dense with campfire smoke, and pits are everywhere—troughs dug into the earth, gravel heaped along the water's edge and beyond.

Barker can't stop looking around. There's a sawmill, a gristmill, a saloon, a travelers' rest, and the ever-present general store, all set back from the water, stationed against the backdrop of darkening woods. She hears someone playing a fiddle, a harmonica singing its mournful tune to laborers and peddlers skulking around the cooking fires, the latter plying their wares; no one seems to pay any attention to them. She glimpses one or two women too, but not many, not enough to create a sense of safety. One of them has dropped to her hands and knees along the riverbank next to a preacher, it would seem, in his fine black suit, both crouching at the water's edge, swirling their iron fry pans, the preacher's Bible abandoned in favor of gold panning.

The preacher is not her father.

And the Indians! They're here as much as anyone, here with their horses and dogs, some in their hunting frocks and their headdresses and their heads shaved bare on the sides, others dressed in the clothing of white men. If the lottery is supposed to be kicking the Cherokee out of Georgia, someone hasn't yet told these men.

As she and Higgenbotham ride toward the toll bridge, Barker spies a Cherokee fisherman hunting along the shoals of the Chestatee. He glances up as they pass by in the twilight. He carries a bow and arrow and fishing net; he wears a rifle frock and deerskin leggings. He straightens when he sees Barker, noticing her noticing him. Barker flashes a smile—can't help it. He's near her age; he's handsome; he has an interesting face.

He salutes her playfully, federal soldier–style, as she and the colt jog by, and Barker salutes him back. He raises his bow and gives her a wave. She twists around in the saddle to see him silhouetted against the spreading night, slowing down Birdie for the sight. When Higgenbotham turns around to learn the reason for her delay and sees the two of them ogling each other, he mutters, *Good Christ.*

—Keep riding, he tells her.

Past the bridge, they head west on the Upper Alabama Road and stop at a trade store open late for travelers. Four men in fur hats and heavy cloaks are playing cards by lantern light on the long front porch. Higgenbotham hears German spoken—or is that Swedish? They're not Clarke County militia; that's all he needs to know. He makes his way inside the store while Barker stays outside with the horses.

One of the cardplayers notices her and calls out, asks her in English how she likes the goldlands. Another player invites her to come down from that colt and join them. These are professional rushers, men who cut their teeth in the gold mines of Europe and South America before making their way by sea to Georgia.

When Higgenbotham hears them addressing her, his face pops up, frowning, in the store window. But Barker steers clear of the men; she doesn't leave her seat on Birdie. The colt is burly and snappish enough to keep away most strangers.

When he returns outside, Higgenbotham leads the horses a good distance away before handing Barker a pair of canvas trousers, a cotton tunic, and a cap of felted beaver. The only light available to them is coming from the trade store's distant lanterns.

—Disguise yourself, he says. —When we stop for the night. From here on out, you're a thirteen-year-old boy.

She looks at the clothing with suspicion. —I'm fine as I am. And I'm fourteen.

—It's not a suggestion, Higgenbotham replies. —And you claimed to be sixteen when I met you. If you've discovered how to turn back the hands of time, I'd like to know it.

While he adjusts the pony's stirrups, lowering them as far as the straps allow, Barker rummages through his saddlebag, inspecting his other purchases: tinned goods, a loaf of bread, stomach bitters, a new bottle of whiskey. Her head lifts, and she scowls at him.

He regards her evenly. The sky behind them is a blackened indigo.

She reaches into his saddlebag one last time and pulls out his final purchases, a gleaming new pistol and a box of lead shot. She opens her mouth, then shuts it, surprised into silence.

—I thought it necessary, given the company you're attracting, Higgenbotham says, glancing back at the cardplayers from lands remote, still playing their game on the porch. —Though my hand's not as steady as it used to be.

She nods once. —Drink less, aim better, she tells him.

They take late lodgings at a stagecoach inn past any settlements or outposts worth naming, a long low building with a darkened front porch and no ale or liquor sold inside. It's the only stop they've found that Higgenbotham deems safe from the militia.

He would have preferred to sleep outdoors or take shelter in an abandoned barn or storehouse. But he's chilled and teetering on unwell, too many hours on the road. Best to dry off, warm up, eat a hot meal.

He acquires their room and pays for it in coins. Seated behind a wide oak desk, the proprietor asks Higgenbotham if Barker's his daughter. It's the first time anyone has asked the pair what relation they are to each other.

—Granddaughter, Higgenbotham says, inventing on the spot. —She's my granddaughter. My daughters all passed.

Barker directs a glance at him but doesn't speak.

They eat a late meal in a narrow dining room that smells of fried fish and burned toast. Over their heads, glowing lamps hang from hemlock beams along the ceiling. They sit elbow to elbow with a handful of other late-arriving travelers, the only sounds the clink of cutlery, the scraping of plates as people eat. Higgenbotham notices each patron's face, studies them one by one, surveying. No militiaman worth his salt would tolerate a dry hotel like this one. To be honest, he can barely abide it either. But one cannot be too careful. Not when he has a girl gouger to deal with.

Barker's spirits perk up with their meal. She grows talkative, tries to make conversation with him. She asks him what it's like to be a messenger for the land lottery.

Down the table, several men lift their heads when they hear her question. Higgenbotham whispers at her to keep her voice down.

She has changed into the clothing he bought for her, though not the felted cap, which she has rejected as too large for her head. The breeches are big too, but she has solved that issue by tying a piece of string around the waist. The tunic fits her and is a butternut hue that she likes. Not in a million years could she pass for a boy in this outfit. Higgenbotham has only made the problem worse.

—Being a messenger must be some adventure, she says.

He sips from a cup of water, grimaces. His stomach is not well; he needs his nightly whiskey. —That's one way of putting it, he says.

—You don't like being a messenger?

—No, miss, he replies. —No, I do not.

—Well, you're giving away Indian land, she says as a couple of men down the table look over at the pair again. —Maybe that's why you don't like it. Maybe you've contracted scruples.

Higgenbotham picks up his fork, stabs a hunk of trout. —The *State of Georgia* is giving away Indian land. The politicians and the lawyers are giving it away, with the backing of northern bankers. I'm merely the vehicle of notification.

She considers this statement. —Who gave them the right? she asks. —Who gave those men permission to do that?

—They gave themselves the right, he says. —They searched their consciences and found gold waiting.

The dining room door opens. The innkeeper's wife appears in the frame to announce the end of the meal; she tells the patrons the kitchen's closing.

Higgenbotham sets down his fork. —Granted, there are laws, he adds. —But most men in these parts aren't inclined to follow them.

—Ain't you a man of these parts? Barker replies. —Ain't you lived here longer than I've been alive?

Higgenbotham lowers his head, contemplates his barely touched meal. It's true—he's resided in the South so long, he can remember when Georgia stretched all the way to the river Mississippi.

And he was supposed to have parted ways with this child by now; he had hoped to leave her behind once he escorted her across the Chestatee. Well, here they are, and he hasn't made a move.

—Time makes mincemeat of us all, he says. He pushes the unfinished pieces of trout away and lays his napkin like a shroud over them.

8

THEY HAVE LEFT the stagecoach inn the following morning when it begins. At a stop to water the horses, Higgenbotham dismounts and abruptly bends over, his hands finding his knees. He vomits into the dirt so violently, the liquid splatters the pony's flanks. He straightens, wipes his mouth on his coat sleeve, and meets Barker's gaze, his countenance ashen.

—Mister! she says. —You've taken sick.

He lifts his hand to wave her words away, downplaying the incident. —Something I ate—

He convulses again, so hard the force doubles him over. Bile, clotted and pale, issues from him; it's like nothing that's come out of him before. When he regains his composure, he notices a stain darkening his breeches. Wild fear takes over his expression. —I've—he says. —Never in my life have I—

He doubles over again.

There's no doctor back at Leather's Ford so they must ride toward the federal road and the next settlement to find one. Higgenbotham drags himself up into the saddle, and sensing an emergency, the pony snaps into compliance; westward it is, he won't fight the direction. He trots obediently forward. The snow has all but disappeared; the road is mud and corrugated sandstone.

They ride a mile, then another, in silence. The next village has to be near, just over the next rise, he says. When Barker asks how he's feeling, Higgenbotham says *better.* A lie if he ever told one.

Barker was on the circuit with her parents back when her mother fell ill. It was in muggy Columbus, in southwest Georgia. She remembers her father praying on his knees by the bed, her mother sweating, coughing bilious blood into a basin. Later, blood began hemorrhaging from her nose and ears, saturating the sheets. The doctor placed poultices on her abdomen, administered cup after cup of some foul-smelling, murky potion. For two weeks, Barker and her father had to sleep on the floor of a stranger's house, a young lawyer who had heard Barker's father preach and took pity on them.

Higgenbotham doesn't have a pitying lawyer on hand. And Barker's mother died despite their efforts.

—Go on, she says to Birdie and the pony. —Faster now.

The colt plunges through tendrils of fog into new-growth forest. Behind him, the pony has galloped straight into a patch of springtime blackberry. Thorns catch in his voluminous mane and tail; he squeals and comes to a halt. Higgenbotham manages to free the animal but is sick again afterward; he dismounts and staggers into the trees, is gone several minutes.

When he returns, his complexion is ghastly, the color of smoke. He weaves on his feet like a sailor newly landed; he cannot keep his balance. They've stayed south of the Etowah so far, but the river is close, its dull roar reaching through the trees.

Barker climbs off Birdie and takes over. She grasps Higgenbotham by the elbow and leads him to a patch of moss under a fatly sprouting oak. She arranges her coat on top of the moss and has him lie on it. Her bedroll will suffice for a pillow.

She offers him water. He declines; he can't keep down his own saliva. A blood vessel in his neck pulses so rapidly, she briefly wonders if his heart will explode. He asks her to bring him his saddlebag, then rolls onto his side and vomits again.

Barker fetches his bag. Slowly Higgenbotham hauls himself to his feet and moves into the privacy of the woods. He returns to the clearing several minutes later wearing a different pair of breeches. He won't look at Barker; he's humiliated by his weakness.

—I'll fetch help, she says. —Lay back down. How far's the next stop?

—We should've met it by now, he says raspingly. —We might be off course.

—How do I right us, then?

Higgenbotham lowers himself heavily back to the ground. —West. Just keep west.

Barker looks up through the oak's limbs. The sun appears nowhere; it has hidden itself behind fallen clouds.

—Keep the river on your right, he says. —Reach the federal road, and you'll see a sign for Scudder's, in Hightower. That's the place. Ride fast. Don't let anyone stop you.

—What if I can't find it?

—You'll find it, he says.

A shotgun blast silences the forest. It comes from the east, through the mist, past a stand of oaks and chestnuts. Another blast follows, a perfectly lit flint exploding.

Higgenbotham elbows himself up from the moss. Barker, squinting, spies movement at the edge of trees—a figure shifting and disappearing in fog, then forming again.

It's not one man; it's several. Faint outlines, moving shadows. A company in motion at the other edge of the woods.

—What is it? Higgenbotham whispers, pulling himself to his feet, standing unsteadily. —Who's coming?

Another blast. A screaming squeal erupts, followed by shouts.

Thataway, it went thataway. Hurry, now, don't lose it. Get it, now. G'on, get him, you dumb devil—

—They're boar hunting, Barker says.

—They who? Who's *they*? What do you see? Get me back on that damn pony.

Barker glimpses a uniform, tattered and mismatched, and the arrogant glint of a bayonet. She doesn't need to see more. She seizes Higgenbotham's sleeve, tugs him into motion. —Right now, hurry! Their dogs'll smell us.

—What's that he's got wind of—

—Look, he's wantin' to chase the—

—Hey, he got a whiff of somethin'—

—Well, what you got wind of, boy?

—Dogs— Higgenbotham starts, and Barker yanks him by the arm, cutting him off. She pushes him over to the pony.

—We have to ride. Can you ride, mister?

—Yes, he says, and promptly sinks to his knees.

The pony turns his head, nudges Higgenbotham encouragingly. Barker grabs Higgenbotham's hand, grips his cold bones through his cold skin. She pulls him again.

—Get on Birdie, then. Get on him, not the pony, she says. —We'll ride together. Come on, mister, climb on up, it's all right. I'll boost you. Birdie's big enough to hold us both.

Her voice is calm, which he appreciates, and she sounds older than her years; her voice is like cool water on a hot forehead.

She helps boost him up, helps him slide and gasp into the colt's saddle. Then she hoists herself up in front of him as Higgenbotham lists to the side. She reaches around and steadies him, instructs him to hold on, to stay still, stay upright.

He apologizes for his invalid state. Barker snaps the reins twice, and the colt springs into motion; they're off.

—My mama was sick once, she says. —I've seen worse than anything you're likely to throw at me.

One of the hunting dogs howls through the woods. Another joins, barking his excitement. As the colt begins running west, the pony hangs back, seemingly incapacitated, terrified by the baying.

—Those aren't dogs, Higgenbotham says. He grunts as the colt gains speed. —Those are something else.

Barker calls over her shoulder for the pony. She calls him again, but it's no use; the little animal is still back there, paralyzed by alarm or indecision. The colt flies forward. Higgenbotham's eyes meet Barker's.

—Wolfdogs, he says. —Those are wolfdogs making those noises. Then he remembers something. —My pistol. It's in my other bag. The one on the pony.

Barker starts to say they can't retrieve it, can't backtrack, can't take that chance. But just as she opens her mouth to speak, the pony rushes into motion. A blur of black and white speeds through the trees, galloping in the colt's direction. *Don't leave me!* The pony sprints through the forest, short legs pumping mightily.

A whistle sounds. *Suuuueeeeet!* And another, longer and sharper, shrill enough to stop the wolfdogs' barking. Someone is calling them, summoning the hunters back to camp. Barker glimpses one of the animals slinking through the trees, a flash of silver and gray, ears flat against a large skull.

—Damnation, Higgenbotham breathes; he has seen the wolfdog also. —What a creature.

The pony doesn't share his admiration. As Birdie slows, the pony blows past the colt, racing into a wide hollow, a meadow dipped in fog. He's faster than Birdie now, faster than anything his barrel chest and short legs would seem to allow. He'll await them at the next settlement, away from those dreadful howls in the forest.

Barker points. Strapped to the disappearing pony's side is Higgenbotham's saddlebag holding his newly purchased weapon.

—There goes your pistol. Speedier than any shots you're likely to fire from it.

At Scudder's, the dreaded diagnosis: cholera. How contracted, no one knows. Maybe drinking from a contaminated stream, maybe a visit to a foul privy. Maybe late hours, damp quarters, never-ending winter, or overlong mental exertions. The prospecting towns are filthy; gold rushers wash nothing but silt and pebbles, and they toss their refuse in the roadways when they're too drunk to dispose of things properly.

Scudder's men bring Higgenbotham into a weatherboarded cabin behind a village inn. This settlement is knee-deep in miners and vagabonds all crammed together and working for Jethro Scudder, mill and mine owner, war veteran, enslaver. These are men without means, bunking under tarps and in bark shanties, peering out from their shacks to observe the encampment sprawled and growing around them. The place is loud with pickaxes; grunting oxen hauling sleds; snatches of song, whistles and ballads; shouts as miners pour river water into rocker troughs.

Higgenbotham's belongings, his clothing, hat, stockings, and all, everything that can be cleaned, everything that can fit into a washtub, must be boiled in lye. His foodstuffs must be discarded. Barker may not visit him; she's placed under quarantine in an upstairs room at the inn, put under a wait-and-see.

—The only town in gold country that's not seen cholera cases is Auraria, the doctor says that first night as he draws a blade across Higgenbotham's forearm, his labors illuminated by the light of a single lamp. Blood trickles into a porcelain basin. —They've set up a board of public health. Brand-new town, he says, flushing at the thought. —I'd like to live there.

Higgenbotham can't track what the doctor's saying; he's too busy dehydrating. Diarrhea has taken over his life. He's a riverbed, not a person, no fluids left to expel, but that's all he exists to do now. His thirst is extraordinary. He asks for water, for a rag dipped in water that he can suck.

—Not tonight, the doctor says. He soaks the patient's feet in pails of warm water, adding mustard powder and salt to the bath. He's a busy doctor, earnest and worried; cholera is his least favorite disease. He produces a jar of leeches, dips into it, and places the slugs, one after another, on Higgenbotham's stomach, bleeding him a second time.

Higgenbotham passes out, revives to find the leeches removed, is given chamomile tea mixed with opium. Under the influence of that draft, he apologizes to his late wife for failings unnamed.

Scudder's washerwoman turned nurse arrives just after daybreak. While the doctor sleeps in a chair, snoring lightly, she chases Higgenbotham's clothing around the washtub with a paddle as determinedly as Higgenbotham's old schoolmaster used to chase wayward pupils around the yard with a rod. When she finishes beating the garments, she hangs them in the sun to dry, draping his shirt and breeches over a clothesline strung between two Carolina silver bells. Next she turns to the patient, administers a dose of calomel, and hands him the water-soaked rag he needed while the doctor shifts in his chair and continues snoring. The rag tastes sour, but Higgenbotham sucks on it anyway, as grateful and helpless as any newborn.

In the afternoon, the doctor leaves and the nurse adopts extremer measures. She stirs together a clyster of starch, warm water, and laudanum. Higgenbotham wants to ask her what it's for, but he can't form words.

—You'll soon see, she says, reading the question in his face, her dark eyes boring into his. —It's to save you.

Using a hog's bladder and a pipe, she empties the cloggy mixture up into his bowels to block them up, to keep him from shitting out his life. She repeats this reverse purgative every half hour until Higgenbotham's rectum is afire and he begs her to stop, until he tells her, slurring from the laudanum roiling through his veins, that death would be preferable.

The nurse settles into a rocking chair in the corner as the afternoon light wanes. She brings out needlework to keep her hands occupied. Her face is in shadow, her hair wrapped in a cloth head covering.

—Now we wait, she says, and Higgenbotham remembers saying much the same thing to Barker in the Athens alley not so very long ago.

Not long enough is his last thought before unconsciousness takes him.

In fever, he travels backward, to his days as an employee of the US Post Office Department. New postmasters and post offices were springing up everywhere in those years, and the number of postal routes multiplied. Higgenbotham was a good mail carrier. He knew the rates by heart: eight cents per sheet if sent forty miles or fewer; ten cents if sent forty to ninety, and so on, topping out at twenty-five cents per sheet if sent over five hundred miles. He delivered on time; he rode his horses hard but humanely. If he traveled at night, he would light a torch and hold it high to keep his mount from tripping over tree roots. Reaching his designated post office, often a mere hut at the forested edge of a settlement, Higgenbotham would drop his bundle of letters at the door and be off as fast as his horse could carry him. He kept his nose out of people's correspondence; he followed departmental policy: *Do not open or read the mails. Never lose sight of the mails for a moment. See that the mails are protected from the wet and kept safe from injury of every kind.*

But who protected the letter carrier?

After they lost the triplets, Ruth Higgenbotham returned to Savannah, where her parents lived. Before she left, she asked her husband to stay in their Milledgeville home and not come after her. *Don't follow me,* she told him. She said she needed time to mourn alone, to grieve her loss in private, though she didn't explain how she could accomplish that task with both of her parents present.

Higgenbotham didn't press the matter, didn't question her. He did ask Ruth to write to him, and he remembers her promising to do so. He told her he would wait for her; he would not leave Georgia, even though the only reason he'd moved down here was to be with her; the only reason he called Georgia home was that Ruth had called it home first. They had met a few years before, when Ruth traveled to northern Massachusetts to visit an aunt who happened to be friends with Higgenbotham's mother. The two older women were both religious, both widows with a liking for strong coffee. After Ruth left her aunt and returned home to Savannah, Higgenbotham wrote to her, and she wrote back. Six months later, after a flurry of letters sent and received, he traveled south to see her. They married in her parents' house the day before her twenty-second birthday. That was the end of Higgenbotham's life in New England.

But after the triplets died and Ruth left him, the weeks ground by and then the months, and then a year passed and still he heard nothing from her. It was as if the marriage had never happened. Her parents had swallowed her back up. Here Higgenbotham was, a Vermonter turned Georgia letter carrier, a mail bearer with a prized star route, drowning in correspondence from all seventeen states in the Union, yet no letter from the one person he wanted to hear from.

He even went to Washington City and visited the Dead Letter Office. He asked the clerks if he could look through the stacks of abandoned and unclaimed mail that awaited sorting. Maybe Ruth had not addressed her letter to him properly; maybe she'd somehow mailed it to the wrong state, forgotten the name of Milledgeville, misspelled his name; maybe she had addressed herself to another Matthew Higgenbotham.

He found nothing.

If he reflects rationally—and, granted, Higgenbotham is not rational right now, granted he is pouring sweat, tossing, blazing on this straw-filled mattress, his nurse turned tormentor stabbing her embroidery hoop in the corner—if he reflects *honestly,* he can say that in hindsight, most of his life has been absurd. For a mail carrier to spend twenty-nine years hoping for a letter that never came!

But he also loved the road. That must be said; that was part of the equation. He loved the hemlock forests, the waterfalls and singing brooks, the passenger pigeons that flew in thick clouds over the Georgia foothills, streaming so densely, they shut out the sun. He felt at peace outdoors. When he first started as a carrier, his mail route was simple, just a long northward trek to Augusta, looping west to the small settlements of Georgetown, Greensboro, Washington. As the postal department grew, however, his route did too, and over time he journeyed farther north, added stops at Oglethorpe, Athens, Jefferson, Watkinsville. Still later, he ventured into Cherokee country; he delivered the first mail ever received at Vans Town, and years later, in 1825, he was delivering to Talking Rock, Coosawattee, Rossville.

The mail was a hopeful sign in those days. It was a sign of Georgia's potential. Back then, Higgenbotham believed maybe there really was room in this state for everyone.

He no longer thinks that way.

He tosses and turns on his sickbed, flings an arm toward the packed-dirt floor. He isn't very religious anymore, but he does have something in common with Barker's father: a passion for the road, a compulsion for continuous transit. Lorenzo McRae has been on his circuit so long, he can't figure out how to get off it, how to stop riding. That's Higgenbotham's guess, anyway. And Barker's father hasn't come back for his child because he *can't*, because he's caught, snagged on a route that won't let go of him. The road and its mandates, the road and its solitary seductions, have bound him up and won't release him.

That's Higgenbotham's opinion, anyway.

His eyes flutter open. His black nurse stitches on in the winking light of a smoky lamp. In his febrile state, Higgenbotham mistakes the smoke for campfires burning. He hears the fire's crackle, hears men's laughter, the jingling gear of horses, the lowing of tired cattle. He sees himself sharing that campfire with wandering minstrels like he used to do; he's back somewhere in the old woods, bartering for wax to waterproof his tent, purchasing smoked fish or popcorn from Indian traders, or bandaging the blisters on the feet of an enslaved man fleeing middle Georgia, an elderly fellow so terrified of every white person he encountered that Higgenbotham had to ply him with jokes to persuade him that he really was from the Free North and would not send him back to his captors.

Q: What are the four seasons called in New England?

A: Almost winter, winter, still winter, and three months when my sled don't work.

Q: What do you call a Massachusetts man who cuts down trees?

A: A Boston lager.

He rolls over, nearly falls off his sickbed, rolls back again, sweats through his bedding. The compress his caretaker has placed on his stomach slides to the floor.

As a boy growing up in the foothills of the Green Mountains, Higgenbotham once found a litter of orphaned wolf pups in the hollow of a rotting oak, no sign of the pups' mother anywhere. He fed those little wolves for five days, filching milk from the family cow, lying when his mother asked him if he'd taken the milk. He lied so vigorously that his mother sold the cow for slaughter because she believed the creature had stopped producing. Higgenbotham confessed the truth, stricken with guilt. In response, Mathilda Higgenbotham took her switch to him. It was just the two of them at that stage; his father had died a few years before from an infection following a tooth removal.

The next morning, chastised but undeterred, young Higgenbotham hiked back to that wolf den, this time bringing leftovers of roasted chicken. But no pups remained to be fed. He searched and searched, circling the oak's base and nearby, in a grove of hemlocks. There he found evidence of slaughter: blood spattered over dry hemlock needles, tufts of fur, and four baby-wolf teeth, tiny as apple seeds, on a bed of shelf fungi.

Higgenbotham never learned who the killer was. A hunter? A bobcat? Or, a more unsettling prospect, his own mother teaching him a lesson.

Teaching him that there are things in life you cannot control but will be held responsible for anyway.

That second night, the men of the 221st District come through Scudder's settlement. A dozen militiamen take over the long porch, the entrance to Scudder's inn for travelers. They show up armed with knives, rifles, that treacherous-looking umbrella—and now also cholera, which has felled more than just Higgenbotham.

Jethro Scudder strides outside and demands to know the company's business. The mine owner dislikes three things and three things only: taxes, abolitionists, and sick people. He refuses to allow any of the men to enter once he hears two in their midst are ill. He tells them to try one of the roadside establishments west of his village. Cherokee proprietors run those, he says.

The militiamen decline to pursue Scudder's suggestion. They're not headed back on the federal road tonight; they're certainly not boarding at a place run by Indians. They're tired, hungry, and their sick men need a doctor.

Scudder offers a deal. They can camp along his stretch of the Etowah for one night, two at the most, but they'll pay for the privilege. And while he'll send the doctor to check on those who are ill, none of them are to set foot in his inn or his tavern during their stay.

—The infirmary shack out back's occupied, he says when one of the men asks about it. —Cholera beat you boys here. You'll sleep outdoors.

Higgenbotham has no idea the militia have descended. He's delirious, perspiring under quilts in his sickbed. But Barker knows; Barker from her third-floor quarantine sees all and misses nothing.

She observes the men loitering around the inn's front door, smoking and conversing as stable hands lead their horses away. Two of the horses pull a farmer's sled that carries the carcass of a boar. She sees wolfdogs skulking around the hitching posts, three of the creatures, with rough gray coats and pronounced ribs, their hip bones so sharp, the animals look levered up on the back end. Downriver, a bobcat hisses, loud enough that the wolfdogs momentarily stop in their tracks: They have a challenger.

Then Barker sees something else. It takes her a while to figure out what it is. At the far side of Scudder's tavern, a covered wagon, waiting in the darkness, with someone seated on the driver's seat. Two people, if she looks closely—a black driver and a white man beside him. A meaty white man in a threadbare uniform, clapped in blinders like a horse.

It's her uncle.

She shrinks back from the window, astonished but not surprised, astonished but also numb, thinking everything and nothing at once.

How Wiley Wood has made his way here in his present condition, she has no idea. How fast did he travel? The desire for vengeance must fuel him. Either that or its opposite—his desire for her attention, his unflagging, unwavering *need.*

Barker pulls a blanket tightly around her. From her bed, she listens to the sound of the river and the men below her window.

That whole second night at Scudder's, she will struggle to sleep. The fantasy of her father swooping in to help, miraculously appearing, doesn't once occur to her. She notices the fantasy's absence, isn't sure what to do about it. Her father is becoming less a person than an ideal, an abstract hope, like the eschaton or gold at the end of a rainbow.

Higgenbotham had better hold off on dying, she thinks. At least for a while, at least until the 221st Company rides out from this place.

She waits for the light of morning.

9

WHAT ELSE DOES it mean to be the circuit rider's daughter?

It means trying and trying to make your father smile, to draw him out of his ruminations, and once in a while succeeding but more often falling short; more often you cannot.

It means praying for his relief, for an end to his inward sufferings, but your prayers provide no respite for him.

It means asking God to lay your father's burden upon you, to let you carry it. You're strong; you're younger than Lorenzo is; you can shoulder it for him.

God says no. God says He's saving you for other sacrifices.

Tallulah Gorge was one of the last places you saw your father preach. The Niagara of the South, the tourists call it. Spectators gathered along the rim trail of a rivered canyon to gawk at the view and take in your father's sermon. No one was saved that day, and only one backslider came forward. These were well-to-do Europeans and English visitors, uninterested in letting the Holy Spirit slay them. They brought their easels and oil paints to the trail, their spectacles and spyglasses for sightseeing. Your father amused them; he was local color, something to write home about later. When he finished preaching, they applauded politely and went back to their plein air painting.

These tourists didn't cling to his words, didn't need him like the farmers and laborers and poor Georgia sorts did. Their faces went blank when your father spoke of the worms that human beings are: *We should be amazed at the privilege, that we who are worms of the dust should be admitted to the blessed sight of God to all eternity—*

Not these holidaymakers; there was not a single grub among them.

In the aftermath, you went and sought your father out. You came across him sitting on the rim trail alone, looking out over the river's chasm, which plunged nearly a thousand feet. The tourists had gone, retreated to their inn for pastries and imported delicacies. The Tallulah River coiled and glided below, the roar of multiple cataracts resounding in your ears.

You sat a few feet from your father on the trail. He didn't notice you. He was hatless, clad in his battered black suit, his necktie untied, his shirt rumpled. His boots were worn too, the soles nearly gone, the same fine boots he'd received from that bedridden woman he'd visited. He sat, lost in reverie, rocking slightly. Over fifty people had come to salvation the prior week when he had preached at humble Loudsville, where he spoke about redeeming the time because the days were evil. One wouldn't know that earlier triumph by looking at him now.

You wanted to help; you wanted to save the one who saved other people. Your father's melancholy baffled you. Why was he so sad? Your mother had stayed back at the campsite a half mile down the trail. She was busy packing supplies, stacking leftover Bibles in crates, preparing for the three of you to ride on. She worked all day long, harder than your father did, if you were honest. If anyone had the right to feel morose, Sarah McRae did. But she rarely let you see her sorrowful.

You rose and walked closer, then stood on the edge of that trail, trying to catch Lorenzo's eye, balancing on one foot, hopping and skipping. You were trying to make him laugh, to snap him out of his brooding. But you lost your balance, as show-offs will, and your father had to scramble to his feet and pull you back from the ledge.

He was irate. He yanked your arm, hard. He asked what you were thinking. —What foolishness is this?

He had to shout to be heard over the river below. Or maybe he just wanted to yell at you that day. —Do you want me to have to clean up daughter parts from the bottom of the ravine? he demanded. —Can't you see I'm at my wit's end already?

These agonies came over your father after revivals or when he was fasting. He was so tall and lanky and bruised-looking beneath the eyes that, on this day at least, the canyon winds seemed capable of blowing him away. It struck you in that moment that one good gust could cast him over those rocks and down into the waterfall.

You explained that you were only trying to make him smile, but Lorenzo wouldn't hear it. He told you to return to camp and help your mother finish packing the wagon.

—Let me be, he said. —I'm trying to pray. I'm trying to find God's face.

—Why are you trying to find God's face? you asked him, worried because of the look on *his* face.

—Because He has hidden it from me, he said, his eyes meeting yours, beseeching, supplicatory. —I am back in the night again; I have lost the witness of the Spirit. A small sound escaped him. —The silence, I cannot bear it, he whispered.

You could say a few things to your father today. You could speak to him with greater understanding of what it is to be forsaken. But these days, he is nowhere to be found.

Maybe he doesn't want to be found; maybe he's actively avoiding you. Maybe God's face will shine on Lorenzo McRae only if he rejects all earthly loves, if he surrenders everything he cares about, everything and everyone he adores, and pushes them over that cliff into the river's mouth.

Maybe you should have flung yourself off the ledge that day; maybe then your father would have noticed you.

Scudder has no interest in what brought the men of the 221st Company into his mining camp. Militia groups and Georgia Guardsmen are constantly coming and going, spending money and buying trouble, descending on the stores and stands along the federal road, this dirt-paved toll-way managed largely by Cherokee. Scudder's a businessman, South Carolinian by birth, Georgian by the grace of God, he likes to say; he respects perseverance and not much else. And it's not clear to him that this ragtag assembly on his front steps has worked hard at anything beyond drinking and hog chasing.

He offers to have their boar butchered and smoked, for a price. He'll also charge them for the doctor and any burials they might require. The two choleric soldiers will die overnight and their bodies will be buried in Scudder's graveyard—no crosses, no stone etchings, just a cairn of river rocks marking the spot, both men laid to rest in the same hole.

When the militiamen show Scudder their handbill and ask if he's seen the girl in question, Scudder feigns ignorance. He sees no reason to help them. Despite his near delirium, Higgenbotham managed to pay the mine owner upon his arrival, coins for a physician's care and also to ensure Barker's protection from anyone who might harm her. Higgenbotham didn't mention what Barker had done to put herself in danger, and Scudder didn't ask him.

—Girl? What girl? Not seen a red-haired girl in months round here, he tells the soldiers when they ask. —Though I wouldn't mind, if you know what I mean. He winks.

The men set up camp along the fringes of the settlement. They spend that night in their tents, snuffling and coughing. They spend the following morning burying the two in their midst who expired overnight, tying bandannas around their noses and mouths for protection.

In the afternoon, they take themselves to the porch outside Scudder's tavern and loiter and gossip, wondering who else in their group might fall ill, complaining about not being allowed indoors. There are barmaids inside; they haven't seen a pretty woman in days.

Scudder takes a good long look at the assembled company and decides that the horseman wearing a yellow kerchief is the only sober, well-kept one among them. The blind one hiding off in the wagon has announced himself as their captain, but to Scudder, Captain Wood appears unwell, theatrical, prone to tantrums. He's more impressed by the one nicknamed Kerchief, mixed blood though the youngster is.

By late afternoon, the men still haven't left the porch, and Scudder has had enough. They're scaring off his other customers. He chastises the company for their uncleanness, for their laziness; he tells them to go wash themselves in the river or he'll not let them camp on his property a second night. If they want to find that missing girl, they'd better pull themselves together, start acting like soldiers and not derelicts.

Kerchief crosses his arms and stares at the mine owner like he'd like to put a bullet in him.

—Yourself excluded, Scudder tells him, inclining his head. —You're the only one here who keeps himself up, who keeps himself looking like a man ought to. He waves the rest of the company off his porch. —Now it's down to the river, baths for all of you, or no tents on Jethro Scudder's land tonight.

That night a fight breaks out, and all because of the bathing. It starts with comments made to Wiley's group by two Cherokee horsemen on their way to Blackburn's, a roadside stand west of Scudder's. When the Cherokee behold Clarke County's finest buck-naked and scrubbing themselves in the river, a joke is made, lobbed into the twilight, half in Tsalagi, half in English, but clear enough to get the message conveyed, something about how pale and soft the militiamen are or, more specifically, how their sad, pale white asses could vie with the moon for how glowing and round they are.

The men of the 221st District take offense, naturally. One soldier wades out of the shallows and positions himself in the Indians' way, blocking their ponies, his arms outstretched, thrusting his naked hips at them in a crude gesture. Another soldier reminds the horsemen that the whites' asses might be pale and glowing, but Georgia's takeover of Cherokee country is the brightest light of all.

—'Tis a flame perpetual, he calls out, and spits at one of their ponies.

A brawl ignites. The Cherokee dismount, and the bathers leave the water to defend themselves. The fighting spreads, awakening the riverbank, summoning men from Blackburn's as well as Scudder's. More Indians arrive on the river in dugout canoes, and the chaos spreads. Within minutes, thirty or more men are in a full-scale mutual assault, white miners and half-naked militiamen trading blows with more than a dozen Cherokee. Several barmaids emerge from Scudder's tavern to watch the melee. One of them sings a song as she leans provocatively over the porch rail:

All I want in this creation
Is a pretty little wife and a big plantation
Away up yonder in the Cherokee Nation

The fight continues for nearly an hour. Rolling in mud turns the fighters all the same color, makes them all the river's children. By unspoken agreement, no one fires a gun, but other weapons are fair game. A coffee grinder sails through the air and connects with one man's head. From her quarantine window, Barker watches a Cherokee man strike a miner in the jaw with a fry pan. The crack of metal on bone is loud enough that she winces.

Kerchief is in the mix too; she recognizes the militiaman with the yellow bandanna whom she saw outside the Athens alley. The young man is caught in the middle—he's militia, but with Indian blood in him. He starts kicking whom he will, punching left and right at anyone who threatens him. He grabs the arm of a white miner who has struck him from behind and twists it until the fellow's shoulder pops and dislocates. What are they fighting about? Nothing, everything, all of it. They're fighting about land; everyone wants a piece of it, every settler wants to shit gold. The Cherokee want to be left alone. *Intruders!*

A doctor is summoned, the same physician who's been caring for Higgenbotham. Along the river's edge, he tends to the men's dislocations and lacerations, lines his patients up in order of the most badly beaten. He offers his services to the whites only. One by one, the Cherokee glide off into the night; they'll tend their wounds down the road at way stations operated by their own people. Kerchief will stay with the 221st Company, try to be all things to everyone.

Barker leaves her quarantine room and heads downstairs to forage in the kitchen—she's feeling famished. But Scudder's wife, a plump sentinel in a sky-blue dress, confronts her at the dining-room entrance. The older woman seizes Barker by the arm and directs her back to the stairs. Her grip is strong, and she wears a sheathed knife tucked into her apron.

She gives Barker a pointed shove. —Upstairs. Don't you come down again, young lady; it ain't safe. There are savages afoot.

—Yes, ma'am, Barker says. —And some Indians too.

That night she can't sleep. She peers out the window, observing the riverbank, watching the last stragglers from the fighting. The injured have formed a column waiting for the doctor's services, some the worse for wear, all appearing surprised, blinking, offended by their own wounds.

Barker has often thought men complain more than women when they suffer pain. Women have just come to expect it. And she has seen her share of suffering women.

Her mother on the day she died, for one. And the women on her father's circuit, in cabins and huts along the Blue Ridge Mountains, whom she and her mother used to help with childbirth, women far from a doctor, racked with labor pains. Barker's mother had no formal midwifery training, but she had experience; she had seasoning. She used to make Barker fetch implements—a pan of boiled water, clean cloths, and, once, kitchen tongs for a breech she hadn't been able to turn.

Watching that breech birth made Barker wonder why God had doomed half the human race to such agony, to such ripping pangs. If these travails were unavoidable, why didn't God assign childbirth to men, the supposedly stronger sex? Why didn't men bear the children if the duty was that hard and that important?

No one answered that question for her.

Then there was the time Aunt Elma managed to lacerate her thigh in a barn mishap, opening a four-inch gash so deep, it gave way to a profusion of blood and exposed tissue. Barker never found out exactly how it happened—something to do with a dropped tool, a rake or scythe dislodged from its station on the wall. She only witnessed the aftermath, Elma washing herself at the well behind the barn, stanching the bleeding, skirts hitched as she propped her booted foot on the stone wall. Chickens bobbed by her, heedless of the emergency, pecking for ants in the dirt.

If such an injury had happened to Wiley, the entire town of Watkinsville would have heard about it within five minutes—that's how loud he would have hollered—and the next few days of Barker's life would have been consumed by ministrations, by bandaging and compressing, coddling and checking. Not so for Elma. She tended her wound alone and without a sound, like any other wild animal, though in the moment itself, Barker did approach her, did try to offer help. The expression on her aunt's face quickly stopped her. Elma had paused from cleaning the wound and was gazing down into the well, into that dark water which stays invisible. She looked as if she could see something or someone down in there, as if some unknown element beckoned.

When Barker called her name, Elma looked up blankly, not seeing her niece at first. —You're hurt, Barker said. —Bad, it looks like.

—It's not so bad as it looks, Elma replied. And then she said something else, barely audible: —*Get out.*

Barker didn't understand what she meant. Get out of her presence? Get out from this farm? Get out from under Wiley? Was Elma talking to Barker or to herself? Was she expressing a wish or a directive?

But regarding that injury, your aunt never made a sound.

In the morning, before dawn, Barker creeps downstairs and heads outside before Scudder or his wife have risen. The makeshift medical station by the river has been abandoned. A few signs remain from last night's brawl—a plank of wood half buried in mud, a torn coat, a used bandage roll. No one is around.

She checks on the horses. In the stalls, she feeds Birdie and the pony she now calls Pistol. She doesn't stay long, can't risk it, keeps scanning her surroundings. She can see the silhouettes of tarps erected by her uncle's men downriver. She tells the animals they'll all be back on the road as soon as Higgenbotham has recovered enough to stay upright in his saddle.

Leaving the stables, Barker glances up and sees someone watching her. It's not a militiaman. It's one of their wolfdogs, escaped from the company's camp. He's young, and his silver-brown fur is coarse and spiky, lending him an air of adolescent dishevelment. He's scrawny and tall, with a large skull and amber eyes, his ribs visible through his coat.

—Get gone, she says, shooing him back with her arm. —Scram!

The wolfdog's ears prick up. His tail wags.

Barker hasn't seen her uncle since that glimpse of him in the wagon outside Scudder's tavern two nights ago. But she hasn't gone out searching either—she has stayed hidden.

—Leave, she says to the animal. —You can't tag along. I got to get back.

She throws a handful of dirt his way, to scare him off. In the stables, the horses shift and bump against the walls, restless at the scent of a predator. The wolfdog slinks away but doesn't disappear. He follows Barker in the pale predawn back to the inn, staying a few paces behind. Occasionally he darts ahead, sniffing the ground. Barker makes her way inside the inn and shuts the door on him just as daylight breaks.

She eats a bowl of cold grits in Scudder's kitchen, standing alone by the counter. Then, through a back window, she sees the wolfdog appear again, his oversize head poking up, his tongue lolling as he watches her. He must be even hungrier than she is.

She fills the bowl with more grits and goes back outside through a rear door that leads to a dead vegetable garden.

—Only this once, she tells him, and places the bowl on a stone in the dirt. The wolfdog noses the bowl, turning it over, splattering the grits. He devours them with great eager gulps, consuming silt, grubs, gravel; whatever touches a corn grit is going into this half-wolf's mouth.

Mid-meal, he pauses, those amber eyes lifting up to Barker. His tail wags so hard that his bony hips swish.

—All right, but I don't trust beggars, she says, and walks away from him.

Higgenbotham will live, but the doctor doesn't use the word *recover*. The patient's gastrointestinal symptoms have eased over the past three days, but his heart rate remains elevated, and he's sleeping eighteen hours a day. The washerwoman turned nurse watches in silence as the doctor bleeds him again. If it were up to her, Higgenbotham would be prescribed clysters and nothing else. A person is saved not by what comes out of him but by what stays in him—that's what this washerwoman would say. But no one has asked for her opinion.

—You're past the worst of it, the doctor tells Higgenbotham. —But a toll has been taken. You won't be the same man you were previously.

—Might be a blessing, Higgenbotham mutters, though only the nurse hears him.

The militiamen depart that same morning. Still bruised from their night of fighting, they break camp slowly, sniping and quarreling as they outfit their horses. The wagon bearing their captain is the last to pull away.

From her third-floor window, Barker watches the mule-drawn vehicle turning onto the road. Her uncle has retreated inside the wagon bonnet, but she can see the driver, whose expression beneath his low-brimmed hat contains both fear and irritation.

That afternoon, the doctor allows her into the infirmary hut to visit Higgenbotham. She brings the patient hotcakes on a plate from Scudder's kitchen. She peers into his eyes, his ears. She asks about his night sweats, his water consumption, his bowel movements. She interrogates him about his sleep.

—We got to get you well, she says. —We got to get me out of here.

Barker informs Higgenbotham about the militia, their arrival and stay in Scudder's settlement, the two men they lost to disease. She tells him about the wolfdog eating grits and her sighting of her uncle Wiley. The soldiers have left, she explains, but when they rode off, they headed in the same direction she and Higgenbotham need to be traveling, along the same road they need to be taking to the revival meeting at Mary Franklin's mine.

—So they're ahead of us? Higgenbotham asks. —So now we're following them?

His head falls back on the pillow.

An hour later, he's awake again, sitting up higher, complaining that the straw in the pillow has left his neck itching.

It's a good sign, his complaining; it means a little fight has crept back into him.

—They're chasing the same man we are, Higgenbotham says to Barker. In sleep, he's done some thinking. —They've rightly deduced that wherever your pa is, you'll follow. They caught wind of the same revival you're headed to find, and they're going to beat you to him.

He reminds her that his original plan was for the two of them to part ways at the Chestatee. She snorts. —At the very least, he says, let's change the route or come up with another destination.

Barker refuses. She won't entertain any alterations to the itinerary; it's her father or nothing.

Higgenbotham scratches his neck. He tells her she needs to prepare herself not only for danger but also for disappointment. When or if he's found, Lorenzo McRae might not provide the warm reception, the hearty embrace, that his daughter anticipates.

—I spent years trying to win my own mother's love and attention, God rest her soul, he says. —Not until I was long grown did I realize how much time I wasted.

—Wasted how? Barker asks.

—Some parents can't be pleased, he says. —And some are so worried about their own eternal standing, they forget they have children to raise.

Barker bristles.

—Well, what would you have me do? she says. —What would you have me do out here? With no home? In the middle of gold country? Would you have me stop looking for him? Would you have me stay with Jethro Scudder?

—*I would have you* come up with a plan, he replies. —Something other than chasing a phantom. You need to protect yourself, Miss McRae, and not just from your uncle.

He's not in the right frame of mind to be speaking to her. Four days of fever have left him irascible.

—And *I would have you* leave me to my house in the Green Mountains, he goes on. —Let me head north before it's too late. In Vermont, I'll never have to talk to anyone from the South ever again.

Barker's eyes widen.

Higgenbotham sighs, tries to recast things. —That's the cholera talking. That's nothing but an old man's self-pity.

But when he heaves himself up to a standing position, puffing from the strain, he finds her sturdy little self right beside him, balancing him upright, her arm circling his waist like an old friend's.

Barker looks up at him, steadying him like he'd fall over without her. Truth be told, he might.

—We'll head out tomorrow, she says. —And you can stop talking to me anytime, I won't mind.

10

YOU WENT TO her a couple of times, several times. Surely a solution could be found. The two of you could come up with a plan together. A woman couldn't live staring down into a well forever. *Aunt Elma!*

You tried to talk to her about him, tried to say what you could. But the words arrived garbled in your mouth so that your speech sounded vague and indirect, largely useless.

—Maybe we keep him from strong drink, you said. —Maybe we send him into town when he's ornery.

Maybe, maybe, maybe. Your aunt just blinked at you. She couldn't handle this conversation straight on. You would have to come at it sideways, let her listen and think while she kept at her sweeping or baking.

You tried quoting scripture at her. *For I know the thoughts that I think toward you, saith the Lord, thoughts of peace, and not of evil.* You looked at her. —That means He wants you to prosper, you said. Elma looked at you like you'd sprouted three heads, like you'd become three people and none of them appealing to her.

You revised your approach. You reminded her that God *wanted* to help her, that God loved Elma Wood too, not just Wiley, that the Lord cared most especially for the humble and vulnerable. —Look how He helped the Israelites, you said. —He brought them out of Egypt. We could be brought out too.

—Forty years, Elma said as she sat on the stoop and shelled peanuts in her apron. —It took forty years for them to leave there.

—We'd be faster, you said. But your aunt shook her head and continued shelling.

You tried again later, after Elma accidentally overcooked a chicken and Wiley, inebriated, shook her by the shoulders so hard her teeth knocked. He said she had done it on purpose, to make him go hungry. In private, you tried to tell your aunt that it wasn't her fault, and she gazed right at you when you said it, her eyes large and full of feeling, but then she just went on as usual.

You also tried to tell her what Wiley did to you sometimes in the night, things that had no words. But you couldn't get that part of the truth out.

Aunt Elma! you finally said, or maybe you just thought it. *I hate you!*

And you did. Her acceptance of her lot made you mad, drove you to fuming. Her lot and yours along with it. The Bible called women to be helpmeets to their husbands, but it also said husbands should love their wives the way Christ loved His church. And to the best of your recollection, Christ loved His church by dying in agony on the cross for it. Wiley wasn't doing any dying for anyone. And Elma was a lost cause; she was letting him trample her. She was nigh unto mute.

If you argued with her, your aunt would halt whatever chore she was performing, her arms falling to her sides, her gaze directed to the floor, while she waited patiently to hear what she had done wrong this time, then she fluttered away once more. It was like arguing with a mourning dove. How does one argue with a mourning dove? Easier to leave her alone, to abandon her to her endless chores, to her canning and jarring and shelling, her stitching and mending and washing. To this passivity she had and had not chosen.

—Never mind, you said when you saw her shrinking from your questions, from your effort to propose plans. —Never mind, Aunt Elma, don't feel bad, it's all right. You didn't do anything.

But that was also your point.

You wrote to your father. *There are trials and tribulations in this house,* you declared, writing cryptically, hoping he would grasp the message. *There is not a spirit of mercy. Please come back for me.*

The Holy Spirit was giving you things to say, things to say and write and *do*. You had the energy for an exodus, or for planning an exodus, at least, for thinking your way out. You asked your uncle if he could mail the letter to your father when he next went into town.

—That would require us knowing where he's at, Wiley said. —That would require your pa sending us word, making his whereabouts known like a good pa should. And he ain't done that.

Your father's absence pleased your uncle, gave him an opportunity to point out the failings of a man other than himself. But by then, you were angry with your father also. Why hadn't he written? Surely God could spare him for an hour; surely God could release Lorenzo from his preaching duties long enough to write to his daughter, to pen a single note to her on a single piece of stationery.

They're still there, those letters you wrote to him, tucked under your straw mattress in the loft back at the Watkinsville farm, back in the dogtrot with Elma. They were never mailed. Wiley never took them.

Elma's still there too, you presume, knocking around in that kitchen by herself, alone except for the chickens and hogs out back, the most peace she's had in ten years.

She's probably praying Wiley never finds you. She's praying that her husband stays away on this hunt until accident or fever takes him.

But Elma Wood isn't wholly helpless, you have also learned. She's not without recourse. She can do more than pray if she's pushed.

At Franklin Mine, there is no revival; there is no camp meeting and no gathering throng, just a wooden preaching platform on a grassy knoll perfumed by wild ginger, overlooking the Etowah River. The platform stands ten feet high with a pine roof. Two traveling preachers have climbed up to sit on it, their legs dangling from the side. They're the only clergy within three miles. One of them glances up as Barker and Higgenbotham ride by.

The wolfdog has followed the travelers here, crossing the Etowah at Blackburn's Ford right along with Barker and Higgenbotham, swimming beside the raft when the ferryman wouldn't take him. Barker tried to send him back, waving and shouting at him to go home, but Higgenbotham told her to let the animal be. The wolfdog made it across the river and onto the bank faster than they did. He shook himself off in the sunshine and waited for them, tail wagging, watching the raft bob toward dry land.

—Bless'd be His name, one of the preachers sings out now from his perch; from the look of him, he has been blessing the Lord all night. It's Sunday, the fourteenth of April.

Higgenbotham guides the pony past the men without comment, but Barker brings Birdie to a stop, and the wolfdog stops too, beside her. Shielding her eyes from the sun, she gazes up at the platform. She knows those words; she knows that call-and-response. These are her kind of people.

I salute you in the name of our Lord! she calls up to them, and the men say back, in unison: *Of whom the whole family in heaven and on earth is named.*

They smile at her, and she beams back. Does she know "Come All Ye Mourning Pilgrims"? one of the preachers asks; they could use a harmony. Barker nods eagerly at them, ready to sing.

—Don't you dare, Higgenbotham says to her. He reaches out and thumps the colt on the rump. The wolfdog barks as Birdie jumps forward, jostling his rider. —Keep on the road, Higgenbotham says. —No preaching and no singing.

Barker gives him a look. —But—

—Not even if the Lord himself alighted on that platform, Higgenbotham says. —Not on my watch. Now, gird yourself: It's time for the Widow Mary.

He pats Pistol on the neck. —She'll know where the traveling circus went.

Mary Franklin's mine is a gamble in progress, a smattering of pine huts and hemlock cabins southeast of Ball Ground, along the river. Set back from the water looms a white-columned house and behind it a blacksmith's hut and a small store for goods and trading. Widow Mary employs a workforce of transient southern whites and enslaved blacks, with a few Cornish miners from across the Atlantic thrown in for good measure.

—Placer mining's the game around these parts, she says to Barker and Higgenbotham. —That's the search for gold you can see. Mary has just begun expanding her operation beyond streams and hillsides to veins of ore deep in the earth, digging for the gold you *can't* see.

—The future lies in tunnel mining, she adds. —All the easy gold's been snatched up already.

She leads her visitors downhill, toward the river. Mary Franklin has a bountiful head of flaxen hair, a robust figure, and a slyly upturned nose. She does not look her forty-nine years. She wears an elaborately ribboned hat and carries a fan made of turkey feathers; she uses that fan as a pointer. She talks over the rumble of a water-powered stamp mill, which she presents to Higgenbotham and Barker with pride as they reach the river, explaining how the machine operates. When she speaks, her voice reveals a faint tremor, a laryngeal hesitation that makes her sound more in need of aid than she is.

—Hard-rock mining's all underground, she says as they continue walking. —Requires equal parts planning and madness.

She steps aside to let a pair of oxen pulling a sled trundle past. The ox driver tips his hat when he sees her. Mary's cheeks lift in a smile. —We're in the lead out here, and I owe it all to *you*, Matthew.

She rises on her toes and plants a kiss on the lottery messenger's cheek. Higgenbotham blushes. Barker watches this exchange with interest.

—I'll take y'all on a tour, Mary declares. She turns to Barker and claps her hands. —No one ever visits me. Y'all have time for a tour, don't you? What brings you two here, anyway?

Her eyes land on Higgenbotham hopefully.

Barker steps forward. The river is loud behind her. —Where's the camp meeting? she asks. —Where're the evangelists, Mrs. Franklin? There's supposed to be a week of preaching here. We heard about it back in Gainesville. She pauses, studying her surroundings. —Where *is* everybody?

An amused sound escapes the widow's throat.

—Oh, child, Mary says in a drawl marking her as south Georgia–born, so far south as to be nearly the swamps of Florida. —Oh, you strange little girl. She reaches out and fingers the boy's tunic that Barker wears. —They changed the plan. They moved the preachers up to Lumpkin County. I kept telling them my mine wasn't the place for it.

She laughs again, a sound that dissolves into the river behind her. —The only God people worship around *these* parts anymore is gold.

A tour they must take; Mary won't have it otherwise. She loops her arm through Higgenbotham's and steers him along the riverbank and uphill, past heaps of turned earth and rock piles, oxen and men laboring against a backdrop of rises scarred from ditches.

Until a year ago, Mary tells them, she was dirt-poor, the widow of a beet farmer who died from cutting down a longleaf pine that responded to its murder by falling on him. At the time her husband passed, Mary didn't have two copper pennies to rub together.

—Then Matthew Higgenbotham showed up at my door, she says.

Higgenbotham tries to extricate his arm from hers but cannot; the Widow Mary has him in an iron grip. She's a petite woman, not much taller than Barker, but she's strong.

Within a week of receiving her good news, she had twelve offers on her new property. She turned them all down. She traveled north by mule to view her winnings in person—she wanted to see what the fuss was about. She found twenty squatters on her acreage, rogue rushers from Tennessee and North Carolina. These men were scouring her section of the river and its tributaries and coming away with gold nuggets the size of black-eyed peas.

—What'd you do? Barker asks her.

—Hired a man to whip those squatters off my property, Mary says. —Then hired a dozen more, each fellow larger than the next.

She employed some miners, rented or purchased others, and launched her own mining camp. She recruited lumberjacks, cattle drovers, and blacksmiths, the toughest men she could find. She wanted them to serve as armed guards as well as miners. Then she brought in two black women to serve as overseers. She gave these women authority to run the place as they pleased, though she did not see fit to give them their freedom. This pair now managed the daily operations of Mary's mine with such efficiency and severity that the miners lived in dread of them—

Higgenbotham cuts her account short.

—We can't stay, he says, peeling her hand off his arm. —Have any Clarke County militia been by here? They're seeking the same camp meeting we are. We're giving them a wide berth.

—Haven't seen any militia, Mary says. —But if any show up here, my men'll know what to do with 'em.

Higgenbotham asks if she knows where exactly they moved the camp meeting—Lumpkin County's a sizable area. He gestures at Barker. —Her father's a circuit rider; we think he'll be there.

—Ah, Mary says, nodding. —One of them damn shouting Methodists.

—Yes, Higgenbotham says. —But we still need to find him.

Mary laughs, taps him on the chest with her fan. —I can tell you where the camp meeting went. What's it worth to you?

She bats her eyelashes at him. She's going to make Higgenbotham pay for this information, compensate her with the currency of time and flirtation. But hearing a sound, she turns, banter momentarily forgotten. —What in the world's *that* thing?

The wolfdog has trotted up the path behind them. His ears and forehead are covered in burrs from some thicket he has battled, an invisible opponent he has conquered. He lifts his head, training his sights on the trio as they regard him.

—He's a tagalong, Barker says. —He don't belong to us.

Higgenbotham disagrees. He's been waiting for a wolf to call his own since his mother likely did away with those pups in that rotting oak.

—His name's Scout, he says, improvising. —He'll stay out of your way, Mrs. Franklin. He won't harm anyone.

He whistles for the animal to come to him, but the wolf-dog skitters away, darting briefly toward Barker before running off again.

When they reach a scaffolded cave entrance along a low hillside, Mary stops, hands on her hips, and faces her guests. The sun is directly overhead. No one's leaving her encampment today; she's demanding that her visitors stay the night, at least.

—Now, she says brightly. —Who wants to see what it's like to live underground?

Mary's building her hard-rock mine using slave labor, twenty-five field hands carted up from a Marthasville plantation, the men on loan between planting seasons. She recently lost half the team when a caving structure collapsed on them, the timbers giving way, killing more than a dozen souls. That happened just a few weeks ago, she informs her visitors now, but the tunnel has already been rebuilt.

Barker glances at Higgenbotham. The widow wipes at her eyes, which aren't tearing.

—I'll never forget it, Mary says, and fans her face with her turkey feathers. —Terrible day. Peanut, you in there? Come on out, I need you to meet some people.

Stooping, she peers into the cave entrance.

The enslaved miner known as Peanut is Barker's age or younger. Round-cheeked, with dusky skin and a sorrowful, know-it-all gaze, he ducks to exit the cave and confront the newcomers. In his hands he carries rope, a lantern, and a pickax.

Mary instructs him to take Barker and Higgenbotham into the tunnels and show them around.

—Not for me, Higgenbotham says. —I'll sit this one out. Barker can do it. When Mary protests, he raises a hand. —I don't need to head underground. At my age, I'll be there soon enough.

The widow chuckles, again looping her arm through Higgenbotham's. —You ain't old, she says. —You're just the right amount of seasoning, by my reckoning.

Higgenbotham reddens again. Barker can tell he does not like this woman. He quizzes Mary about the sturdiness of the scaffolding, the composition of the soil, miner safety. Digging lower than the water table has proven impossible so far; Mary wants to find a way around that obstacle.

Barker follows Peanut into the cave, forgetting the outside world, marvel overtaking her. Past the entrance, the tunnel opens, and she can stand upright. Peanut wields his lantern high as they walk into the darkness. Barker stays close behind him. He rounds the corner quickly, heading deeper into the bowels of the hill. As his silhouette vanishes, she hurries to catch up with him. When she hears running water, she stops. A dark spring flows past her feet, the air wafting up moist and fungal. She walks forward, stepping carefully, rounds another corner. She ducks to miss the tunnel ceiling, which has lowered again.

Peanut reappears; he has circled back to fetch her, but he's moving fast, doesn't see her, and they bump into each other. He pulls away with a snort. He's impatient; he finds this settler girl slow and cumbersome. He loves these tunnels; he wields as much command over these corridors as he does over his own musculature, its curves and springs, tendons and cords. In the flickering dark, he points. The lantern reveals a narrow shaft plunging deeper into the earth.

—There, he says. He ties his rope to a stake and lowers himself into the waiting hole, gripping the lantern handle with his teeth as he drops down.

—It ain't deep, he calls up as he disappears. —It ain't so deep as it looks. Take the rope when I'm through; it'll hold you.

He reaches the shaft's base and tosses the end of the rope up to the surface. Barker hesitates for only a second before stepping forward. She'd twenty times rather be in this underground tunnel than back in the kitchen at the dogtrot fetching sweet breads for Uncle Wiley. She grips the rope and imitates her guide, stepping backward, descending. The shaft narrows as she drops jerkily down.

When she reaches the bottom, Peanut's lantern briefly blinds her. Then he lowers the lantern, and the tunnel reveals itself. —Welcome to the goldlands, her guide says.

Barker takes in the shimmering expanse around her. She's standing in nearly a foot of mud and subterranean water. The shaft walls have been reinforced with planking, but the sides of this tunnel are slick with trickling water. Light from the lantern streams outward, bouncing off the walls. Peanut swivels around, inspecting.

He tells Barker that they're finding ways now to extract ore from the earth's stomach, that the men use pumps and barrels to clear water when it rains and these tunnels flood. He tells her he'd rather work in a cave like this one than be back in middle Georgia threshing hay or hanging tobacco. He says he lost two cousins in the mine collapse last month but that hasn't put him off the work.

—Why not? Barker asks.

He tells her that the Widow Mary lets her workers, including her enslaved ones, pan the river and its tributaries at night for their own profit if they have the energy for it. Whatever they find between midnight and sunrise, they can keep for themselves, as long as, if they sell the gold, they sell it to Mary at her preferred rate.

—I'm saving up to buy my freedom, he says, thrusting out his chest. —Should have enough in four years.

—You don't feel afraid? Barker asks, thinking of this young man's cousins, of the cave-in, this unpredictable earth, these walls saying *No trespassing*.

—No, ma'am, Peanut says vigorously. —The Lord don't send lightning to the same place twice.

Barker looks down at her feet, at her uncle's boots half immersed in groundwater. Twinkling beneath the water is light, an iridescent pinprick, first here, then a glint elsewhere. Flecks of gold wink on and off in that water like stars. The more she looks, the more she sees, the expanse widening, sparkling, the goldlands in miniature.

Peanut looks down, sees what she sees. —It's everywhere, he says, nodding gravely. —This land, it's enchanted.

She reaches down and scoops up a handful of silt and mud. Flakes swim in the sediment, minerals and mica, not all of it gold, maybe not even a quarter of it. That doesn't matter. She would stay down here all night if Higgenbotham and the Widow Mary would let her. She would be all right here, she thinks, just her and the quiet, just her and nothing. Maybe Peanut for occasional company.

Yes, she could build an underground house here, preach to bats and beetles, proclaim to them the existence of sunlight; they'd never believe it. That would be enough. Wouldn't it?

For a minute, she's not sure she wants to see her father again.

Barker stays in that shaft until Peanut tells her the lantern's dying. —Time to head up, he says. —Mrs. Franklin's no friend to the tardy.

Mary insists they spend the night, won't take no for an answer. She feeds them trout dredged in cornmeal, dried peaches moistened with cream and honey. She lacks the supplies to whip up something fancier. There's gold in her river, but not enough meat or dry goods to feed her workers. She's had to ship in bacon and flour from Tennessee, pork from Kentucky. Soon she'll have to ship in corn too, she complains, if farmers around here don't start planting more of it.

She blames these shortages on gold fever and its distractions, gold fever and an influx of hungry newcomers. —Though I have as bad a case as anyone, she says. —I'm aggravatin' the problem. She laughs.

Higgenbotham escapes to a spare room for sleeping, while Mary takes Barker to her own quarters: a spacious bedroom with a red, white, and blue rag carpet, a rocking chair, and a four-poster bed. On a bureau, a half dozen candles light the place.

Mary ushers Barker over to her bed and pats it, motioning for her to sit. She says it's time for some woman talk. She wants Barker to explain how she came to be on the road at such a tender age.

—Clearly you're on the run from someone, she says. —Who is he?

Barker takes her time replying.

—I got into it with my uncle, she says. —Him and his men came after me. Now Mr. Higgenbotham's helping me find my pa.

—Why'd you get— Mary starts to ask what prompted the dispute but stops herself mid-question. —No, don't tell me. I believe I understand.

She pulls Barker to her, swaddles her in a lavender-scented embrace, crushing Barker's face in the bosom of her silk nightgown.

—You *endure*, Mary says when she releases her. She reaches for her handkerchief; this time, her eyes are genuinely watery. —One day, you'll look back on all that and feel *nothing*. You'll look back on whatever happened, and it'll be like someone else's life.

Barker tells her about her winning lottery ticket, the rights to forty acres she's received, and Mary nearly levitates. —Show me those papers, she demands.

Barker hands them to her, and the widow smooths the pages out on the quilt. She traces Higgenbotham's signature with an admiring finger.

—Well, ain't you the lucky one, she says. —You might be almost as lucky as I was.

She lights a pipe and proceeds to smoke it as she studies the papers. She removes the pipe from her mouth just long enough to look Barker up and down and ask if she'd like to be five thousand dollars richer.

—Ma'am? Barker says.

Mary offers to buy the rights to that gold lot off her right then and there. She says she can pay half in US money, half in scrip printed by her own company. —It's recognized by any bank in Georgia, she says proudly.

Barker takes the papers back, slides them into her saddlebag. —It ain't for sale, she says. —I can't sell those rights to you.

Mary takes another puff on her pipe, her eyes narrowing. She tells Barker that seven thousand dollars—yes, she's raising the offer—would allow a young woman to do whatever she pleased.

—You could buy horses, she says, her voice more tremulous than usual. —Or start a missionary school if you so desire. You look like that type. You could help your pa preach to the heathen; I bet he'd love that.

She scoots closer, slides a confiding arm around Barker's shoulder. She smells of tobacco and that lavender and, beneath those scents, something faintly oily.

—Or you could join my mining company; you could live here with me, Mary suggests. —We could expand the Franklin operation. We could carve out the mountains together. And if anyone tried to do ill to you, if your uncle showed up at my door, I'd have his stomach bayoneted through.

She smiles again, baring small white teeth. Barker declines a second time.

Mary presses harder. —Women have as much of a head for business as men do, she argues. —We could have such adventures, you and me. I'm all alone out here, she adds wistfully.

—I can't, Barker says. —I can't stay here, and I can't sell that gold lot to you. It ain't mine to sell. She pauses. —It's not my uncle's, but it's not mine either.

—You mean it's your pa's?

—No, Barker says. —It's the Indians'. Everybody knows that.

Mary's mouth tightens. She removes her arm from Barker's shoulder. —Well, look at you, she says. —The little moralist.

Barker meets her gaze.

—Look at you, Mary says again after a pause and takes a draw on her pipe. —Running from one man, chasing another, and trapped in the company of a third. She breathes out a plume of smoke and continues. —That third one might be better than the rest, but he's still a man, which means he's still trouble. That Matthew Higgenbotham is shuffling toward decrepitude.

—Then why're you so friendly to him? Barker asks.

Mary uses a small tamper to extinguish what's left in her pipe. —You need to own yourself, Barker McRae, she says. —Take charge of your life, of your future. Then you can speak to people however you choose, friendly or unfriendly, however it suits. That's what I always say: *Own yourself.*

—Do you say that to Peanut too? Barker replies. —Because I think he'd like to own himself more than almost anybody.

Mary hauls off and slaps her, a move so sudden it shocks them both. She's wearing a gold ring that cuts Barker's cheek, drawing a spot of blood.

—Watch yourself, the widow says.

11

TO LUMPKIN COUNTY, then. To the relocated camp meeting, which has hauled itself north with its tents and its crates full of Bibles, with its singers and criers and shouts of *Glory be*, a traveling theater for the soul. Away from Mary Franklin and her stamp mill and her slap to Barker's cheek, away from her tunnels collapsing on human beings. North by northeast they're headed, toward the Blue Ridge Mountains.

They set off in a wagon bonneted in canvas and pulled by two gray nags heaving unhappily in their traces. No more Pistol and Birdie—Mary refused to let them leave. She said the animals needed more rest and Higgenbotham a mount more befitting his standing and dignity than a pony. She placed the animals in neighboring stalls in her stable and promised to have her men care for them until Higgenbotham returned. She seemed intent on ensuring that the lottery messenger would have to see her again.

—And apples, Mary added as Barker eyed her suspiciously. —I'll give your horses apples every day you're not here.

Mary tried to kiss Higgenbotham farewell, but he managed to avoid most of it, receiving from her a glancing peck on the chin and a look that said more was owed. After a quick bow, he hurried away from her.

Higgenbotham uses a light hand on the grays now. It's a balmy morning, bursting with signs of spring, the pollen in the air dusting the horses yellow. Barker, who has hay fever, retreated to the wagon's interior, and from it come the sounds of sneezing and honking. Higgenbotham sits warm and dry up on the bench, immune to the nuisances of the season, the first time he's felt well in days.

He's snugly cosseted in a new overcoat, courtesy of Mary, and a full load of supplies fills the wagon interior, also thanks to Mary. He'll benefit from her affections even if he doesn't return them. Three bottles of whiskey rattle in a wooden crate, a comforting sound, and there are oats for the horses, blankets, and freshly washed ground cloths for sleeping. A second crate holds tins of salted meat, crackers, rye bread, dried apples, more dried peaches. He has never been so well outfitted. People will think he's digging in his heels in gold country rather than doing all he can to finish his job and get out of here.

Oh, Vermont, he thinks. *Wait for me!*

Higgenbotham spent the previous night in the open. He didn't wind up staying in Mary's spare room, even though she'd had the sheets aired and beaten for him. He felt uncomfortable indoors, on guard, wary of a potential late-night knock. Besides, it was a mild night, the first truly balmy night of the season. He walked outside and laid his bedroll in a clearing a hundred yards from Mary's house under a chestnut tree overlooking the river, far enough removed that he wouldn't be found overnight, even if the widow suffered a bout of loneliness and came looking. After a while, Scout came over and flopped down a few feet from him. Higgenbotham didn't mind that company. He didn't mind a wolfdog at all.

He awakened several hours later to find Scout pressed up against his side, snorting in his sleep, and a sprinkling of pollen over the blanket. For a moment he thought it had snowed gold. He reached over and rubbed Scout's stomach. The wolfdog started awake and righted himself with a look of surprise and embarrassment. His belly, Higgenbotham glimpsed in the starlight, was scratched raw and flea-bitten.

—Look at you, all chewed up, he said. —Now, how'd you go and let that happen?

Scout's tail thumped. Higgenbotham began to fuss over him, pulling tufts of winter fur from his hindquarters.

—Good Lord, they've bitten you raw, he said, and Scout's tail thumped harder.

Midmorning, Barker pokes her head out of the wagon's canvas closure and surveys the road. She has braided her hair tightly into two obstinate plaits. Her nose is red from sneezing. She's wearing the breeches and tunic Higgenbotham bought for her back at Leather's Ford. They're all she wears now; she prefers them. She has adapted too well. Scout pokes his head out from the bonnet beside her, ears pricked, watching crows fly overhead. He hitched a ride in the wagon this morning.

—Get down, Barker tells him, but he doesn't budge from her side.

She calls out to Higgenbotham. She informs him that she doesn't want anything tagging along after her that she has to worry about keeping alive and feeding. Wolfdogs are a distraction from their mission.

Higgenbotham nods briefly, doesn't look back over his shoulder at her. —Good luck, he says. —Good luck telling the universe your preferred terms and conditions for what it sends in your direction.

On the road, they pass Cherokee farms and homesteads, chicken coops and corncribs, shaded paddocks, fields being readied for planting. By summer, there will be wheat and oats here, or corn, and indigo everywhere. Modest cabins dappled with sun and shadow come into view along the way. Two colorfully dressed women cross the road leading a red and white steer. They swing a young child by the arms between them, letting him skip and kick. The boy wears a blue jay feather in a headband, a waistcloth, and not much else.

The child releases his caretakers' arms long enough to stick his thumbs in his ears and waggle his fingers at Barker. She leans out the wagon bonnet and waves at him. The boy makes a silly face; she makes one too, imitating his. He squeals with delight until one of the women grabs his arms and barks an admonition at him. He begins to cry. Barker and Higgenbotham travel on.

When they've passed the farmland, Higgenbotham speaks to Barker with some severity.—Stop that, he says, calling back to her from his driver's seat. —Stop bothering the Indians. They have enough troubles already.

She reaches out and taps him on the shoulder. —Troubles you and your lottery helped hand 'em, she replies.

Onward they ride.

That night, in woods razed by the clearing fires of settlers, they make camp beneath the charred bones of old pine trees and do not speak. Higgenbotham prepares biscuits and corn grits flavored with roadside oregano. Barker's hay fever has left her without an appetite, so he consumes both their portions. He falls asleep by the campfire, dreams of Ruth, his long-ago wife, wonders if she is living or deceased.

Barker stays in the wagon with the bonnet drawn tight. She does not let Scout sleep with her. She dreams of foul acts that have no words, the first time she's dreamed about the events of Maundy Thursday since she fled Watkinsville. She awakens sweating and gasping for breath.

In the morning, they quarrel over the right way to fold and pack the ground covers. Then they disagree over whether Scout needs to be fed from the tins or if he can hunt down breakfast on his own. Barker holds the latter opinion.

—We'll make him soft, she says. —He'll forget how to fend for himself.

—Too late for that, Higgenbotham says. Scout has bounded over and nosed her hand, pushing with more insistency when no food is forthcoming. He gives up and trots over to Higgenbotham, receiving a biscuit for his efforts. He stays by Higgenbotham after that.

Next they argue over whether Higgenbotham has drunk too much coffee. —First the whiskey, then the coffee, he says. —What else am I doing that vexes you? Do you want to draft a list?

Barker spends the morning on the driver's bench ignoring him. The sun slides above a burned ridgeline. She reads the Bible in her lap. Later, she dives back into the wagon, finds paper, quill, and ink in one of the crates Mary provided. She settles in to write a letter, this time to her aunt. She gets as far as *Dear Aunt Elma* before giving up.

When she returns to the driver's bench, she produces her Bible and reads again for some time, muttering under her breath. After a while, Higgenbotham asks what she's doing. Barker tells him she's memorizing scripture. She says that in her experience, the Bible is easier to listen to than the opinions of most people.

—Don't let me stop you, he says. —I'll be over here not speaking.

The grays groan north, grooved scars visible along their shoulders as Higgenbotham guides them forward. Hard labor, months spent hauling rocks on hickory sleds along the Etowah in service to the Widow Mary, has ground these horses down.

By midday they have climbed into low hills abundant with deer and greening with the season's first ferns. Near the top of a rise, they come upon a postal coach that has stopped to correct a loose back wheel. The driver says he's headed to Lumpkin County, specifically to Dahlonega, a name lifted from the Cherokee that means *the place of yellow metal.*

—Those Injuns, the postal driver says. —Someone ought to set 'em straight, tell 'em it's a mineral. They think gold's a point on a map. They think it's a location.

He keeps his eyes on Barker the whole time he's talking.

Higgenbotham helps with the postal wagon repair for old times' sake; he tells the postman he used to be a carrier. He asks who the driver might have seen coming and going; he inquires about militia riders. The man tells him he did see a company of some sort on the road headed toward Dahlonega or the town immediately south of it, Auraria.

—Were they militia? Or preachers? Higgenbotham asks. —There's a revival coming.

—They weren't men of the cloth, the postal driver says. —They might've been Pony Club. They had a lot of horses. Though who knows any more. Nowadays everyone's looking for a good ride, for a fast filly.

He winks at Barker.

—That's enough, Higgenbotham says to him.

Later, after the man has moved on, Barker resumes her seat beside Higgenbotham on the driver's bench. She asks if he wants to know what parts of scripture she has been memorizing. She's ready for a recitation—she wants to practice on him.

The wagon sways as he declines her offer. This road is rocky, increasingly unreliable, he tells her; it's consuming his attention.

—I have my hands full, he says. —This road's treacherous.

Barker looks doubtfully at him. The road has been bad the whole time, and he wasn't worried about it earlier.

—Also, Higgenbotham adds, because he knows he's letting her down. —Truth be told, matters of religion aren't my favorite subject.

He lifts his hat far enough to scratch his hairline. —To think that someone's up there, watching all this mess down here, he says. —And doing nothing about it!

She slouches against the wagon board. Higgenbotham taps the reins, maneuvering the grays around a knot of tangled tree roots in the middle of the road.

—I could've made seven thousand dollars, you know, she says after a minute. —I could've earned seven thousand dollars from that widow and been free of you. She wanted my lot number.

Higgenbotham shrugs. —Go right ahead, he says. —Her offer likely still stands. You want to do business with the Widow Mary? Be my guest. But she's a hard driver.

He points at the welted scar tissue across the grays' shoulders. —*Caveat emptor.*

—Stop swearing at me, Barker says.

They sleep outdoors again, along a wide flat creek interrupted by silver boulders. They can't risk staying at the two travelers' rests they've seen. Wiley's men could be there. Anything along the general route toward Dahlonega and the revival is unsafe, in Higgenbotham's opinion.

That night, he can't keep awake, despite his intent to stay alert. Light rain comes and goes and settles into a listless drizzle. He sleeps on his ground cover under a tarp strung between two flowering rhododendrons. Rain drips steadily from the leaves, like a ticking metronome. When the rain passes, the temperature drops again.

Barker stays in the wagon with Scout; she has given up trying to send him away. She has surrendered. He's warm and furry, and she's cold and not. The two of them curl under a blanket together, huddling close.

Lying nearby on his ground cover, wearing his coat for warmth, Higgenbotham dreams of the night, years ago, when he stopped to camp in southwest Georgia and discovered a mass of muscled fur and flashing eyes snarling down at him from the branch of a nearby tree, a quartet of fangs bared in the flare of a match lit by his own trembling hand. It was a panther, as velveted and unfathomable as the sky.

He awakens from the dream in a cold sweat. Residual fever? Mourning for bygone days, more likely. European bounties on predator animals have wiped out Georgia's wolves, foxes, wildcats of several varieties. He suspects he will not see another panther in his lifetime.

Hours later, he opens his eyes to find daylight spreading across a cloudy eastern sky and the grays gone. Thieves have stolen Mary's horses; they severed tethers from stakes and led the pair off. The Pony Club has finally touched him. All these months, all these years he has spent on the road, and at last it has happened.

Barker emerges from the wagon hugging her chest, her hair slipping out of its braids. She stares at the place where the grays should have been. —What happened? she cries. —Where'd they go?

—If I knew the answer to that, I wouldn't be standing here like a man with one leg, would I, Higgenbotham replies. —They're gone, that's what's happened.

At least it wasn't his own horses, he thinks; at least it wasn't faithful Mandy or newcomer Pistol. And maybe the grays wanted to run away; maybe they wanted to try their luck with a captor other than the Widow Mary.

Barker sneezes. She wipes her nose on her sleeve, a habit he would like to train out of her. Scout roams along the creek, belatedly checking for a scent trail, tail high and switching. The wolfdog slept too soundly last night; he failed to wake up when the horse thieves visited. He was too cozy under his blanket, too securely nestled up against this girl, this child, who, to the wolfdog, smells of loneliness and cinnamon.

Higgenbotham takes a long breath. Their journey has just become that much harder.

—What'll we do *now?* Barker asks, thinking the same, longingly gazing at the wagon seat and, inside, the crates filled with supplies, too numerous and heavy to carry. —We were supposed to reach the camp meeting today.

Higgenbotham lifts his face to the blank sky. Pony Club men are outlaws through and through; those bandits would as soon stab a man as learn his name. And what they'd do to a girl he'd rather not think about. He won't pursue them.

—We'll do what people the world over have done for centuries, he says. He hears his mother's tone as he speaks, is surprised by it. —We'll walk. A good brisk walk never hurt anyone.

He tries to moderate his tone, finds he cannot. —Or is that too much of an imposition on you, Preacher Barker?

By foot now, through trail and trace, through coppice and canebrake. By foot, with their saddlebags hefted over their shoulders, stuffed near to bursting. They make slow progress and exchange few words, the promise of mountains in the distance. Abandoned huts and shacks sprawl alongside streams, the doors yawing open on broken hinges, reminders of rushers come and gone, men who found their fortune or more likely did not and moved on, departed for the next futile dream.

By midday, the sun still has not appeared, and the wind blows colder, disavowing the promise of spring. The farther north they hike, the worse the chill grows. Is that frost on the daffodils? Discouragement steals over Higgenbotham. The ferns here have curled like potato bugs braced against an invader.

They make camp early, before dusk, in one of the vacated shacks. Higgenbotham doesn't care to start a fire, even though he's cold. He feels spent; his heart is still beating faster than normal; all that walking has done him in. He would sleep till noon if he could.

He arranges his ground cover on the hard dirt floor, pulls his coat tight and his lone blanket up, and lies there, teeth chattering. Barker flops down on the other side of the hut. It's tight enough quarters that if they each reached an arm out, they could touch. They don't reach their arms out. Scout creeps back and forth between them, checking one person, then the other, finally settling down to lick at his paw. Barker's so quiet that when Higgenbotham closes his eyes, he can pretend he's alone, back on his old postal route, back when a man could ride for days before he reached Georgia's western border, though his route rarely took him that far. Outside the shack, a barred owl calls; another whistles back. *Me! Me! Me! Pick me!* The petulant sound of a juvenile.

In the morning, Barker shows him a blister on her heel, as large and round as a silver dollar. Higgenbotham bandages the sore, and they keep walking. Barker hikes with a limp now, with a defiant pioneer hitch. Over their heads, the sky is the color of old cotton.

They pass plantations along creeks and streams, sprawling homesteads that have helped define the Cherokee Nation; successful Indian planters have set up homes around here, intermarried, acquired orchards, slaves, mills, horses, and cattle. None of that will help now that hundreds of thousands of white Georgians have decided they want them out of here. Barker squares her shoulders, keeps marching, Scout keeping pace beside her.

Higgenbotham has had a few blisters in his day. The bad ones are worse than tooth infections. You can always stop eating for a day, but you can't stop walking, not if you're cutting dirt, not if you're on the run and in gold country.

—You can recite your Bible verses to me, he says to her after a while. —If it helps.

She declines with a regal shake of the head, keeps limping, doesn't glance at him. They're still a day's walk from Dahlonega. If they had the horses, they'd be there by now.

Midafternoon, they lighten their load, paring the saddlebags down to the essentials. Higgenbotham will carry the crackers, the coffee grinder and beans, the ground covers, the corn grits, the whiskey, the pistol and shot pouch. Barker will carry the dried apples and peaches, a flask for water, a jar of pickles, one blanket, and her Bible.

—Leave the Bible, Higgenbotham says. —We're headed into a revival. Bibles will be raining from the skies.

—I'll leave my Bible if you leave your whiskey, she replies, which shuts him up.

Any militia uniforms, duck for cover, Higgenbotham thinks but doesn't say to Barker. *Any men with two eye patches, dodge them like your life depends on it. Any preachers with an aversion to performing their paternal duties, run like the wind.*

The question is in which direction.

12

WILEY WOOD'S NOT without recourse either.

Give him time, that's all he needs, time and patience and twelve—no, make that ten—armed men from the 221st District; time and a prayer to stave off infection. An abscess would be the end; pus is the enemy. That and Wiley's own obsolescence. If he can beat those foes and evade the cholera that took two of his men, he wins.

And he doesn't need sight to find Barker.

That's what he tells Scissors, anyway, this neighbor's son, this surly driver to whom Wiley speaks without ceasing as the wagon rattles north. The young man hunches his shoulders whenever Wiley addresses him, receiving each word like a blow, absorbing all, offering nothing in return. Talking to Scissors is like talking to a canyon; all Wiley hears is his own echo. He finds such stoniness aggravating, the indifference almost physically painful; he would like to flog him. But this driver is not his to abuse.

Their journey thus far has not been easy. With the end of that last wintry storm, the roads thawed to mud, and the wagon wheels wobbled recklessly as the miles passed. They crossed one river, the Oconee, and nearly tipped into it, Scissors disregarding Elma's admonition to take the ferry; they forded a second, the Chattahoochee, thankfully shallower. They crossed a third, the Chestatee, by bridge, and a fourth, the Etowah, by ferry. All these crossings in his bonneted throne made Wiley seasick, made him feel like a queasy river lord.

He met up with his men at Scudder's settlement and sent them on ahead the morning they departed. The militia's horses are faster than Wiley's borrowed mules, so he pledged to catch up with them at the camp meeting. He didn't want to slow the company down. The men of the 221st District suspect Barker is headed to the revival, headed for her father. Through inquiries, they've determined that's where the preacher is likely to be. Wiley agrees that Barker is chasing Lorenzo, agrees that wherever Barker thinks her father is, she'll go. Lorenzo's true location matters not in this equation. All that matters is where his daughter *believes* she'll find him. After all, who else does she have to chase?

To pass the time, Wiley asks Scissors how he came by his name. Surely this youth is called that because of his long legs and bony frame. —You must've come out of the womb resembling handle and blade, Wiley says, not unadmiringly.

—I never received no facts on the matter, sir, Scissors replies, and lapses into silence again.

Wiley claps his hand on his companion's shoulder, suffused with passing sympathy. He tells the neighbor's son that Scissors is a fine name. He receives no response. He hears a chorus of buzzing and humming, spring rising to life around the wagon, bees and cicadas and biting flies tormenting the mules, insects that he will hear but never glimpse again. He will never see Barker again either, not even if they catch her. But what a man sees is never the whole truth anyway.

Midday, Johnny Thrasher—the rider everyone calls Kerchief—circles back on the company's route to check on Wiley. Kerchief's palomino gallops up alongside the mules, slowing to keep pace with the wagon. Kerchief talks to Scissors, not Wiley. He asks the driver what supplies he needs for the night ahead, how the captain's faring. They'll be camping again tonight; does Captain Wood require anything? Extra blankets? Water? Bandages?

Wiley strongly dislikes people talking about him like he isn't there. Why does everyone do that around a blind man? He waves Kerchief back to the road. —Go, go! he commands. —I don't need anything. Just the one who did this to me.

Kerchief speaks to the captain directly then. He tells him that the men of the 221st District can't keep running their horses with no decent place to sleep and no reasonable end to the chase in sight. They need a promise that their search is almost over. The militiamen have their own cares, their own jobs at the mill and labors in the field, their own families to feed.

—*They* need a promise? *I* need a promise, Wiley retorts. —I need you to find her. Y'all have a job to do. Every one of you stays on that hunt until I say so. Remember what I offered, Johnny.

Wiley has pledged a reward for Barker's capture. He has promised his company men the rights to forty golden acres—his winnings in the lottery—once they find his niece and deliver her and the grant she stole to him. He plans to give those land rights to whoever has stayed on the hunt, the acreage to be improved, mined, sold, or divided up among the faithful however they want.

Before his injury, of course, Wiley briefly coveted that land for himself; before his injury, he jigged for joy at the prospect of owning forty acres. But that was when he could still imagine looking upon his winnings with his one good eye.

Now he lives in the dark, and all he wants is Barker.

—It's a generous offer, Kerchief says.

The young man's tone doesn't match his statement; he sounds sardonic, not grateful. Wiley notices these discrepancies now that he doesn't have vision interfering with his attention.

—Find Barker, and you'll have your golden acres, Wiley declares, tilting a bit on the wagon seat, mildly lightheaded. —Find her, and you'll be wealthy men.

He recalls Kerchief's lineage, that mixed blood coursing through the young man's veins; he decides to press his point. —And you, Johnny, you'll get back your birthright, Wiley says. —You'll earn back a corner of Injun country. He laughs. —You can smoke a peace pipe on those forty acres, build a wigwam on 'em.

Kerchief clears his throat. This young militiaman has never darkened the doorway of a wigwam in his life, and they both know it. Johnny Thrasher grew up in a house with columns out front and a livery out back, both structures finer than any cabin Wiley ever owned.

—Scissors, Kerchief says, shifting back to the driver. —The men'll make camp away from the river tonight.

The two younger men exchange words about where the company will stop and how long until the mules can catch up. Kerchief thanks Scissors and rides off, his palomino kicking clods of mud behind her as she departs.

—Come back, Wiley calls, demands, to the air, to the road, to his militiaman. —Don't leave; we weren't done! He turns in his seat, addresses Scissors. —Call him back, boy, will you?

But his driver ignores him.

That night, as the company camps in a soggy meadow southwest of Auraria, Wiley has Scissors wash his stitches in gin. —Debride me, he instructs him.

He roars and flails when the alcohol soaks his sewn eyelid. Scissors scrambles away.

—Get back here, Wiley says. —Get over here and keep pouring. It must be done or death will come for me!

Scissors returns to the captain's side, cautiously. He rinses the blind man's eyelid, wipes it, and pours again; he cleanses the wound until the skin around Wiley's eye socket is raw and the stitches drenched and fizzing.

Wiley is obsessed with cleanliness; he fears putrefaction, contaminants, shame in general. And as Scissors puts fresh gauze on the wound and replaces the patch, Wiley, lying on his pallet, finds himself thinking of Preacher Lorenzo. He considers the circuit rider's words that time he heard him speaking before an audience. *We are washed in the blood*—that was what Lorenzo McRae said. Could Wiley be washed in a similar way? Could suffering be redemptive, regardless of what the sufferer did?

He lifts his head long enough to let Scissors tie the patch strings in a bow at the back of his head, neither as neatly nor as tightly as the bow Barker used to tie for him. He can taste gin in the corners of his mouth. The last thing Wiley saw in this world was his niece's face hovering above him. Or was she hovering beside him? Where exactly in the bed was she?

Barker! The girl he rescued, the thief who owes him everything.

Call him what you will, accuse him how you must, but never once in the past two years has Wiley let that child stray from the field of his attentions. Never once did he ignore her or abandon her like her father has done. He has never *not* thought of her.

—Here's your eye, Barker said, her last words to him, to the best of his recollection, that cursed Maundy Thursday. —*Now leave me be.*

Little filth. He cannot live without her.

Several preachers Barker and Higgenbotham encounter on the road to Auraria have seen Lorenzo McRae. Or at least, they know who he is.

He's a living legend, these circuit riders say, slowing their mounts long enough to answer Higgenbotham's questions under a brilliantly blue late April sky. *He brings crowds of a thousand to their knees. Hundreds come away slain in the Spirit every time he preaches.*

But no one has seen him recently.

A Baptist on a donkey remembers seeing him up in Blairsville. A Methodist on a packhorse places him in Carnesville, or Clarkesville, or was it Clayton? A Moravian claims to have spotted Lorenzo in Ball Ground setting up a school for children. A Presbyterian has him with the publishers of the *Cherokee Phoenix* in New Echota.

But where is he *now*, Higgenbotham asks them, circuit riding or missionizing? Saving settler souls or starting Indian schools?

No one knows.

Is he headed to the camp meeting? Is he headed where all the other traveling preachers are going? To the northern part of new-formed Lumpkin County? Can anyone confirm?

Shrugs all around in the bright afternoon sunshine. The road they're on leads past several mining operations and is well trafficked; it's a gamble for Higgenbotham and Barker to use this route, to risk being seen in the open. But Higgenbotham has the gnawing feeling that they're running out of time.

He goes where the Spirit tells him, one rider crowned in a tall top hat declares. Another reminds Higgenbotham that men like McRae take no pay for their preaching and therefore cannot be pinned down.

He's a martyr, a prophet, a radical; you could have called him a saint if the Methodists bestowed such titles, if the Methodist leaders hadn't grown alarmed and discarded him.

The more these preachers laud Barker's father, the more Higgenbotham's foreboding increases. In his experience, men that charitable, that selfless, usually retain some glaring flaw, some morbid or mortal shortcoming. The question is: What's Lorenzo's?

Higgenbotham glances over at Barker.

When she hears the traveling ministers describe their sightings of her father, her smile takes over her face; she becomes ninety pounds of effervescence. She pokes Higgenbotham in the arm. *See!* As if they've been arguing over her father's merits this whole time. Maybe they have been. When a flock of honking geese pass over the road in a V formation, Barker skips high, batting the air, a gesture of hope, of *Finally this walk is nearly over,* however inaccurate that might be. Higgenbotham averts his gaze.

A one-armed Christian Connection minister riding an exasperated piebald tells Higgenbotham that he saw Lorenzo McRae not seven days earlier. —He was near the

Etowah, the preacher says, sawing at the piebald's reins with his one hand. —Preaching to the miners. Warning them the land they're digging up isn't theirs to defile.

—Sounds like Lorenzo, Higgenbotham says.

—He has taken the Indians' plight as his own, the man says. —Some miners beat him for his pains. They didn't care for his words.

The preacher glances over at Barker, uncertain how much he should say in front of a child.

Barker brings Birdie to a stop. The colt whinnies and paws at the road; he doesn't like the piebald, whose irritability is contagious. —Where's he *now*? Barker asks. —Is my pa all right? Is he coming to the camp meeting?

The preacher looks over her head at Higgenbotham and shrugs; his empty sleeve twitches. The piebald pulls at the bit, head tossing.

—Poor child, he says. —To have a father like that one!

He nods at Higgenbotham, tugs his horse around, and rides off.

They walk as long and far that day as Barker's blistered heel will allow. No one offers them a ride—the preachers' mounts can't afford the extra weight. The oxen traveling this road are worn down from carting Bibles, and the horses and mules pulling supply wagons aren't doing much better. Circuit riders are hard on their animals.

Barker and Scout do not tire, trotting ahead despite Barker's blister. Thoughts of her father have given her hope, and hope has temporarily rejuvenated her. She dashes into a roadside field, returns with violet phlox crowning her red hair. She tells Higgenbotham it's for May Day, though the first of May is more than a week away. What day is it, anyway? Higgenbotham can't recall. His head has started throbbing. The winged migrants of spring have been arriving, cuckoo, warbler, whippoorwill, their songs filling woods and sky. Barker's good mood irks him, her eagerness, her belief that her father is near and that he is wonderful.

Higgenbotham tastes something sour. He spits into the dirt.

—I need water, he says. He reaches into his saddlebag and retrieves the one bottle of whiskey he permitted himself to pack. He uncaps it; Barker throws him a disappointed look. He feels he has known her five years already.

That afternoon, he tells her to prepare herself for the possibility that they will not find her father at the revival. Or, worse, that they will find him but he won't take her back. Something hard and bitter has lodged in Higgenbotham's throat. Life does not dole out happy endings the way this girl thinks it does; someone needs to tell her.

—I know you don't believe in him, Barker says. —I get what you think, mister.

—Stop calling me *mister*, he replies.

They make camp outside an abandoned travelers' rest, a rotting clapboard building set back from the road and lined with livestock pens, the setup adjacent to an empty stable and a henhouse. Drovers used to keep their hogs and cattle in those pens, holding the doomed animals in these enclosures overnight while they sought a warm bed and a hot meal for themselves, brief sanctuary from the road and the woods beyond it. Higgenbotham tries the front door of the travelers' rest, but it's latched tight, and he's not up for breaking in. He tries the stable, but rats have overtaken it. The henhouse is ankle-deep in dried bird droppings that fill the air with white dust when he moves inside. He exits coughing. Better to sleep outdoors.

—Is there no one else you can stay with? he asks Barker as they unpack their bedrolls. The sun is setting, throwing the travelers' rest behind them in shadow. Scout has disappeared inside the henhouse. —Any family members willing to take you in, anywhere at all, if we can't find him?

Pessimism has taken hold of him. He fears he will be burdened with this child forever. —Someone on your mother's side? he suggests. —Any other aunts, a grandmother? Or a kind teacher, perhaps?

Barker absorbs these questions, the last hint of daylight slipping away, her bedroll clutched to her chest. —I'll find him, she insists. —I will.

Higgenbotham sighs.

—Barker, he says. —We can't move through life flinging ourselves from one false hope to the next. He pauses; his mother is taking over his words again. —At a certain point, we must face facts.

Barker unties her bedroll and shakes it out, snapping it in his direction. She quotes Romans at him. It's her favorite verse, she announces. *—And we know that all things work together for good to them that love God, to them who are the called according to His purpose.*

—What the hell does that mean? Higgenbotham says.

She stamps her bedroll into place, bends to smooth the creases. In the dusk, her eyes are enormous and judging.

She tells Higgenbotham that if he had any faith, he would understand you had to *believe* those words to make them come true. You couldn't dismiss God's promises and expect things to go the way you wanted them to.

—You have to sink your teeth into them, she says. —God only answers prayers if you believe He'll answer them. If you don't believe, He won't do nothing.

Higgenbotham feels his facial muscles tightening. —Won't do *anything*, he says, correcting her. —And I don't need you to interpret the Bible for me.

—Then why'd you ask? she replies, crossing her arms. —You asked me what the verse meant.

He squats down to empty his saddlebag, takes a few deep breaths. Scout emerges from the henhouse coated in guano dust and sneezing.

—One advantage of having lived six decades, he finally says, is that you come to realize most of life is not in your control. Not even if you pray about it. Maybe *especially* not if you pray about it. People who pray set themselves up to be disappointed.

He pokes around in the bag, finds a cloth, and uses it to brush off Scout. Barker watches him, her lips set in a hard line.

—All I'm saying, Higgenbotham continues as silver-brown fur reappears on Scout's sides and hindquarters, is that you need to steel yourself for the likelihood, the fairly high probability, that your father is not going to take you back. Either he doesn't have the time, or the ability, or the will. It's one of those three. It might not be his fault. But you need to be ready.

He pats Scout on the rump, cleanup finished.

—My pa's a good man, Barker flings back.

—I'm sure he is, Higgenbotham says, nodding. —He might be too good, is the problem. He might have gotten in so deep with his missionizing, he can't go back to being a father.

He takes his blanket and arranges it on top of her bedroll—she can use the extra warmth. They'll sleep far enough apart tonight to be alone but close enough that Scout can lie between them and still think he's supervising them both.

—He'll take me when he sees me, Barker says, her arms still crossed, her expression miserable and insistent. —I know it. I know him and you don't. He needs me.

—Then why has he gone so long without sending word? Higgenbotham reaches back into his bag and produces his whiskey bottle. —You haven't heard from him in almost two years. You weren't living on an ice floe. There are riders; there are coaches. There are so many postal routes these days, your pa could hail a letter carrier anytime he stopped to water his horse.

He uncaps the bottle. There's a tin cup around here somewhere, but he lacks the patience to hunt for it. —He could have written, he continues. —He could have found out if your aunt and uncle were handling you fairly. He never did. You were in danger. That much is clear to me, even without you imparting details. You were not well treated. And he never checked.

His volume is rising. This isn't his mother talking anymore.

—He couldn't send for me, Barker retorts. Her cheeks are aflame. She reaches down and picks up her bag. —You don't know what it's like on the circuit, mister, what dangers and trials he endures.

—There is no trial greater than that of a parent separated from his child, Higgenbotham thunders. He hauls himself up to his full height, all six aging feet, bottle still in hand. —A good father would cross an ocean by raft to find his child. He would journey through a wilderness filled with wildcats. Your pa was fortunate enough to have a child? It was his duty to care for you. He pauses. —There's nothing so difficult standing in his way, after all, nothing except a forest and a doomed nation.

He takes a swig from the bottle. He's not sure if he's referring to the Cherokee people or the Georgians who invaded.

—You don't know him, Barker says again, whispering.

—I know enough, Higgenbotham says. —I recognize when a man like Lorenzo McRae is on a fool's errand. Which means you and I are on a fool's errand also.

She throws down her bag and stalks into the woods. Higgenbotham watches her leave. He sets about gathering twigs and leaf litter to build a campfire, to do something, anything. He takes another pull of his whiskey. To pace himself, he boils ground beans for coffee. Then he pours the whiskey into the coffee, and he drinks that down too.

When she returns, her face is red and blotchy, but she's pleasant to him, or at least pleasanter than before. She helps him stoke the campfire and fry up corn fritters. She says nothing about what Higgenbotham said, words he regrets already. She says nothing about his drinking either. He drinks more, to provoke a response from her. Still nothing. She's so agreeable, it alarms him.

They eat by firelight while listening to tree frogs chirping from poplars behind the travelers' rest, the amphibious chorus so loud that even if Barker and Higgenbotham were on speaking terms, they wouldn't have been able to hear each other talk. Barker places her plate, her dinner unfinished, on the ground and tells him—nearly shouting—that she's tired. She asks if she can wash her plate and fork in the morning.

—Don't worry about it, he hollers back. —I'll take care of the washing.

She lies down under the blanket he gave her. Higgenbotham cleans their forks and plates and rinses them in a nearby stream. The frogs begin to quiet down. When he returns, her back is to him and the fire. She's so small under that blanket, she might as well be a rabbit. Yes, that's what he has gone and done—he has gone and crushed a rabbit.

—Do you want to play a game? he asks her. Higgenbotham detests games, but he's uneasy now; he's disconcerted by how silent she is. —Chuck farthing? Button whizzer? I have buttons and twine.

—No, thank you, comes the polite reply.

—Well, good night, then, he says.

Barker echoes the phrase back. —Good night.

But it doesn't sound like her; it sounds like that damn rabbit, if a rabbit could use words.

Higgenbotham's heart catches on something.

That night he hears chittering and hooting, screeching and snuffling, creatures moving through dense forest beyond the clearing, above the trees and below them, in the brush. He hears a wolf howl in the far distance, its cry anguished and piercing. Scout, startled awake, lifts his head and wails a reply, a lungful of time and sorrow. When he finishes, the wolfdog blinks in surprise; he didn't know his own voice. From deep in the trees, the wolf howls back.

For Higgenbotham, the sound conjures up moonlit roads, dead hemlocks, unmarked graves, bones in clay; lost faith, charity, hope. He brings out his pistol and loads it, though he could never shoot a wolf. If true danger came from that source, he would fire into the air, nothing more. To keep Scout from bolting, he puts him on a rope and loops the end around the trunk of a nearby sourwood. Though he wonders if the wolfdog *ought* to bolt; he wonders if finding a new pack might be better for him.

—Pick your friends with care, he tells his canine companion, which is something innkeeper Thrasher, his old friend Thrasher, used to say to him.

He awakens to a spent fire and a morning fog as dense as steam from a kettle. The earth smells of worms and millipedes and other crawling things. He putters around the dead campfire, rekindling the embers. He checks Barker's bedroll and blanket—she's not in them. He grinds more coffee beans and boils his coffee. Then he waits; she must be doing her private business. He'll give her time. He drinks his coffee.

A hawk screams overhead, invisible in the fog. Higgenbotham finds four strips of bacon wrapped in paper and lodged in the bottom of his bag, a pleasant surprise. He sizzles the bacon up over the fire, frees Scout from his lead, and feeds him half the bacon. No dog, not even a wolfdog, will have to hunt for breakfast when he travels with Matthew Higgenbotham.

Scout gobbles the scraps and lopes off. Higgenbotham sets down his cup. He scans the line of poplars. Still no Barker.

Then he notices that the pistol he placed beside his bedroll last night is gone.

—Damn it all, he says.

Swiftly he tamps out the campfire. He ferrets through their supplies—the dried apples, the pickles, the pistol and shot are all missing. What else? Her Bible. Of course. What exactly did he say to her last night? He said she shouldn't expect to have a father waiting for her. He said that even if Lorenzo McRae was found, he likely wouldn't take her.

Oh, Lord, he's done it now.

Higgenbotham makes his way up to the road. His throat is in a vise grip. He strains to see past the fog, the whirling condensate so thick, he's like a man walking through a spiderweb. Dimly he can make out the narrow curving lane headed north. Barker's not on that road.

Think, he tells himself. *Repair this.*

She must have left hours ago, in the middle of the night. She could be at Auraria by now, or even Dahlonega; she could be at the revival. Maybe she's finding her happy ending after all, her beloved father waiting for her, welcoming her with open arms.

Or maybe not. And Wiley and his militia are still out there.

Scout zigzags across the campsite, rounds the travelers' rest, runs to the road, and comes back, tail high with concentration. He's trying to pick up Barker's scent, but he's not a bloodhound; that's not his specialty. His talent is pack life and protecting. He trots in agitated circles.

Go to Dahlonega? That's the question; that's the only question Higgenbotham needs to be asking. Should he chase a disappeared child who doesn't want to travel with him or view her departure as a blessing in disguise? He glances down. His coat and vest are worn through, no longer capable of providing much warmth. His stockings are more holes than fiber. His boots have another week or two before they give up the ghost. And higher up's not much better. His hat is hardly a hat anymore, the felting rubbed thin, the brim permanently slouching.

He could head south if he wanted. He could deliver his last four lottery notifications, collect his final payment from the commissioners, and get out of Georgia, flee the goldlands while he still can. Leave before it's too late, before he's too old to travel, and he's eventually buried in some roadside Methodist or Baptist cemetery without a single tree to shade him.

Scout nudges Higgenbotham in the knee and whines.

—I know, Higgenbotham says. —You'd rather be with her than me.

Scout whines again. *How do you know that's what I mean?*

—Because it's obvious, he says. —Because who wouldn't feel that way.

The fog is closing in on him. An eastern phoebe plummets from the overstory, lands in a bush, and chides him. He waves the bird back into the trees.

The image of his poor Ruth comes to him then, the three wax dolls he did in fact make for her, his quiet memorial to their lost infants. He remembers that after opening the basket in which he had carefully arranged them, his wife pushed the offering away. She pushed so hard that the basket tipped off the table, and the dolls fell out. One of the waxen heads broke off and rolled under the stove, where it might remain to this day, for all he knows; Higgenbotham left that house in Milledgeville a few weeks after Ruth departed. He's never been back. He's been a man of the road ever since.

His hand reaches for the bottle.

Don't, he tells himself. *Don't. Old man, get on with it.*

He shoves the whiskey into his bag, shoulders it, and whistles for Scout. They walk north.

13

YOU PREACHED IN front of him once. He paid attention to you then; he couldn't avoid you. This event took place a couple of months after his failed sermon at the Tallulah canyon, the sermon where he lost God's face afterward.

It started when your father suffered a coughing fit in a chapel in the west Georgia town of Columbus, near the Chattahoochee headwaters. You had just turned twelve. You were in the front row of a spacious, newly built sanctuary, watching him. Your mother was not at the service—she wasn't feeling well that morning.

Between coughs, your father asked for water and gestured for the congregation members to forge ahead and sing a hymn. Grumbles rippled to the back of the meeting room. This Columbus crowd didn't countenance delays, didn't like the visiting circuit rider any more than he liked them. These were bankers and shipmasters and lawyers with their wives in tow, powerful men who had cleared the Creek Indians off the waterfront to begin their moneymaking in earnest. Lorenzo had come to put the fear of God in them.

Before he could cough out another word, you walked up to the front of the chapel, stood beside him at the pulpit, and spoke.

It wasn't a planned action. It wasn't a conscious decision. To this day, you feel the choice was made for you. You remember what you said. In a voice loud enough to carry to the back of the chapel, you called out:

—*Blessed are the meek: for they shall inherit the earth!*

The bankers went quite still. Two women in the second row began murmuring to each other behind their fans.

But you were ready. The Beatitudes are like peach cobbler; no one dislikes peach cobbler. No one except bankers and lawyers, you learned that day.

Sallying forth, you continued to speak as your father stood to one side and stared at you, dumbfounded, still racked with half-suppressed coughs.

You told those congregation members that your sermon that day was about what it meant to be poor and what it meant to be rich. The poor on earth will become the rich in heaven, you said; whatever is the case here on earth will be reversed up in heaven.

—So you all had better get ready, you said. —Because you're about to become eternity's paupers lest you repent.

The bankers gazed back in cold silence. Lorenzo gripped the sides of the podium, waiting for a glass of water that never came. Had it resided in you all this time, he must have wondered, this reservoir of his own convictions? When had his daughter learned to read his mind?

But you didn't have to read his mind; you just had to listen to him. You'd attended nearly all of your father's sermons for the past four years, since he'd started taking you and your mother on the road. You'd observed his style, his performance, his cadence. You'd seen when he dipped into a story and when he resurfaced. You'd watched when he wept, when he railed, when he shifted to reading or reciting the Bible. You'd noticed how he paused to gauge his audience, measuring their readiness, their state of attention. You'd absorbed everything. And now it was your turn.

After the service, your father didn't say much. He said he needed to pray. He didn't take any supper either. He waited until the following morning to address you.

That conversation took place in the dining room of the guesthouse where the three of you were staying. Over pancakes, your father asked you what it had felt like, preaching up there, delivering the Gospel to a sea of angry faces. No one had come up to the altar rail when you invited them. You hadn't minded. All that mattered was being up there, talking and walking and even wheeling around once or twice, your chest filled with fire, with conviction, with truths that needed to be heard. *Blessed are the peacemakers: for they shall be called the children of God.*

—It felt like the words were a string of beads, you said to him. —And someone was pulling that string out of my mouth. And I had no hand in it save to wait for the beads to present themselves and name them one by one as they passed.

Lorenzo set down his fork.

Upstairs, in the guest room, your mother was shivering under blankets, sweating, newly afflicted with the fever that would take her life just three weeks later. That morning would be the beginning of the end for your family.

—You could never be ordained, of course, your father said after breakfast ended and the two of you made your way back upstairs to pack. —You would need to carry letters of endorsement from male clergy wherever you went so people wouldn't turn you out.

He placed a hand on your shoulder as you climbed. He was considering the idea, the possibility that his daughter had inherited a calling not unlike his own. He was struggling with his response. He was a radical, open to new voices, to new forms of God's revelation, but if one of those voices was his daughter's—well, that was something else.

—Itinerancy is a difficult life even for men, he said. —I know very few women who have attempted to preach. If you choose this life, Barker, if you become a female exhorter, you will never marry.

—I don't care to be married, you said. —And you ain't ordained either.

Your father laughed. —True enough, he said as the two of you reached the landing. —I nearly was once, but now it's anchors aweigh; now I sail unfettered!

He bent and kissed the top of your head, a gesture he didn't often make. Outside the guest room, with his hand on the door handle, he paused to look back down the hallway and landing at the lodging house ornamented in the morning light. Sunshine streamed through the windows, shining on the boarders on the first floor as they bustled about in their finery, their walking sticks and peacock-feather hats. Through those windows, you could see the shimmering Chattahoochee and a long, winding road, and not a traveler on it, at least not yet, not that early in the morning.

—This life, Lorenzo said softly. —This life, Barker, it's almost glorious.

Then he opened the door.

She sees the smoke from the campfires first, drifting over a slope of sawed forest. Then she sees a sign tacked to an elm tree, block letters carved into a placard: ENTERING AURARIA.

On the road, a turkey drover calls out to his flock. Hundreds of the birds waddle past Barker, streaming around her, noisy and gobbling, the males arrogantly spurred. She stops to slip a few of their dropped feathers into her bag. Cleaned, they'll make good quills for writing. The old man might like one, might enjoy the offering. But he's not here to receive it. She has left Higgenbotham behind, him and his whiskey and his naysaying.

She walks on under a noontime sky. The Blue Ridge Mountains have reared up to the north. Closer by, prospectors wade in a stream as speckled trout and redbreast sunfish flash in the shallows. Along the Chestatee River, she sees five men lowering a diving bell, a floating caisson, by rope into the water. More men along the bank shout instructions to the two divers crouched inside. These rushers have run out of gold along the creek banks, have resorted to searching for it underwater.

Along the river, nailed handbills flutter from the trunks of trees:

CAMP MEETING AT YAHOOLA CREEK. ALL WELCOME.

Who lived here before the gold men came? Everyone knows; no one cares. Barker strides faster, still limping. She has stuffed leaves in her uncle's boots to protect her blister, but it isn't helping.

Her last mile into town, she accepts a ride on a mail coach after the driver won't leave her alone. He's the same postal man with whom Higgenbotham spoke earlier, the one who looked at Barker the whole time he was repairing his wagon wheel.

He slows his horses as he comes upon her, waves at her as two cattle drovers shout their herd forward, bringing the stench and sound of livestock driven toward an unhappy future.

—Limp-a-lot, the postman calls out to Barker. —Hey, girl! Don't let those beasts trample you.

Bending from his high seat, he studies her with undisguised interest. —What's the matter, don'tcha talk? Where's your grandpa? Didja lose him? You can't be on your own out here, girl.

—I'm all right, Barker says. She hikes faster, to no avail. Cattle are in front of her, blocking the way forward. The mail driver's horses are breathing down her neck. He pulls closer. He tells her he has two daughters back home and would never be able to sleep nights if he knew they were walking unchaperoned on a road like this one.

—Not even if they was dressed like you, he says. —Trying to be a boy, now, are we? He laughs. —It ain't working.

Barker limps forward, stepping into steaming cow patties, making little progress. The driver natters on, keeping pace beside her. If she won't ride with him into town, he says, he'll just travel along with her; it's the only way he can protect her from the scoundrels lurking around every corner. And protect her he will, he announces.

Barker gives up. Against her better judgment, she climbs into the postal wagon and perches on the driver's seat as far from the postman as possible. She hugs her saddlebag close as he snaps the reins. His team heaves forward, maneuvering left around the herd, passing the drovers. They have entered Auraria at its southern end. She can hear the clanging of the tin chuck-a-luck from games being played in the roadside taverns.

—Whaddya say? the postman asks, turning parental now that he has a captive audience, turning admonitory. —Don't be rude, little one. Whaddya say when someone lends you a hand?

Barker mutters *Thank you.* She dislikes this man, but she'll do whatever it takes to reach her destination, to transport herself home more quickly.

Home. But where is that? More to the point, *who*?

The postman tells her people call him Compass, for how well he knows the roads. He shares the story of an Indian boy who recently found a large piece of gold outside Auraria, very close to where they're now riding. As he talks, he slips an avuncular arm around Barker's shoulders.

—'Twas the size of a lemon, he says as his horses swerve to avoid a farmer's oxcart. —I'll bet he bit into it, thought it was one, maybe busted his tooth on it.

He chuckles at his own story.

Traffic is teeming in this boomtown. Auraria storefronts with slatted wooden porches rise up on either side of the road, and Barker glimpses law offices and saloons, a bank, a dentist, a bakery. Two Indians on the roadside are selling jars of honey and smoked fish wrapped in paper. She slides as far away from her postal companion as she can. He prattles on.

He tells her about a drunken settler outside town who killed his wife before hanging himself. —Both of them now lie in the same grave, he says. —Imagine that!

Barker stays quiet.

The town of Auraria was born of a forty-acre gold lot drawn by a family of orphans just last year, he says. The children's guardian took over the process and decided to sell the land for them.

—If he'd let 'em keep it, Compass says, those orphans'd be rich now. Look what's sprung up around here!

—What happened to them? Barker asks, instantly curious. —What happened to those orphans?

Compass shrugs, not interested. —They didn't tell that part in the newspaper.

He removes his hand from her shoulder long enough to point out the building that has given him these stories, the *Western Herald* office, the same newspaper Uncle Wiley once brought home. Barker gazes at the street. She sees a man begging, a barred owl perched on his shoulder, chained. Nearby, a peddler hawks gold maps, pushes his cart up and down the walk. *One dollar, just one dollar to find your fortune, get it while you can!* Auraria's a town built on rumor, fueled by discovery, springing up overnight on a ridge between two rivers. They built the law offices before they built the churches. They still haven't built the churches; they're too busy seeking treasures on earth.

Compass's hand tiptoes back to Barker's shoulder. Sanitation crews are out here too, sweeping the street, shouting at a woman on an upstairs balcony, warning her not to empty that slop bucket in the road. The woman shouts something down at the crew and pours the bucket into the street anyway.

Compass shakes his head.

—Everyone's in it for himself here, he says, steering his horses to miss the woman's deposit. —Count no one your friend in Auraria.

When he guides his team to a stop outside a general store, Barker takes the opportunity to part from him.

—I'll be going now, she says. —I can find my way from here.

Compass tells her not to be a silly girl. She can't walk to the revival alone. The men in this county are ruffians and the women not much better. —Present company excluded, of course, he adds, and reaches out and pinches her knee through her breeches.

Barker flinches. She starts to climb off the wagon seat, but Compass grips her arm, holding her firmly. All at once, her pulse is in her ears, strumming.

—Now, here's the plan, the postman says with a broad reptilian smile. —I drop off the mail and then I drive us out of here. We'll have an adventure, you and me, yes, we will. The two of us together.

His head nearly touches hers. The faint odor of diseased gums, rancidity, is on his breath.

—I'm going to the camp meeting, Barker says firmly, leaning away from him. —My pa's there. He's expecting me. He'll miss me if I don't show up, mister.

—Sure he will, Compass says, and releases her arm to pinch her knee a second time.

Barker hauls off and shoves him. It's a solid push, almost a tackle. She knocks him so forcefully, she surprises herself—she didn't know she could do it that hard. He loses his balance, topples from his coach seat, and lands, groaning, in the middle of the street.

She's free; she has dethroned him. She's in trouble now. *Run!*

She springs off the far side of the coach. Compass clutches his lower back, cursing; she grabs her saddlebag and flees. She's fast and she's young and she doesn't have a bad back, and that will be enough to get her out of here; it has to be.

She ducks off the main street and turns down a side lane. She runs past a boardinghouse with a sign out front: NO SPIRITS SERVED HERE. A stern-looking matron sweeping the walk looks up to watch Barker fly past, a girl following the revival handbills. CAMP MEETING THIS WAY, SIX MILES. ALL WELCOME.

She lopes down one road, then another. The handbills continue. The signs all lead northward, past the town's end. She keeps going.

Barker's pace slows as the daylight wanes. Gradually, the sky darkens. She's back in the forest again. And she's spent, the sore on her heel burning.

A red-tailed hawk dives into nearby brush, and a squeak follows, a rustling in the holly. She didn't know they hunted at dusk. How can she have been alive for fourteen years and not known that red-tailed hawks hunt at twilight? She looks back over her shoulder. No one's coming after her. She sees no postman and no one else either. But if someone was following her, she might not know it out here. Sometimes she no longer trusts herself.

When it becomes too dark to see, she finds an eroded dugout in a hillside, a nest of roots and moss, sized for a girl. She arranges herself and her belongings inside. She eats the dried apples and one pickle, then curls up on her side and tries to sleep.

Soon voices begin floating in her direction, the sound of nighttime travelers back on the road, headed down the same route she has been traveling, north toward Dahlonega, possibly toward the camp meeting. Preachers? She peeps out from her lair.

She can see their outlines at the base of the hill, darkened figures against the trees and an inked sky. She creeps out from her hiding place, wide awake now. She shoves her supplies in her bag and starts walking behind them. She'll follow those silhouettes to her destination; their torches are enough to see by. She'll sleep once she reaches the camp meeting. She'll borrow their light in the meantime.

But these travelers aren't headed to hear the Gospel.

When the path leads by rushing water, Barker peers forward again and glimpses the figures wading into the shallows of the Chestatee. One of them, holding a pine torch aloft, calls out to another. She sees a flash and the glint of a long spear, and then another torch flares up, illuminating another segment of river, and a third. Soon a dozen or more twirling lights bob and dance alongside the water, which reflects and multiplies their spark.

Barker crouches by the river, transfixed. She hasn't been following preachers. She's been following Indian hunters and fishermen. They'll seek deer out here by torchlight; they'll spear trout and shad and sturgeon, their flames waltzing into the night. The Chestatee River was named for these midnight hunts of theirs: *place of the lights*. She didn't know they still went on them. She didn't know so many Cherokee still lived and made their lives up here.

Stand up, a voice says. It takes Barker a few seconds to realize the voice is coming from inside her. *Stand up and keep walking. You're nearly there, nearly to the camp meeting.*

She's no longer sure if she wants to be.

Close to midnight, she reaches the campground in a cove forest. Stars appear from behind a bank of clouds, and the night air hangs heavy with pollen and the scent of pine. Yahoola Creek bisects the cove, splitting the campers into two halves. Circuit riders and missionaries have set up their tents and canvas tarps on both sides of the water, seeking level ground wherever they can. They're finding their rest before the crowds come.

On the creek's near side, rough-sawed pews in rows await tomorrow's congregants. A makeshift preaching platform, hammered in haste, rises six feet. It won't last the week.

Barker tries to look for her father's tent, but she can't see in so much darkness. It's impossible to tell if he has camped here; the night is all-consuming. She steps down to the creek shoals and looks around, peers up. On a low ridge, through the woods, she dimly glimpses shadows passing—figures riding? She can't be sure. She rubs her eyes, and when she looks again, the shadows have vanished.

The creek as she wades in is shin-deep and freezing. Slivers of reflected starlight bob on the surface. After crossing, Barker climbs into a clearing, her boots squishing creek water with every step. She finds more tents and tree stumps in all directions, the sleepers' tarps drawn tight for the night, no movement within. She'll have a better chance of finding her father, if he's here, in the morning.

A Moravian woman spots Barker limping by the tents and motions for her to come over. She takes her by the hand and leads Barker to the remains of a campfire. —*Sitzen,* she whispers, motioning again. The woman's eyes are dark, her cheeks so drawn, they appear sucked in. She's the only soul still up and about at this time of night. Her sleeping family, a husband and three children, lie nearby, blanketed, under a tarp strung between two hemlocks.

Barker sits and removes her wet boots and stockings. The woman sees her bare feet and exclaims, her hands going to those concave cheeks. Barker's right heel is a puddle of raw tissue.

Using soap and water, the Moravian woman cleans the wound while the rest of the camp sleeps. She dries Barker's foot with a cloth before tying a poultice of garlic and herbs around it. Then she takes off her own shawl and wraps it around Barker's shoulders. A cup of lukewarm soup soon follows, and a plate with a slice of ginger cake. Barker can't believe her eyes. Cake, out here, in the middle of nowhere!

Uncle Wiley would have been pleased. Him and his sweet tooth.

—I can't, she says when the woman offers the slice to her. —It's yours. It's your family's.

—*Nein,* the woman says, thrusting the plate at Barker again. She will allow no protest.

After Barker eats, the woman pulls a spare pallet from beneath the tarp. She checks it for fleas, places it on the ground near the campfire, and gestures for Barker to lie down. Then she covers her with a blanket. Barker thanks her, and the woman retires under the family tarp to sleep.

Barker lies on her stomach, chin cupped in her hands, and watches the campfire dying.

Hurry, sun, she thinks. *Hurry, dawn. Get here so I can preach.*

The thought takes her by surprise. She came all this way to find Lorenzo. Didn't she? But maybe she came for something else too, something as vital and impossible as a father.

That night she dreams of standing before a crowd of listeners, mostly men at first, militia and preachers and innkeepers, but soon some women appear in the audience also, missionary wives and Indian mothers and inscrutable aunts, a hushed gathering at the base of an umbrageous mountain. Before long, there are women everywhere, taking over, filling the cove with their petticoats and bonnets, their colorful wraparound skirts and shawls, more women in one place than she has seen in her life. *Where have you been?* she wants to ask them.

In the dream, she's alone on a preaching platform surrounded by towering hemlocks. She starts to ask the crowd where her father is, what has taken him so long to find her. But then she hears thunder, bold and fierce, drumming from the skies, and rain starts falling through the needles of the hemlocks; the women before her in the audience begin shuffling and dancing, lifting their hands, some opening their mouths to catch the raindrops.

It takes Barker several seconds to realize that the thunder is her own voice. She's not speaking in words; she's speaking in rain.

But when she wakes up, she can't remember what her speech contained. She cannot remember what she, as rain, was saying.

They arrive for her in the morning.

Barker scrambles to her feet as dawn breaks over Yahoola Creek, first light filtering through the trees. Wiley's company must have slept on a nearby ridge. Those figures she glimpsed moving through the woods last night? They weren't phantoms. Her uncle's men have made their way here. They've reached the same cove forest and are headed for the clearing now, launching their search among the ministers and missionaries. Even from afar, Barker registers how worn out the militiamen appear, how thin and haggard, as tired as she is and for much the same reason—chasing a mirage can be tiring.

She has about one minute.

Feverishly, she shoves on her stockings and boots, still damp from her creek crossing. Her blister has improved overnight; it's sore but not excruciating. She tugs on her coat, reaches for the saddlebag, and retrieves Higgenbotham's pistol, which is still loaded, which was loaded when she stole it from him. She shoves the weapon into her waistband. Has she fired a gun before? Yes, thanks to Wiley. Her uncle taught her one afternoon when he stayed home from the mill, having decided it was a good day for killing jackrabbits. Barker didn't hit any jackrabbits, but she hit a pail he set out on a stump for her, earning a pat on the back and not much else.

—Pa? she calls out now, trying not to be too loud. Any dreams she had of preaching will not come true at this camp meeting. —Lorenzo McRae! You out there?

A last-ditch effort. Her father isn't anywhere in this clearing. She feels his absence in the morning light, that familiar hollow, that ache behind her eyes. His tent is nowhere.

—*Pa?* she says, more loudly.

She should have known he wouldn't be here. Lorenzo's too special to share the stage with other circuit riders. He's too distinctive, too anguished. If a religious gathering is organized, he needs it to be all Lorenzo or nothing, all his own sacrifice or none at all. This camp meeting is too crowded with other men of God for his liking.

—*Lorenzo McRae!* she shouts.

Louder now, and useless. Several circuit riders poke their heads out of their tents to stare at her. The Moravian wife stirs, springs into alertness. The militiamen picking their way down the ridge have nearly reached the far side of Yahoola Creek. They have horses; they'll ford it easily.

She calls out again, a final attempt. She's drawing too much attention.

—*Pa, where are you!*

She's giving herself away; she's leading them straight to her. But they were already headed to her; they were going to find her anyway. She can't keep running forever. The rider wearing a yellow neckerchief has homed in on her; Barker remembers him from the Athens alley. He's the youngest, the most agile. He sits tall as his golden horse steps across the shallows. When his eyes find Barker's, they stay on her.

The Moravian woman rushes forward, nightcap askew, black hair unbound. When she sees the horses splashing through the creek, she issues a stream of words at Barker, an urgent question in her native German.

—I can't find him, Barker says, turning to her, ignoring the language difference. —I can't find my father. And those men are comin' for me.

She reaches into her bag, this time retrieving the lottery papers and her Bible.

—*Vater?* the Moravian woman asks, brow etched with worry.

Barker slides the papers into the Bible and claps it shut. Then she thrusts the book into the woman's hands. —Here. Take it.

The woman looks down at the Bible, then back up at her, blinking.

—It's land, Barker says. —It's forty acres of goldlands in those papers. I won't let my uncle have it. Take it so he don't get it.

—*Nein*, the woman says, suddenly panicked, pushing the Bible back at her. This missionary wife knows about Cherokee land and the battles over it, Cherokee land and the great white intruders. She wants no part of this business either.

—Please, Barker urges. The men have reached the creek bank. —You don't want the papers, burn 'em. Just take 'em so he don't get his hands on 'em. She reaches for the woman's arm, squeezes. —I got no one else, she says.

The Moravian shakes her head but acquiesces. She accepts the Bible and the papers inside them, clutching the book to her chest.

—You have showed me great kindness, Barker says as the soldiers raise a shout, pointing at her, their object in range at last, their horses heaving up from the creek, neighing, awakening the campground. —And if a lottery man called Higgenbotham comes through here, tell him the 221st Company got me.

She fires off a single shot, but the recoil throws off her aim, and the bullet lodges in the trunk of a hemlock. The men surround her, pry the weapon from her hands, wrestle her arms behind her back, knot a rope around her wrists. One of them boosts her up onto his horse.

Barker fights back. She bites at their hands, their fingers; she slides off the horse, loses her footing, regains it, hits the forest floor running. One of the men catches up to her and cuffs her with the back of his hand; the Moravian woman cries out. Barker stumbles and falls, scrabbles back up; they surround her once more. She kicks and writhes. She frees her hands, which weren't tied sufficiently tight; these men don't know how skinny a girl's wrists can be. She scratches their faces, aiming for noses, ears, eyes.

—Easy there, Kerchief shouts, and Barker lashes out at him this time. Another horseman seizes her, twists her left arm until her shoulder is screaming. The Moravian woman is shouting German things. Briefly Barker blacks out, then revives, then nearly blacks out again; she can't feel her arm for several seconds.

—Tie her again, Kerchief says.

He steps away, touching the spot on his neck where her scratches drew blood.

The Moravian woman runs after the men, issuing invectives, a river of accusations. She shouts at the company in her native tongue, curses their horses, yells at her own husband. She rouses the entire camp. This woman should have been the preacher, not her bearded spouse; she would have struck fear in the heart of every man. Other missionaries and circuit riders climb out from their tents to take in the ruckus. Militia everywhere, and a girl on a horse, and a woman afoot—a Moravian off her rocker!

The soldiers tie Barker's hands and boost her up into the saddle again, this time on Kerchief's palomino. The Moravian woman wheels around to her husband, who's awake and climbing to his feet though still sleep-laden, still groggy. She shouts at him, a message from wife to husband: —*Stehen Sie nicht nur dumm rum, tun Sie was!*

Don't just stand there, do something!

—This here girl's wanted for multiple crimes, Kerchief calls out to the woman as he hauls himself into the saddle behind Barker. —She took out her uncle's eye. She stole his horse. She's a fugitive.

For reply, the Moravian spits at him.

The men grab the woman and shove her to the ground; her husband cries out. Finally, he's fully awake; he's stepping forward. But the woman can hold her own. She beats her fists against the closest soldier, sits up and pummels him in the nose with Barker's Bible. She would like all their eyes out, she bellows in broken English. Whatever that girl did to her uncle, he deserved it.

The missionary husband intervenes; he steps forward and wraps his arms around his wife's shoulders. Apologizing to the militiamen, he physically removes his spouse from their reach; he pulls her back toward their children. She still holds Barker's Bible, the land grant tucked away in its pages. She has not let go of it.

—*Nein,* she shouts again.

In the saddle, Barker kicks back and connects with Kerchief's shin. She repeats the action, rams him with the heel of her uncle's boot. Kerchief grunts, loses his hold on her. Again she scrambles off the horse, but it's no good; when she hits the ground, she lands hard, and she can't move like she should, can't catch her breath. She drops to her knees. One of the horsemen comes up and lifts the butt of his pistol above her. In the corner of her vision, she sees it coming down.

Like cracking an egg, she thinks dully as blow meets skull, and her thoughts fly off into blackness.

Part Three

Yonah Mountain to Tallulah Gorge

14

THE DAY WILEY Wood first touched you was the day you were delivered. A new birth, for better or for worse, a new creation tapping out of its shell. Fully formed in secret, like a chick hatching.

—Well, look what we have here, he said that first time, lying next to you in the loft, hip to hip, stroking your collarbone. You couldn't move—you couldn't think—he whispered, *Nuggle in.* His thumb played with your lower lip. Then he slid that thumb in and ran it along your teeth.

—Well, would you look at that, he whispered. —The girl of the hour.

His other hand slipped beneath the sheets.

You would like to go back to being whatever the chick is before the egg cracks. Yes, that's what you'd like—to be complete, without entrance, without an opening. A sphere.

An egg needs no one. No parent, no guardian, no savior. It has its own food and drink. Everything it requires for sustenance dwells within its shell and casing. Nothing can touch it. All it needs is a little warmth while it waits.

He made a chair for you later, a rocker for the covered passageway, a place to sit and shell beans in your apron while surveying the pumpkin patch and thinking up ways to leave him. It took him a week to make that chair, seven nights to sand, whittle, weave. During that whole time, Wiley did not touch you once; he did not come your way at night, not even for a peck on the cheek. Carpentry had taken the place of violation for him.

When he finished the chair, you asked him to make two more. When he completed that task, you suggested he make ten.

—Start a chair mill, you said. —Make a hundred. I'll chop down the trees myself.

But he made only the three.

What else? What else did you say to manage the unmanageable, to corral the uncorrallable?

Yes, Uncle, yes. I can fetch your boots.

Yes, Uncle, I'll read that newspaper to you.

Uncle, you look sore tired, you need to lie down.

You worked so hard today; you work so hard every day; me and Aunt Elma, we're so lucky to have you. (No, not that last line. You better not have said that last line to him.)

Uncle, your headache, is it coming back? Do you need a powder?

Have some more gin, Uncle Wiley. Have so much you fall asleep early. You deserve it, don't you? How hard you been working.

Have so much you lay your head on that table and die in your own vomit, will you?

He baked a cake for your thirteenth birthday, another for your fourteenth. He took the day off from the mill for both occasions. He said Elma's cakes weren't as good as his own. He bustled about in her apron, shooing you out of the way. He sifted flour and beat eggs, grumbled when he couldn't find the vanilla.

Your aunt didn't know what to do with him.

Elma spent each of your birthdays mostly outside, hoeing the garden, and it wasn't hoeing season. She came back in at afternoon's end, her dress darkened with perspiration. She cast a glance your way as she untied her sunbonnet.

—He's fine, you said to her, answering her unasked question. How you scorned her in those moments! —You spent the day outside for nothing. He's happy today; he ain't tormented.

Elma set her bonnet down, looked doubtfully at you, and walked away.

Your father never made you a cake. Lorenzo barely knew where the oven was, couldn't have said where your mother kept the flour if anyone asked him. He wasn't home often enough to know.

Also, your family didn't have an oven most years. Your oven was the campfire, the kitchen in kind Methodist homes, the hearth in travelers' rests off the federal and Alabama roads.

But your uncle.

You could write a primer on how to gauge which version of Wiley Wood you and Elma were likely to encounter. Sometimes he was Mill Worker Wiley, flecked with sawdust, reeking of sap and labor. Mill Worker Wiley, when sufficiently fueled, would turn into Drunken Wiley—slurring, petulant, potentially explosive. Other times, Avuncular Wiley showed up. He was wheedling, wistful, and charming. Avuncular Wiley whistled while he stirred the cake batter.

And that cake recipe was easy. One part butter, two parts sugar, three parts flour, four eggs. A dash of vanilla if Elma had it. Three eggs would suffice if the hens were in a slump. Stir it all together, fold the batter into a pan, bake until a knife inserted came out clean.

And later that night, baking complete, he would come up the ladder to your sleeping loft again, come to you with that lone pleading eye, that sorrowful parasitism.

On good nights, on the best nights, Studious Wiley would appear and ask you to help him with his reading. Studious Wiley was an eager pupil. He plowed forward into waves of grammar and spelling, sentence after sentence, his forehead wrinkling whenever a line upended him. Determined to stay afloat, word by word, your uncle progressed, often complaining. You ignored his protests. You were the authority here—you steered the ship in those moments.

Wiley's mouth formed an *O* of surprise when you corrected his pronunciation, when he focused intently on the page. He seemed to like it, to like your reigning over him; he enjoyed not being the master in those moments.

—Again, you used to say, severely. —Read it again. Concentrate, Uncle!

When he improved, when one day he correctly read aloud a long list of items for sale at the Watkinsville store, Studious Wiley whooped for joy, his fist in the air, couldn't stop grinning.

Cocoa and Brazil nuts!
Patent medicines!
Cigars both Spanish and common!
Shoeblack, paste and liquid!
Fancy cake and ball soap!
Sugar and coffee!

He seized you around the waist, twirled you through the cabin until your skirt belled; that's how joyful reading turned him. Elma looked up from her embroidery, her eyes on her on husband, her eyes on you both, as he roughly spun you like a top.

—Anything you want, Wiley said to you. —Anything you want, I'll buy you. My tutoress!

Meanwhile your aunt stretched her embroidery cloth tighter and tighter on its hoop before stabbing a needle through it.

Belligerent Wiley was the one to avoid. Of all your uncle's variations, he was the worst, or close to it.

Belligerent Wiley would come home from the mill in a foul mood. Sometimes he would kick something, like the pumpkin in the passageway, the pumpkin with the smiling face you'd carved into it. Your uncle would jam his toe, of course, and curse, then barge into the house and demand his supper. You remember those times like they're ongoing, like they're still happening inside your chest, your thoughts, your memory. Maybe they are.

When he sees you washing the pot beside the stove, Belligerent Wiley recalls that you disobeyed him yesterday. He remembers his frustration but not your earlier offense. What did you do to set him off? He can't put his finger on it. Didn't smile? Didn't listen? Listened with a distracted air? Spoke too little? Spoke too much? Had red hair? Hair not red enough?

If you let him brush your hair, as he likes to do, it might help his mood or it might not. And next thing you know, he'll be angry about his weakness, about wanting to touch something soft again.

Maybe you didn't answer his question. Or maybe you answered without answering it, which incenses Belligerent Wiley like nothing else, which turns him into a whirring hornet. Maybe you didn't bother to greet him when he came home from his long day at the mill, where he mans the up-and-down saw that cuts wood only on the downstroke, a contraption so slow, he complains he could grow a new beard in the time it takes to produce a single board.

Maybe you didn't wash tomorrow's shirt for him, or didn't listen when he summoned you, or didn't appear sufficiently interested in his daily bloviation. Wiley rails against the US Supreme Court, its recent decision to back Cherokee sovereignty. An insult so miserable, he claims, that the State of Georgia might as well break off from the rest of the country, start up its own nation. No one understands the Indian problem until he has lived and abided among them, he will say.

Once, unable to stop yourself, you replied. —When's the last time you talked to a real live Indian, Uncle Wiley?

For that comment, he backhanded you.

Whatever you did or didn't do, your refusal to placate him, to apologize, now consumes your uncle's attention. Red-faced, he will write the necessary lesson down for you on torn pieces of stationery. He'll scribble it with painstaking care, each word on a separate scrap of paper.

—Is that so difficult? he will sputter, glancing up, berating you and Elma both; in these moments, the two of you merge for him, the two of you become one entity: the specter of a difficult woman. —Even *I* can say I'm sorry when I need to, he goes on. —Is it so hard to repent of your wrongdoing?

He'll write *I, AM,* and *SORRY* on those pieces of ripped stationery, and he'll pin the scraps on the wall beside your loft bed; this message is for you and you only. He wants you to have a good long look at those three words as you head up the ladder in the evenings. He wants you to take them on as your own.

Whatever you say or don't say will be the wrong thing, of course. That's how this particular incarnation of your uncle props himself up; that's how he stays Belligerent Wiley.

Sorry, not sorry; laughed, didn't laugh; meant it, didn't mean it; listened, didn't hear a thing—you cannot win. He will set all his points swinging at the same time and differently paced, like a room with multiple clocks ticking. Small wonder Aunt Elma walks around with her hands over her ears sometimes. There's nothing you can do; those rods are gonging and swaying all over the place, different weights, different lengths, different pulleys and striking mechanisms. Try to repair the arrangement, and a pendulum bob might brain you.

But the day Matthew Higgenbotham showed up at your uncle's farm, something changed.

The day lottery messenger Higgenbotham arrived with those papers in his satchel, something in your own mind turned over. You saw not just your uncle's cruelty, which you already knew, but his dim-wittedness, which you had not fully grasped until another man, a stranger, stood and addressed him, stood and looked him over.

You saw Wiley's clumsy manner, his uncertainty masked by bravado, and you stopped being afraid of your uncle in that moment.

For those few seconds, peering through the dogtrot window, watching him dance his oversize-leprechaun jig while Higgenbotham shifted on his feet and averted his gaze, you decided it was worse to be harmed by a stupid man than a clever one, and you vowed not to be caught in the clockworks again.

When you withdrew from the window, you found Elma standing beside you. She was watching her husband too, watching him in a way that was new to you.

Her expression suggested that she understood. It suggested that at one point in her life, Elma might have felt those same things you were feeling. She, too, saw his weakness, his need, his fiery ineptitude.

But she didn't speak it aloud. She didn't say a word to you.

Question: Can an eyeless man look surprised?
Answer: Yes.
Question: How will he weep? How will a man without eyes cry?
You haven't come up with the answer to that one yet.
Blind him. It wasn't planned. It was an explosion.
Blind him so that in the light of day, he cannot find her.
But he has found her now anyway.

She awakens to a long winding road and the rolling motion of a horse beneath her. She is seated behind Kerchief, bound to him with a rope, her hands also tied, her forehead resting against his shoulder. The road below them is traversed with gnarled tree roots.

Ten horsemen head east toward a horizon ringed with azure mountains. Under his breath, Kerchief hums a ditty, a song Barker might recognize if she could think clearly. She tries to position herself higher in the saddle, but she can't move without pain. When she blinks, her vision doubles. She blinks again, and it briefly corrects.

And her bladder is full nearly to bursting.

She bumps Kerchief with her chin, forcefully, and again a second time, so he knows it wasn't an accident. He has gagged her with the same yellow bandanna that gave him his nickname; she can taste salt and dirt on the cotton.

He slows his horse and twists around, tugs down the gag. Barker tells him she needs to relieve herself. Then she tells him something's wrong with her eyesight.

—I keep seeing two, she says. —Two skies, two palominos, two yous.

—Ain't you the lucky one, Kerchief says.

—Something's wrong with me, she insists.

—Well, you should've thought of that before you took your uncle's eye out, he says.

He loosens the rope binding her to his midsection. He dismounts and helps her down, unties her wrists, points her toward a cluster of magnolias. —Go on, now. Do your business. If you run, I'll have to shoot you.

He waits on the road, giving her privacy. When Barker relieves herself, though, her stream hits the dirt so loudly and lasts so long, her captor hears and makes an amused sound. A mockingbird in one of the magnolias swoops close to her head as she urinates, squawking angrily.

—Leave me be, Barker says, waving the nesting bird away, fuming at Kerchief's amusement, at everything. Hurriedly she pulls up her breeches and returns to the road.

Thrasher's nephew takes her by the wrist and leads her back to his horse. He helps her into the saddle, reties her, works the bandanna back into her mouth.

—Lest you bite me, he says with a shrug. His hooded eyes are as keen and unfathomable as an eagle's.

They ride on. Barker falls asleep again, sagging against Kerchief's back, the rough fibers of his coat scratching her face. Her headache from the pistol butt's blow has taken over, has expanded in her skull. Her shoulder is throbbing. Kerchief breaks into song, and snatches of lyrics wend their way into her dreams—if they can be called dreams, if they aren't just thoughts trying to hold off what's coming.

When she opens her eyes again, it's dusk, and the regiment men are advancing single file along a rocky trail lined by flame azaleas barely in bloom, the horses slowed to the pace of exhaustion. They've been riding since shortly after dawn. This is Habersham County, deep in wilderness, vestiges of past storms visible. Once-towering trees lean or lie toppled, sturdy pines snapped mid-trunk, a feeling of surprise to how they've fallen, a soundless bewilderment. Barker works the bandanna far enough out of her mouth to ask Kerchief about their destination.

He throws a glance back at her. —We're headed to Wiley Wood.

—This ain't the way to Watkinsville, Barker says, momentarily forgetting she spotted her uncle back at Scudder's, momentarily forgetting a lot of things.

—Wiley Wood's not in Watkinsville, Kerchief says.

Mining caves and seasonally habitable overhangs lie scattered throughout these hills, shelters built and borrowed over the years, used by runaways, thieves, bears, vengeful uncles. Wiley, Kerchief explains, is waiting for her in one of them, at a location the company knows. A dugout in the shadow of Yonah Mountain.

—He didn't want all those preachers staring at him, he says. —Didn't want 'em getting excited at that camp meeting, trying to work their miracles on a blind man. So he went on ahead to wait.

—All the way out here? Barker's head has not stopped pounding. —He can't be out here on his own. He can't get no further than from his bedside to his rocker anymore.

—Tell him when you see him, Kerchief replies, shrugging, and tugs his worn coat tighter.

Near dark, they enter a valley with a narrow brook along the eastern edge. The men stop to water the horses. They light their pipes and mill about, puffing and drawing, spent, not saying much. Hickory and black walnut trees line the valley perimeter. Kerchief dismounts to check his horse.

—Where're the lottery papers? he asks Barker offhandedly, too offhandedly to be spontaneous. He glances up as his palomino lowers her blond head to the water. —What'd you do with that lottery prize? It in your bag?

—No, Barker truthfully replies. —I don't have it. What do you want with it?

—What do you think? the young militiaman says.

The sky is blackish blue. The palomino straightens, water dripping from her muzzle.

—You know he's ashamed of his appearance, Kerchief says, changing the subject. —He's been traveling by covered wagon, sits in it all day, keeps the flaps drawn. He's ashamed for anyone to see him in his condition.

He gives Barker a righteous stare, turns away.

—Well, he should've thought of that before he put a hand on me, Barker replies, the words coming out before she can stop them.

Kerchief looks at her hard in the encroaching darkness. The regiment men have remounted and started moving. They hold torches to light the way along the trail. Kerchief starts to say something but stops himself. He gets back on his horse, taps her side, and squints into the night.

—Get on, now, he says to the palomino. —No rest for the weary.

The next time Barker awakens, it's dawn, and she's lying at the base of a massive granite outcropping, a lone mountain of resistant rock separated from its companions by erosion. Her hands are tied in front of her, and her saddlebag has been placed under her head for a pillow. Someone has left a cup of water on the ground beside her.

She takes the cup in her bound hands and raises it, drinks thirstily. The weather is pleasant, almost warm, with clouds the color of fire painting the sky.

The men emerge from their tarps and tents, barely awake, hungover from the road and whatever they drank yesterday evening. Kerchief goes over and squats by a dead campfire, spoons tinned beans into his mouth. He's fully awake and ready to travel, the only one of these men with any vigor or vitality remaining. Behind him juts a rock overhang, a sheltered lair under the shadow of the mountain.

Barker rises to her feet. She doesn't like the look of that overhang, dark and gaping and so large she can't see all the way into it. Kerchief sets down his tin of beans and watches her. The first rays of sun reach around the escarpment as he stands and makes his way over.

—What's that? she asks him. —What's in that hideaway?

—The one who don't travel, Kerchief says as he unties the twine around her wrists. —The one who can barely make it from his bedside to his rocker.

The young militiaman's look is not without sympathy, but his voice as he addresses Barker is unyielding: —Time for you to plead your case, he says.

15

TIME TO SEE him, then. Time to face it and move forward. You can do this. Nothing can be as bad as before. All you're doing now is dreaming.

That's it; slant your thoughts in another direction. Today's just a dream, nothing more, just a long bad dream in the eastern half of the goldlands. You'll wake up soon.

Not soon enough.

Wiley Wood lurches into the morning light, two leather patches covering where his eyes used to be. Ten men look up from their camp chores in unison. No one says a word.

Maybe they're impressed by the sight of him; more likely they're embarrassed. Their captain spent the night under that granite overhang, snoring mightily, liquor his preferred companion. His men have waited until morning to wake him, to let him know they've arrived and have his prize to hand him.

Wiley uses a cane as he leaves his lair, tapping before each step. He advances slowly. Scissors has stayed with the wagon, at a safe remove, nowhere within ordering distance. Wiley's footing is tentative, a bitter shuffle. Barker could die and have it out with her Maker in the time it's taking her uncle to travel fifteen feet.

—Captain, Kerchief says, starting to lift his hat, then stopping; the gesture isn't needed. —How'd you sleep?

—Where is she? Wiley barks. —Where's my niece, Johnny?

Kerchief looks over at Barker, a question in his eyes.

She can't speak. All she can do now is keep breathing.

That's sufficient, isn't it? That's enough, that's plenty. She'll think of something to do besides breathing in a minute. She'll think of something besides this man, her uncle, shambling toward her; she'll think of anything but him.

How about preaching? That could do. Yes, she'll think about preaching. A woman can preach if God tells her to. A woman can preach until her lungs burst, until she explodes into flame, if the Holy Spirit asks it of her, even if she can't perform all the rites an ordained man can, even if she can't baptize, marry, bury, or administer the sacraments. Barker doesn't care about those things. All she cares about is the sermons.

She read about a female preacher once in one of her father's books. This preacher called herself the Public Universal Friend. She drew audiences in the thousands from Massachusetts, New York, Connecticut, Rhode Island. This Public Universal Friend didn't let being born a woman stop her from sharing the Gospel. She didn't let being a woman stop her from not being a woman, if that makes any sense. To Barker, it's starting to.

She takes a breath. Her uncle is steps away.

And now she can't think of the Public Universal Friend or any other brave person. Now all she can do is look at him.

There's his throat, that meaty neck protruding above his puffy white shirt. He always did like that shirt; he wore it on special occasions, to funerals and the gaming house. His chest hairs are visible in the shirt's opening.

And there's his paunch, not quite so round and full anymore, and his legs, those bowed parentheses, the legs of a man too many years on horseback.

And his breeches—why, Barker has hung those ratty things on the clothesline a dozen or more times; she has resewn the stitching on the seams. Same with the repairs to his shirt. She sewed a new button on that white shirt not two months ago, after the old one popped off and he told her to mend it for him.

—*Barker!* Wiley stumps forward into full daylight, swiveling left to right, straining, listening. —Is that you? Johnny, where is she?

—Maybe we let her eat breakfast first, Kerchief suggests, glancing back and forth, suddenly saddled with competing claims, competing duties. The line between captor and protector, for him, might be starting to blur.

—No. No more stalling. Bring her over, Wiley says.

He can sense where his niece is standing; he can smell her. *Tap-tap*—he tiptoes in her direction, across the graveled earth, his mouth parting with concentration. Barker has stopped breathing again. Two of the militiamen come up behind her to stand guard; they will watch her in case she tries running.

Kerchief steps forward also. He leans in and speaks into Barker's ear, lightly, so no one else hears.

—Whyn't you go talk to him. That's all he wants. Just go talk to him a minute. Maybe tell him you're sorry?

Barker shakes her head. She has apologized to Wiley Wood too many times already.

She'll think of something else, something new to take her mind away from here, something that doesn't answer to

Uncle, that doesn't shape-shift. She'll think of Higgenbotham and that wolfdog.

Yes, that's it. She'll remember their recent miles on the road, the odd trio the three of them briefly made. Those times were not as difficult as she'd thought when she was in them.

—Bring her to me, Wiley bawls, fed up with delays. —Johnny Thrasher, bring her over right now or you'll no longer be in my army.

—Wasn't aware it belonged to you, Kerchief says, but quietly. Barker looks up at him. He might be only five years her senior. He gives her a brief smile, one eyebrow lifting slightly.

It's a passing expression, no more, but it's for her and no one else. It means she's not entirely alone here; she can take another breath, maybe two. She can hook this bad dream onto something not so terrible, onto someone outside herself, at least for a moment.

What is that called in the normal world? A friend.

Back that first time? That very first night, when Wiley crawled into the loft bed and pulled the sheets over both of you? The loft *contracted.*

You remember this part. The cabin grew smaller and smaller, and your uncle swelled larger and larger; in a single instant, the known world shrank to the diameter of your uncle's eye, that pale blue iris he kept trained on you the whole time.

—I'm sorry, he whispered, caressing your throat, the skin of your neck above your nightgown. Your limbs began trembling; your skin began crawling; your body began sounding its alarm.

It's a warning that has not stopped since. That alarm, that clanging, has continued without ceasing, in one form or another, since that first night. To your dying day, part of you will always hear it. Part of you will forever be listening to it, like a heartbeat or some other measurable, unyielding rhythm.

—I'm sorry, little one, but, oh! You have done this to me; I cannot help it—

They take her by the shoulders. She cries out. They let go, take her by the elbows instead, shove her forward. Barker lifts her eyes to the heights. Yonah Mountain soars up in front of them, round and hulked like a sleeping bear, a rock abandoned, thrust up from the surrounding fields. It's the only mountain within shouting distance. Maybe it called out to its own parents for help when it first fell away from them, but they were too busy to hear. Maybe this mountain's parents had already gone, disappeared into the spine of the Appalachians, leaving their granite orphan behind them.

Kerchief tells Wiley they haven't found any property papers on Barker. —We searched her belongings and her person, he says matter-of-factly. —There's no gold rights. No papers for forty acres. She won't say what she's done with them neither.

Wiley waves this information away. —I don't care about the land. Barker, come here.

The men exchange frowning gazes. *They* care about the land. The right to mine forty acres at the confluence of two mountain creeks was to be their payment for services rendered, their recompense for this chase through gold country. They're Clarke County men; they don't work for free. Who is this milksop who calls himself their captain, this weakling they used to take pride in following?

But all Wiley wants now is the girl.

She's close; the militiamen push and prod her forward. Wiley's hand finds her face, her cheek. His hand travels to her neck, her upper arm, her forearm. He feels her bound wrists. Then he squeezes her fingers. When their fingertips touch, Barker shudders.

Wiley rubs her thumb between two of his fingers.

—You, he says. —What you did to me.

She wrenches away, but he has her fast; he grips her tightly. She can smell his breath. The sun is bearing down on them; it's no longer dawn.

Wiley's going to exact his recompense. She can feel it coming. He's going to break her thumb, her wrist, or both.

She shuts her eyes and steels herself.

What comes instead is worse. He goes back to touching her face again. Violence is not his current state. Forlornness is.

He takes one of Barker's braids and lifts it to his nose. Her breathes in the scent of her hair. Then he buries his face in her neck as his men gape at him. When Barker opens her eyes, she sees two uncles. She blinks, trying to clear her vision, but it doesn't work; he's still two people. She's seeing double Wileys.

He pulls her to his chest and rocks her back and forth; her head is pressed against his sternum. She can feel his heart ramming in his chest. The men look on, confounded. They came all this way to find a girl who gouged their captain's eye out—for this? For hugging?

—You, Wiley says to Barker again. His voice has changed; there's no hardness left, only tenderness and poignant sorrow. —Now, why'd you have to go and do what you did? he croons. Barker struggles, trying to free herself, but he has her in his mill worker's grip.

—Don't you remember those cakes I baked you? Don't you remember that chair I made?

He's crying now; tears trickle from beneath his twin patches. So, the capacity to weep remains.

—Why'd you have to go, he murmurs, and ruin everything?

16

THE WORLD GROWS wilder. Higgenbotham crosses a trading path that, if he takes it south, leads to civilization, to his final lottery notifications, his final payment from the state commissioners. He doesn't take that route. He's headed to the camp meeting, a man and his wolfdog, a man and his last hurrah. The road wends through rhododendron and laurel before descending into a meadow brushed with blooming trillium.

He passes clapboard shacks that have seen the gold frenzy come and go, vacant huts along streams turned to sludge, sites overworked by men who thrived here once but no more, rushers and the provisioners leeching off them. They're seeking newer veins elsewhere. Feral hogs with their flared snouts have turned up clumps of soil along the road, corrugating the earth, their efforts vigorous enough to be mistaken for human digging. Scout stays quiet and keeps pace with Higgenbotham, ignoring the scent the boars leave. No hunting for him this time; he's on a mission. *Find Barker.*

They walk into nightfall. They do not walk alone. Past sundown, Higgenbotham comes across a nomad leading a bear by a rope, the animal wheezing and mange-afflicted, pink skin visible beneath its balding coat. Scout steers a wide berth around it. Higgenbotham cannot bring himself to look at the poor creature. Another man, a beggar with a famished appearance, walks behind him for a mile or more, plying Higgenbotham with songs until he relents and gives him a few coins; the beggar inclines his head and lurches on. Soon

Higgenbotham comes upon a rooming house of questionable purpose, its windows covered with waxed paper. A shirtless man steps through the open door wearing a copperhead around his neck, the snake coiling around his bare shoulders. The man calls out when he sees Higgenbotham: *Two pennies, two pennies to see the copper god dance!* Higgenbotham inclines his head and keeps walking.

Scout's tail droops lower and lower. The wolfdog doesn't understand why they haven't stopped to rest yet, why they're marching under the light of the stars. Barker fled when he was leashed and couldn't follow her; she ran while he was fast asleep, truth be told, so unnerved by the sound of his shadow kin, a wolf roaming the distant wilderness, that he plummeted into unconsciousness. He has failed as both a guard dog and a wild animal; on both callings, he has come up wanting. When Higgenbotham offers him a piece of apple, Scout takes it in his mouth but drops the slice at the old man's feet, returning the gift uneaten.

Near midnight, they hike up a long hill dotted with roadside graves. Gold rushes are cyclones—they touch down, kill where they please. There are so many ways to die out here, Higgenbotham's sometimes amazed he's still breathing. Cholera, of course, doesn't he know it, but also typhoid, gunshots, knife fights, accidents in the mines, drownings in the rivers. Then there are the snakebites, boar maulings, confrontations at toll roads, drunken melees, overturned carriages, bucking horses, infections, gangrene. And fever, always—fever, from all manner of illnesses, kills more people than anything.

He keeps walking. A few of the roadside plots have headstones, but many don't; most of the dead out here must settle for rocks, cairns, or nothing. A copper kettle crowns one grave; on another, a saucer holds a set of false teeth. Higgenbotham sees two headstones side by side draped with Grand Union flags from the days of the Revolution. Scout starts digging at one of them.

—Leave it, he says, and the wolfdog veers back to the road again.

Higgenbotham glances down. One of his boots has separated from its outsole, which flaps every time he steps forward. He brushes off his coat. Grime and dust are in his beard and along the back of his neck. Maybe there's gold in all that dust; maybe his beard is worth more than his life is. He trudges on. He wonders if Barker will see her father again.

When they reach Auraria—silent storefronts, taverns lit by lanterns, lawyers' offices locked for the night—he stops at the first travelers' rest he can find. He must sleep a few hours or he'll not survive. Two women are having their way with a miner on the porch, piano music tinkling from inside as they coax the man's coin purse open. They kiss and paw at him until he pulls away with a sharp bark of a laugh.

Higgenbotham makes his way past the trio, shouldering by them to enter the establishment. One of the women says something under her breath as he walks by. She tosses her head, showing her throat in a movement that reminds him of a coiled copperhead. The other woman begins to sing a ballad:

Daylight may do for the gay,
The thoughtless, the heartless, the free,
But there's something about the moon's rays

That is sweeter to you and to me
So meet me by moonlight alone
Meet me by moonlight alone

Good luck, he thinks as he moves past them and heads inside. He lays two pieces of his dwindling coin stash on the innkeeper's desk. *Good luck finding love in the dark.*

Higgenbotham never found anyone after his wife left him, never had that kind of closeness with another person again. Nothing more than stray glances in the night, looks exchanged, silent travelers asking questions without asking them, strangers like passing shadows. Once in a great while, a companionable conversation might take place; once in an even greater while, there might be a nod imperceptible, a brush against another's arm before walking upstairs. Higgenbotham followed the rules of the road—few comforts to be found, and what remained abided only if one never spoke of it. His mother would have sent him to hell a long time ago.

But those days are well past him now also.

In the morning he boards a stagecoach, a brand-new triweekly that originated in Milledgeville, stopped in Athens and Gainesville, and has its final destination in Dahlonega. He could have ridden this coach straight from Thrasher's inn to parts north if he'd known where he was going when he started. But life doesn't allow for such farsightedness; not in his experience, anyway.

Midmorning, the coach runs over a rock and loses a wheel. Higgenbotham and the driver spend an hour on the roadside repairing the axle bed and adjusting the reaches.

Scout lies in a nearby patch of springtime grass, chews on a stick, and monitors their progress. By the time the coach reaches Dahlonega, Higgenbotham is ravenously hungry. He hasn't eaten all day.

He stops for a meal at a public house along the square; he shouldn't take the time to eat, but so be it. This settlement is spanking new. Even its fancy name, Dahlonega, is new; until a few months ago, people just called this area Headquarters. Before that, it was Lot 950 on the surveyors' books—and home to the Cherokee. Settlers and miners have built the town up in just the past year, sawing down the forest oaks, painting storefronts with brightly lettered signs, laying wide-planked sidewalks without a hint of rot yet.

In a dimly lit dining room, Higgenbotham polishes off two boiled eggs, some buttered rye toast, and salted cabbage. He pays what he owes and heads back outside into harsh sunlight, Scout on the front walk waiting for him. A passerby in a lawyerly suit asks him about the wolfdog, offers to pay Higgenbotham for the animal. —I need a good hunter, the man says. —He looks like a hunter.

Higgenbotham declines the offer. After the man leaves, he gives Scout a piece of toast and an egg he smuggled out in a cloth napkin.

—You're too smart to hunt, he says.

Scout gulps down the food, signaling his agreement. They return to the road on foot.

He reaches the camp meeting at the worst possible time—at sundown, in the middle of a full raid by the Holy Spirit. Hundreds of people, men and women and families in covered wagons, mostly whites but some blacks and Indians also, have converged on a section of forest along Yahoola Creek, which is as wide as some rivers, though not as deep. Across the campground, scaffolds topped with pine straw blaze with firelight, illuminating the preaching platform, altar rail, pews. Dozens of trees have been cut down, hemlock saplings hacked to stumps, some of which are several feet high, leaving the speechless look of the decapitated. The surrounding terrain is steep and mountainous. Higgenbotham's throat tightens. Why saving souls requires cutting down a forest first is beyond him.

On the wooden platform, two circuit riders take turns exhorting the nighttime crowd. More preachers stand in line nearby, awaiting their chance to speak. They'll go all night if they need to. None of the preachers is Barker's father, from what Higgenbotham can see. None of them is Barker either.

How few are living for eternity and conducting as they expect to answer at the bar of the Supreme Judge!

How few attend to the moral law—to love the Lord with all their heart and their neighbor as themselves!

The pine beacons sputter and flare. Higgenbotham makes his way through the crowds, squinting to see in the wavering firelight. Scout stays close to him. On all sides, people are praying and flailing, some falling to the earth as if pinned with arrows. Cries for mercy echo across the creek and back again. An old settler woman hits the sawdust trail, falls onto her back, and starts jerking and seizing, her boots kicking up the earth like a stampeding horse. The Holy Spirit is having His way with her. Dozens of faces flash and loom close in the dark as Higgenbotham pushes forward, exceedingly uncomfortable. The preachers are loud and singsong, their summonses strident. *Repent, repent before the end comes!* The crowd weeps and cheers.

Enough, he finally thinks. He leaves the crowd, shoulders through to a quieter corner of the cove; he'll find a place to rest at a higher elevation; he'll wait out the mayhem up here. If Barker's in this crowd, he'll find her in the morning. The preachers are still singing, still exhorting, calling for conversion. Higgenbotham frowns as he listens. A man who thinks he can save another person is a fool. A man who thinks he's irreplaceable is dangerous. Higgenbotham never viewed himself as irreplaceable, not during his mail-riding days and not now either. Nowadays, his replaceability is one of the few comforting thoughts he has left.

When he reaches the top of a forested ridge, he turns and takes in the glittering expanse of the cove below. Sparks from burning pine straw float up like fireflies, and below them the crowds mill and sway and yield. Higgenbotham takes in all those spots of flame, all those lives splayed out before him. Beside him, Scout whines.

—*Oh! I feel the pains of hell in my soul and body!* a man in the throng joyfully shouts, his voice carrying uphill. —*Oh! How I would have despised any person a few days ago who would have acted as I am doing now! But, oh! I cannot help it!*

The crowd rocks and keens.

Higgenbotham hikes back into the cove at daylight, Scout padding loyally behind him. He plans to ask every preacher who's awake and coherent if a redheaded girl, the only daughter of Lorenzo McRae, has appeared in the vicinity. He'll ask if they've seen McRae himself also.

He receives no helpful information for the first hour of his inquiries. But midmorning, working his way along the creek, he speaks to a Moravian minister who seems to know something. The man sends Higgenbotham over to his wife, a woman who speaks so little English that one of her children, a dark-haired girl with the scowling severity of a missionary in training, translates for her.

—She says she tried to stop them, the child says as her mother nods vigorously beside her. The two are seated under a canvas tarp. —She tried to stop them from taking the redheaded girl, but Papa wouldn't let her.

The Moravian woman makes a harsh sound in the back of her throat, a spousal judgment that requires no translating.

Further back-and-forth tells Higgenbotham that a group of county militia swept through the camp meeting two days earlier. They were headed east, and they took Barker with them. One of the men mentioned Yonah Bald as they were leaving.

Higgenbotham looks eastward, envisioning the place. He's traveled past it before. Yonah's a mountain marooned, forever stranded on its way to North Carolina, a hideout for lowlifes and runaways.

—And McRae? he asks. He doubts that this missionary woman will be able to help any further, but he'll try anything. —Her father, Lorenzo McRae. He's a circuit rider. Rangy fellow, long red hair. Have you seen him? Is he preaching here?

The Moravian woman stares at him. She might be the only missionary in these parts who doesn't recognize Lorenzo's name. But her daughter leans over and speaks in their native tongue to her, and the mother issues a verbose response. Their exchange lasts for some time, long enough that Higgenbotham grows impatient, interrupts.

—What is it? he asks. —Do either of you know him?

Straightening, the girl casts an authoritative eye on him, a chastisement for speaking out of turn. —No. But we know another thing, she says.

The mother stands up then, steps forward, and grasps Higgenbotham by the wrist. She presses a book into his hands.

Higgenbotham looks down at what she has given him. It's Barker's Bible, with some papers tucked inside. He opens it. He lifts one of those papers and scans the contents.

—Damnation, he says.

It's his own signature on the page. This is the grant for Barker's forty golden acres, lot 96, his own messenger's flourish verifying the legality of the claim. A small groan escapes him. He's supposed to be giving away these notices, not collecting them. His messenger journey is supposed to be nearing completion, not reversing course.

The Moravian woman glances over at her daughter, who squeezes her mother's hand, encouraging her to speak.

—Please, the woman says, returning to Higgenbotham, entreating him in careful English. —Please to take it from me. Is—how you say it—*ist für mich eine zu große Belastung.*

She looks back at her daughter.

—*Too much a burden for me,* the child says.

Higgenbotham nods. He would've understood without the translation.

—I'll do what I can, he says.

17

EAST, THEN, ON Gold Diggers' Road, on the trail of the Clarke County militia. Past Yahoola Creek, past Bright Creek, toward the Chestatee once again. One body of water after another till they all merge. *Ignore your gluteus nerve*, he instructs himself; *ignore your borborygmic stomach. Ignore that Bible and what it contains, those forty acres you can't get away from.*

Find her. Catch up to Wiley's men, and you'll find her.

But to do that, he'll need a ride. Either that or a horse of his own.

A solution comes in the form of a brass-trimmed buggy hauled by four black stallions flying east. The team slows as the driver leans out of his seat to address Higgenbotham. The horses, muscular and rippling, stand sixteen hands high. Lifting his hat, the driver calls out and offers Higgenbotham a ride. Observing the man, Scout growls.

—Hush, Higgenbotham says to the wolfdog. He doesn't like the look of this fellow either, but he's in no position to be choosy.

He accepts the ride and climbs onto the driver's bench. Scout will keep pace behind the buggy; this man won't let a half-wolf ride in his vehicle.

The driver's name is Templin, and he's a gold broker. He owns a private mint near Gainesville, or so he boasts. He started off as a watchmaker and repairer of keys, but of late he has gone into coining.

He tells Higgenbotham that he's heard rumors a federal mint will soon be built in gold country. If these tales are true, the development would allow miners and investors to change their gold nuggets and gold flakes into official US coins without having to send them to Philadelphia like they do now. Templin can't offer official US coins; he can offer only Templin Mint coins. Miners buy them for the convenience, he explains. He has traveled up here to find out what's going on with the planning, to suss out the federal competition.

—You from these parts? he asks congenially as he whips his horses into motion. The day is warm and clear and hyacinth blue in all directions. Templin wears a scarlet cloak and a patterned necktie; he reminds Higgenbotham of a wrapped present.

—No, Higgenbotham says as the stallions tug forward. —I'm from the Green Mountains originally.

—How many years you been in Georgia?

Higgenbotham has to think. —More than thirty.

—Well, you're a Georgia man now! Templin applies the whip again, the short lash cracking against the stallions' backs. —There's more of Georgia than of Vermont in you at this point!

—I'm not in so much of a hurry you need to flay them, Higgenbotham says, even though he *is* in a hurry, even though he needs to speed like the wind. —You can lay off the whip.

—Oh, they like it, Templin says, smiling broadly. —They wouldn't know what to do without a good tap now and then.

He casts a glance Higgenbotham's way. —My nigras are the same. And a couple of my lady friends. He winks.

When he finds out Higgenbotham is a land-lottery messenger, Templin clasps his hands in delight. He fawns over his new companion.

—I *knew* it, he says. —I knew you were a man of standing.

Again, he lays his whip across his horses, causing the muscles beneath their coats to twitch. The buggy bounces east. Higgenbotham holds on to the driver's seat. Behind them, Scout strains to keep pace, panting as he races in the sunshine.

—Give this land to good Georgia men, I say, Templin continues, sweeping his hand at the meadowed expanse around him. —Allow men to be men again. But I also say, let them hurry at it; the gold's disappearing. That well is running dry. He turns, regards Higgenbotham. —You didn't hear it from me, though.

He laughs again.

They pass peddlers and traders with carts heading west, and miners on foot trudging in both directions. Most of these men appear the worse for wear, if not penniless. They likely earned just enough to spend in the taverns and no more. *They should have sat out this gold rush and kept working in their saw- and gristmills,* Higgenbotham thinks. At least the pay at a mill or lumberyard was stable.

—Give us our forty acres, Templin declares, nodding as his horses fly by the laborers. —If we can't find gold, we'll grow corn, cotton, and a crop of Christians! He strokes his beardless chin. —Well, not me; I'd make a terrible farmer. And a bad Christian; I like my ladies too much. But I'm a fine businessman. And I can take a hunk of gold and turn it into a thing of beauty.

He produces a handful of two-dollar and five-dollar gold pieces from the recesses of his scarlet coat, jingles them joyfully. —Purer than anything you'll get from Philadelphia—

—We'll be reaching Loudsville, I expect, Higgenbotham says, cutting him off, pointing at the road ahead. Yes, he needs this ride, but he also needs to be away from this man. —I'll be taking my leave there. You're headed north now, correct?

Templin returns the coins to his coat. —No, sir, he replies. —I've decided to take you to *your* destination first. Yonah it is. Can't risk the lottery man being waylaid by marauding Indians! Why, you're a man of some importance.

Higgenbotham's temples are starting to tighten; he can feel his pulse on either side of his head. —No, he says. —No, no, I'm just the messenger. He looks over again at the minter. —And I don't think the Cherokees are doing much marauding these days.

Templin ignores him. His eyes gleam, and his hand finds Higgenbotham's, briefly clutches it.

—You're more than a messenger, he says. —You're one of us. You're the gold keeper.

They pass survey markers on trees and stumps, property stakes hammered into dead fields, forests half cleared, springs gummed with sediment. Muddied streams and abandoned ditches are everywhere. The horses, straining, gallop eastward, under a sky now scattered with clouds. Templin does not stop to water them, does not lay off the whip. Scout has fallen behind the buggy, unable to keep pace with the stallions.

In Loudsville, they stop for supplies. Scout catches up, finally, and flings himself onto the ground outside the store, panting, his ribbed sides heaving. Higgenbotham dismounts to give the wolfdog water, which Scout laps from his cupped hands.

Like Dahlonega, this town is brand-new, if it can be called a town, if it's not just a church camp in the middle of Cherokee country. There's a store, a one-room school, a brush arbor for religious services, and a Methodist chapel. *They should've had the revival here*, Higgenbotham, looking around, thinks. Maybe they will; maybe this town will be the circus's next destination. Set back in the hills are Indian homesteads, their smokehouses and cattle pens all silent. Most of the cabins appear empty.

At first Higgenbotham tries not to look at those homes, but once he gives in and directs his attention their way, he finds he can't stop; he can't quit staring at what remains of this Cherokee farmland. He sees a clothesline with a blanket still hanging from it, a multicolored skirt left to molder. Peach and apple trees, once pruned and thriving, are growing untended here, taken over by vines. A yellow dog sits outside a cabin, its ears pricked and alert, watching and waiting for someone to come home. How long that dog has been waiting, an hour or a month, Higgenbotham doesn't want to know. The animal is too far away for him to see closely.

He passes a hand over his eyes.

This is the crop he has sown; these are the deeds he has distributed. This is his handiwork—his legacy: these homesteads slowly emptied out, inhabitants harassed and legislated and lawyered into leaving. Higgenbotham doesn't have heirs; he doesn't have children who will survive him. He has thirty years of waiting for a letter that never came and now this cursed land lottery. And regardless of the fine print, regardless of the safeguards for Native peoples he has tried to maintain, when all is said and done, he has been complicit. He has been a courier of theft and exile and deception.

He looks up at those hillside cabins again, at that lone Indian dog still waiting for its owner. He's about to hear his old Calvinist mother again; he can feel her coming, sense her rising from the grave to lecture him. But when the voice of conscience reaches his ear, it's not his mother's. It's Barker's. It's Preacher Barker speaking to him.

You should have known better!

What happens next seems to take place outside him, separate from his body, divorced from his thoughts. In one and the same moment, Templin exits the Loudsville store, arms weighted down with packages, and Higgenbotham looks down at his own hands, which are—of their own accord—reaching out and grasping the reins, taking the horses over. He hears a whistle: it's his own pursed lips summoning Scout into the buggy. Higgenbotham does not approve of this Gainesville minter; he does not like him one bit. But he hasn't liked himself for some time now either.

—Hop on up, he says as the wolfdog's head pops up along the sideboard. —Hop on up, Scout. Hurry!

With a single leap, the wolfdog sails up and into the driver's seat. A perfect landing—he's been waiting to replace the minter this whole time.

Templin's head lifts as he descends the steps outside the store. When he sees Scout, his carefree smile changes to annoyance.

—Get that beast down from there, he calls out. —I thought I said no half-breeds in my—what are you *doing*, messenger?

Higgenbotham leans in and speaks to the stallions. He'll leave the choice to them; he won't force anything. But it's time he acted. It's time he *did* something. He issues an invitation:

—Leave him. Run if you want to, he says.

He doesn't have to invite them twice. The stallions surge into glorious motion.

—What in the hell are you doing? Templin cries again, starting forward. He calls for his team to stop, but these horses harbor no loyalty to him. They trot directly past him, snorting in triumph, aiming for the road, their regal heads held high. The bells on their harnesses ring out like church on a Sunday morning.

—You can't take them! Are you mad? Templin shouts.

The stallions were fast to begin with, and they're faster with Higgenbotham at the helm. They're better runners when a man doesn't whip them than when he does. Templin never took the time to learn that about them.

The minter raises one fist high. —Round these parts, the penalty for horse thieving is death, messenger!

—Well, if they hang me, at least I won't have to listen to you anymore, Higgenbotham shouts back. Then he and the horses round a bend, and the minter vanishes from sight.

Has Higgenbotham lost his mind? Most likely. Will he pay for it later? Undoubtedly. Does he care? No. Not yet, anyway.

—*Run*, he hears himself saying; he hears joy in his voice; he hasn't heard that sound in ages. Scout sits tall and straight on the driver's seat, though he leans against Higgenbotham's shoulder whenever they take a curve. He leans less out of necessity than for the happiness of bumping up against his new favorite person.

—Go on, Higgenbotham says to the stallions. They'll reach the 221st Company within another day at this pace. —Run! Run, boys!

Scout barks twice.

18

THEY SHOOT A DEER, skin and butcher and roast it, feed themselves around the fire. They bring Barker into their circle, give her a plate, let her eat, then they tie her wrists again. They keep her under guard, away from her uncle in his rock shelter. After drinking what's left of the regimental spirits, they shuffle into the trees to relieve themselves, shuffle back; several fall asleep quarreling. In the morning, they dine on leftover venison and chicory coffee under the shadow of Yonah Mountain.

Again, the men of the 221st Company ask Barker for her lottery papers. Again, she declares she no longer has them in her possession. They form a huddle, aggrieved; they plot and smoke their pipes, complain and seethe. Several want to inflict punishment: Make her straddle a wooden beam and sit on it with her legs weighted, force her to produce the land grant or experience her joints dislocating. But Johnny Thrasher won't let them lay a hand on her.

He and Scissors spend the first part of the morning outside one of the tents checking Barker's injuries. They inspect the goose egg on the back of her head, caused by that blow with the butt of a pistol. It's resolving; no bleeding, the swelling reduced. They test her sore shoulder next, the place where one of the men tugged too hard on her at the camp meeting. Scissors manipulates the joint, testing her range of motion; Barker cries out. —Let it be, Kerchief says.

After Scissors leaves, Kerchief crouches down beside her, by the extinguished campfire, as the sun warms the rocks around them. He speaks in a quiet voice. He tells Barker that she's tougher than most men. He says it's a job he's doing, nothing more, nothing she should take offense at, if possible. He asks her not to hold his capture of her person against him.

—Don't send me back in there, Barker says. —Are you sending me back in there with him?

Kerchief doesn't answer, but he keeps her with him for a while longer.

Midmorning, the men confront their captain. Stooping in his shelter overhang, they demand that Wiley make arrangements for their payment. They'll take coins or even paper scrip if he can't give them the land rights he promised.

—I don't have anything, Wiley says dismissively. —I gave all the money I had to that lottery messenger. He took it all for his fee.

The situation deteriorates. Tempers fray. Wiley has lost his bearings, the men say. He should have thought ahead. They want their golden acres. They're owed payment for this chase. The return of his niece has decimated their captain's reason and concentration.

—Land? Who cares about land? Wiley fires back. He certainly doesn't. What's land to him now, after all? If he can't see his acres, they don't exist. If he can't set his eye on the prize, some princely expanse of evergreen forest, then that forest is nothing to him; it is a no-forest. And if the forest has ceased to exist for Wiley, then it has ceased to exist for everyone.

Hasn't it? Why don't they understand this consideration?

—What do I care about gold either? Wiley adds, sneering, hurling his words at the rocks, this lair that has become home to him. —Gold's useless. It ain't no better than mica or any other metal. He pauses to expectorate. —Gold is a temptress dropped by God into the world to torment men and test their mettle.

He read that line somewhere; he's happy he remembered it. He feels like Barker's father for a moment—silver-tongued, eloquent.

Scissors arrives with a plate of venison, the meat overcooked and half charred. Wiley pushes the food away.

—Bring Barker back in here, he says. She's all he wants today. The men file out of the overhang, weary of him; Wiley calls out after them, tells them to bring his niece when they return. He wants to speak with her again; he wants her to come live in this shelter with him. Where are they keeping her?

No, the men say. Not until you pay us. Barker will appear when their payment for militia services rendered is either made or promised straightaway.

Scissors brings in a basin with water, a chunk of lye soap, and a cloth for drying. He sets these objects on the ground in front of the captain. —For washing, he says, and walks away.

—Stay, Wiley says. But his neighbor's son is gone, ducking out of the overhang, returning to the campfire and the other men. Wiley must strip off his own clothes, scrub his own foul pits and parts until the drying cloth bears his odor.

While he cleans himself, Wiley thinks of Elma. His wife would be tending to him right now if she were here; she would not abandon him to his own grime like his men have done. Wiley loves Elma and he abuses her, in equal measure.

If she would stop permitting his cruelty, he believes, he would stop carrying it out; he doesn't understand why she can't grasp this simple fact. Elma Wood is to blame for his own poor behavior. The mute, birdlike expression that takes over her face every time he threatens to shake or slap her, every time he rattles her bones, that terrified, beaked countenance—she does it to him; she puts on that horrid visage to provoke him. And when he is unable to soothe her, to make that expression go away, he must roar up and make her suffer more, because what else is there? What else can be done in the face of such abjection, such refusal to rein him in?

He will shake the wounded bird out of her.

Wiley sets his towel down. He smells something. He sniffs the air, sniffs again like a bloodhound. The odor lingers, sour and close, akin to curdled milk. He puts a hand up to his stitches, brings his fingers to his nose. The wound? Yes, it might be the wound smelling this way. It is. That's his own scent of rot he's taking in.

—Boy! Wiley shouts, panic stirring.

A poem comes to him from his beloved newspaper days, his adventures in reading, a joy he will not taste again. He remembers reading the lines aloud with Barker's help and not liking the poem, not approving of its undercurrent. The notion of white and black and red men all cavorting about, all free and of the same measure! But the poem has stayed with him:

Wend you to the Cherokee?
Where the Indian girls are prattling;
Where every one is conscience free,
And "chuck-luck" boxes loud are rattling
Where gin by the barrel full is drank—
And whites and blacks are all the same;
Where no respect is paid to rank,
But every one's of equal fame.

He can hear Scissors outside swapping tales with the company men, bickering and gossiping. Men start thinking they're all the same out here in the goldlands; they start acting on the semblance of an equal footing. They'll treat anyone as a friend so long as the fellow can wield a pickax and shovel, so long as he's not afraid to stand in a creek until his feet are numb with cold, his extremities nigh unto frostbitten. By those standards, Wiley's men might find Scissors more their equal now than he is.

He roars for help again.

—My wound, he says when Scissors returns. Wiley can hear the alarm in his own voice; he detests the sound. But aid must be procured. —My wound's infected. Come here and take a look.

—Seems all right to me, Scissors says from the safety of ten feet away.

But when Wiley insists the young man come near, when he calls Scissors a foul word and threatens him with twenty lashes, neighbor's son or not, Scissors steps into the dugout and stands before him.

—Good. Now debride me, Wiley commands.

The youth waits, unmoving, for several seconds before he retrieves a bottle of spirits from beside Wiley's sleeping pallet. Scissors knows the protocol. He's been cleaning the captain's wound since the mules left Watkinsville. This time, he takes a swig from the bottle first. Then, before Wiley can reprimand him for the epiglottal swallow he heard, Scissors takes another liberty. Slowly, deliberately, he pours the gin over the captain's head. He empties the bottle onto him, shaking it until no drops remain, drenching Wiley's hair, his bushy eyebrows, his ears and neck. So much gin pours over Wiley that he splutters and coughs, spirits streaming down his chin, glistening like dewdrops in his beard.

—What're you doing? he cries, waving his arms, trying to lay hold of this rascal, this uppity youngster; he swears he will put the whip to him. —What're you goddamn doing? You blasted—

Scissors puts down the bottle and stalks out.

Outside, the youth confesses what he has done; there will be no hiding it. He admits his deed to the other men as the captain roars his helplessness from the interior of the hideout. The soldiers of the 221st Company are amused by his action. Several clap Scissors on the back for it. One of them gives him a plug of tobacco, though Scissors has no pipe for smoking it.

The militia approve of what he's done. They've had it with Captain Wiley. If a humble mule driver of mixed race wants to take a lesson to him, they'll allow it.

Kerchief stands apart and watches this exchange. When Scissors looks over at him, he pauses, nods briefly. —He had it coming, he says.

A final meeting, then. A final tribunal, in the late afternoon, this time with Barker and Wiley near the center and ten angry horsemen squeezed into the overhang around them. They fit torches into crannies in the rocks to illuminate the shelter, arrange themselves cross-legged in a cramped circle; those who have pipes smoke them.

The men inform Wiley that they'll return to Clarke County without him unless he can procure their payment by some other means. They'll take Barker with them also. What exactly they'll do with her, they haven't decided. But she's worth more at this point than Wiley's word is. He can perish in his private cave without them.

Barker injects herself into the conversation. She informs the assembled group that her father has the claim they seek. Lorenzo McRae has the signed rights to those forty acres in his possession; she's sure of it, she tells them, lying vigorously.

—Take me to him, she says. She still needs to find Lorenzo, hasn't given up; this is her last try at a strategy. —Find my pa, and he'll give you that claim when he sees me. He's got the papers, I'm telling you.

The men gaze at her, then at one another, unsure what to think.

—I gave them to a missionary lady, Barker adds, improvising, reading her audience like a good preacher will. —That Moravian lady at the camp meeting—her husband knows my pa. She told me they'd get the papers to him straightaway.

Half truth, half fabrication. True to giving the woman the papers, not true to everything else she just said. Barker studies the men in the torchlight, folds her arms, and waits. Silently praying, but she won't let them know it.

—A likely tale, one of the men says.

—She promised me, and she's Moravian. And they don't lie. They think lying's the unpardonable sin, Barker says.

—Then you is bound for hell yourself, Wiley retorts, thrusting out his chest as he weighs in. He rises to his feet to address the others. —Even if she did give those papers to a missionary, her pa weren't nowhere near that camp meeting.

—How would you know? Kerchief asks, shifting his eyes to Wiley. —How would you know Lorenzo McRae wasn't near that camp meeting?

Silence follows. Barker's uncle prepares to give a speech. Using both of his walking sticks, he steps into the center of the circle as Barker backs away. One of his patches has slipped partway down his cheek. He has been waiting for this moment, waiting to make this declaration, for some time.

—I know exactly where her pa is. I know where Crazy Lorenzo has run himself off to. I can take you. She's been chasing in the wrong direction.

—You know where he is? Kerchief, incredulous, asks.

Wiley takes his time answering. Until now, he hasn't needed to share this information because they've been chasing Barker and Barker only. They've been going where Barker *thinks* her father is, not where her father actually could be located. But the situation has changed, and Wiley will make the most of it. He can feel sun on his face all at once, until he remembers he's in a rock hideaway. That sensation of warmth must be the return of everyone's attention on him.

—Yes, he declares confidently. —Yes, indeed. I know where he's at. He's been writing letters; he sent two of 'em. That's how I came to possess this information.

A rustle to his left. —*Letters?* Barker, from outside the circle.

—Yes, Wiley says again.

—To *me?*

—You, me, Elma, whoever, Wood announces.

He wants to tell Barker to come sit on his knee, but he manages to restrain himself, to retain his dignity. —They came a couple months ago, he adds. —Written from an inn by Tallulah canyon. I picked 'em up at the post office.

He can hear someone start forward—Barker again, still behind the other men. —*He wrote*, and you didn't tell me?

Wiley shrugs. That bad smell is coming back. Something is stretching, awakening, beneath his stitched-closed eyelid. He dreamed of maggots last night, the slow decomposition of living flesh; he has little time for footling around left.

—Your pa's out there seeking the Holy Spirit, he says. —Out there at the state's end. He wrote to say he still ain't found the Lord's face yet, but he's hopeful he's finally in the right place for it.

Wiley snorts. —You're better off without him.

When she realizes what her uncle has learned, what he has kept from her, Barker plows through the waiting militiamen and hurls herself at him. She shoves him, forcing him back; she pushes again. Wiley loses his balance, staggers, hits granite, lands on his hindquarters. He cries out, less from pain than from surprise—another attack from assailants unseen, another humiliation.

He knows, going forward, that he will be judged in this life less for his deeds than for his debility, for his blindness and his blindness only. The unfairness of that prospect—that unearned pity and scorn—makes him cry out again, hoarsely.

Barker lunges at him a second time. —You told me he never wrote, she says, straining to claw him; Kerchief steps forward, drags her out of the captain's way. —You told me you never heard from him!

—I did say that, Wiley concedes. He picks himself up from the floor, breathing raggedly. His patch has slid all the way down his cheek. The wound is so raw and suppurating that his men look away from him. —I did, surely. And it was true, up till a short while ago. I do concede I withheld the truth from you.

—*But why?* Barker howls. Kerchief has wrapped her in a fierce hold, his lumberman's arms unassailable. Wiley doesn't answer her question.

To Tallulah, then. To Tallulah to propose a trade: One girl gouger for forty golden acres. One stranded child for a father's best offering.

Yes, Wiley said Lorenzo couldn't have been at that camp meeting, couldn't have gotten his hands on the lottery papers directly. But Barker sticks to her story even as Kerchief holds her tight, still restrained.

—The Moravians'll find him, she declares. —They know every missionary in this state. If they haven't yet heard my pa's in Tallulah, they'll figure it out shortly. I bet they're already on their way. I *know* it.

The men half believe her. Or, if not half believe, at least a quarter—at least they can agree Tallulah's worth a try, even if the odds aren't great. The odds are better than what they have here, empty-handed in the shadow of Yonah.

Kerchief nods when Wiley's men state their plan. The gesture is not optimistic. He knows about long shots. Everything in Kerchief's life so far has been a long shot.

He tells the men they'll move out in the morning. He watches while they begin gathering their gear and saddles. Kerchief joined the Clarke County troop out of boredom and a need to belong to something. He stayed because he found acceptance. In the company of these hard-up men, he found laughter and commiseration, hustle and sport. Together they shared the recognition that life was not going to give them what they wanted and the sooner they accepted that fact, the better; the sooner they accepted that in this world there were haves, have-nots, and have-nots-and-never-will-haves, the better off they would be—and they'd take their comfort and satisfaction where they could.

As the men pack their goods, Kerchief walks to the campfire and pours dirt over the remaining embers. He's in charge of the 221st Company now, not Wiley. How and when this handoff occurred, he couldn't say precisely. He's young, but with these men his age doesn't matter. He's become someone they trust.

He directs Wiley to the covered wagon, tells him they'll ride at dawn. What it means to belong to something seems to be the question of the day, the question of the hour, out here in gold country. Kerchief grew up with Cherokee and

Scottish blood on one side, fur-trapping French-Canadians on the other, and a warrior uncle in the middle who did a fair portion of raising him. An uncle he could never compete with, so he eventually gave up trying.

He can't go live with the Cherokee because he's not one of them, but white settlers look at him strangely when he walks into their taverns. *Nothing personal*, they'll tell him later after they learn he's militia. *No hard feelings—we didn't know you was one of us.*

Kerchief helps the captain into the wagon, settles him in with a blanket. He tells Scissors that he's doing a fine job but the captain's wound is infected. Scissors gives him a side glance. —I'll do what I can, he says.

Personally, Kerchief would rather not have joined this cross-country errand. He has never believed anything good comes from chasing someone who doesn't want to be caught. But he'll stay with this company, for now at least; he'll stay with these men who don't care what blood runs through his veins so long as he delivers results and their promised payment.

—We'll see if her pa's at Tallulah, he says to the men as they retreat to their tents for the night. —We'll see what he's willing to pay.

Higgenbotham reaches the bald the following morning less than an hour after the company left. The abandoned campfire is still warm, the horse manure so recent that the flies haven't discovered it yet. In a makeshift shelter, he finds a tin plate with scraps of venison, a dirty bandage, a pair of stockings one of the men forgot or discarded.

He returns outside and studies the road. Barker's captors have headed east, from what he can glean, the evidence of their travel visible in wagon treads and hoofprints. If he hurries, he can catch up with them; his stolen stallions can outpace the regiment's ponies. He squints up at Yonah's hooked peak. Long ago, legend has it, Indians from two rival tribes—Sautee, a warrior of the Chickasaw, and Nacoochee, a Cherokee—fell in love and eloped from this very valley. The bride's father and his men chased the couple down and killed Sautee by throwing him off the side of the mountain. Nacoochee promptly flung herself off the cliff after him. She didn't want to live in a world that her lover no longer inhabited.

What would Sautee and Nacoochee think of their old lovers' leap now, Higgenbotham wonders, befouled by Clarke County men, reduced to a prospectors' hideaway? A place where Wiley Wood can pick his teeth with bat bones. He pulls himself back into the minter's buggy as Scout jumps up beside him. He taps the reins, and the stallions pull east. There are trade paths and old-time buffalo trails along this route, and a toll road jointly maintained by Cherokee and white settlers. Higgenbotham has no idea what he'll do when he finds Barker. He doesn't have his pistol. He has his mind and his sixty-four-year-old body and his apple-paring knife, and that's it; that will have to suffice. If he were a praying man, he would pray about now, or soon. But he's too stubborn to drop to his knees at this age.

The stallions race forward. They pass white oaks tipped silver-pink, shacks nestled against hills in the distance, smoke threading from a brush-clearing fire or cabin chimneys. Past the bald, wild turkeys strut across a field, and an old Indian mound looms up, a burial site from a civilization so old, Higgenbotham doesn't know its name. The turkeys thrust out their heads, jabbing left and right, hunting insects as the stallions move by. A coyote, a rare sight, chases a jackrabbit, the pair disappearing into the field, swallowed up by grass and cane.

Scout blinks up at Higgenbotham.

—That might be your kin, Higgenbotham says to him. He's slightly out of breath. The doctor at Scudder's was right: Cholera has rendered him a diminished physical specimen. —Those coyotes are closer to your kind than anything I've seen. Except wolves themselves, of course, but they're out of your reach.

He reaches for the whiskey, permits himself a sip. It's the last in the bottle, unfortunately. —Go on if you need to, he continues, waving Scout in the direction of the vanished coyote. —Go on, find your people. Don't stay if you have someplace you'd rather be.

Scout remains on the buggy seat.

The air cools; the stolen horses climb upward. They travel past more prospecting camps, quiet in the eventide, far off the road. Higgenbotham sees trenches filled with garbage, hills stripped of foliage, rushers gone feral.

When layers of blue mountains appear on the northeastern horizon, he senses he is almost upon them. The stallions haul up a long ascent, straining. The clouds sink into hollows on either side of the road; the clouds are beneath him. He hears a horse neighing but cannot see it. The wind has kicked up; the day is ending, the treetops bowing, sleep-ready. When he reaches the peak, Higgenbotham stops the horses and takes in the expanse around him.

The first time he saw the Blue Ridge Mountains, he thought they were the most beautiful sight he had ever beheld; he still thinks that, no matter how familiar they are, no matter how many times he travels through these unending layers of indigo highlands. Nothing can compare, not in this life and probably not in the next. That's the truth, that's God's truth, and he's including Vermont in that assessment.

And there they are, the men of the 221st District, in the waiting valley.

Higgenbotham spots a wagon and mules. He counts ten horsemen. One is the soldier with the yellow kerchief, Thrasher's ne'er-do-well nephew. Another has Barker on the saddle with him. The company has advanced slowly, the horses spent and worn.

Barker appears unharmed from this distance. Then again, almost every child appears unharmed from a distance. It's up close that the trouble starts showing.

He brings the minter's team forward gently, quietly. By morning, this region will be blanketed in fog, the far mountains dusted with rime, a spring frost that won't let go of them. The regiment is stopping now, seeking a place to make camp for the night. Higgenbotham will do the same, from afar. He'll stay behind; he'll keep his distance until he understands the plan, their destination. He needs an opening, a stratagem. Ten men against one doesn't work in his favor, even if this time he has the moral high ground, maybe *especially* because he has the moral high ground. In Higgenbotham's experience, taking the moral high ground is usually a disaster.

Give me till morning, he thinks at Barker. *Get through tonight, and I'll come for you first thing. I promise.*

But he is also frightened.

A snake hiding in a bed of muscadine bites Scout while Higgenbotham is setting up camp in the woods. It's a copperhead, a juvenile, born early in the season and more venomous for it.

When he hears the wolfdog yelp, Higgenbotham drops his gear and hurries through the brush toward the sound.

—Leave it! he shouts when he sees them, an incoherent command, because Scout hasn't bitten the snake; the snake has bitten Scout. The wolfdog whips his head from side to side, trying to dislodge his attacker. The baby copperhead flies up, curling, its muscled body snapping, but its fangs stay in Scout's cheek.

Higgenbotham doesn't think. He acts. He reaches for a rock, a Goliath-size rock half buried in grapevines, and rushes over. He brings the stone up and thumps it down, crushing the little snake's tail. Its jaw still doesn't unhinge. Scout bolts, carrying the half-crushed copperhead with him, out of his mind with panic. All it took was one good bite and a rock lobbed close enough to his head to feel like judgment.

Higgenbotham leaves the team and rushes deeper into the woods, following Scout, swerving and ducking through more rhododendron and laurel. He finds the wolfdog in a brook, in water up to his stomach. Scout's drowning the snake, lowering his head to immerse the juvenile in the brook, and doing such a stellar job, he appears to be drowning himself while he's at it.

Then Higgenbotham realizes they aren't alone.

One of the men from Wiley's company has hiked away from his fellow soldiers in the valley, seeking some peace and quiet in the woods. He's watering his horse and taking a long piss into the current. Hearing Higgenbotham crashing through the brush, the man turns, and his stream of urine rotates with him. His eyes fall to Scout and the snake. He's a hundred yards away from them.

—I know that dog, the man says amiably as he shakes his member and returns it to his breeches. He seems unsurprised by the sight of Higgenbotham. —That's one of the captain's hunting dogs. They all ran off a while back; he ain't seen any of 'em since.

Warily, Higgenbotham stands at the edge of the stream, waits to see what this soldier will say or do.

—That one's the worst of the lot, the man continues, nodding at Scout. —He's the one that wouldn't hunt. Least the other two could track a hare. Dumb as a turkey, he is, this one.

Abruptly, the copperhead loosens its fangs, disengaging from Scout's jaw. The flow of water carries the reptile, spinning, downstream. Scout lifts his head, snorting and blowing water, the outline of ribs visible through his wet coat.

Higgenbotham clears his throat. —Well, if he's your captain's dog, you'd best take him, he calls with deliberate indifference. —He's been following me these past few days; I've emptied my tinned beef feeding him. Now he's hurt. He's of no use to me.

The militiaman waves him away: Bluff succeeded. —Don't want no snakebit dog, he says. —Have my hands full already.

Higgenbotham nods, hiding his relief. —Where y'all headed? He's putting on his best Georgia twang, his best *I'm one of you* dialect. —Saw your company downhill a ways.

—Tallulah, the man replies, squinting up at the sky through the overstory, his manner thoughtful and unhurried. —We're chasin' gold in *Tallulah*.

He says the word like he enjoys the rolling *l*. *Ta-lu-lah!* —Or land with a promise of gold, he adds. —Or a preacher with a promise of land.

—That so, Higgenbotham says.

The Clarke County man sighs. His eyes are bloodshot, bleary with beer and travel. —You wouldn't believe the tale if I was to tell you. You wouldn't believe the chase we has been on.

—I'll take your word for it, Higgenbotham says.

After the militiaman leaves, Higgenbotham wades across the creek to retrieve Scout. He finds the wolfdog shivering in the shallows, his left cheek angrily swelling.

Higgenbotham picks him up, but Scout doesn't want to be carried. So he sets him down, then half drags him across the shoals of the creek to dry ground. —It's all right, he says. —The snake's gone. And I didn't mean it back there, what I said to that fellow about you. I was pretending.

Scout pulls away. But a few seconds later, he shoves his wet head against Higgenbotham's knee, trying to be both left alone and held, as if the two tasks could be accomplished simultaneously.

Higgenbotham inspects the wound. He squeezes the punctures, attempting to express the venom. Scout whimpers. A trickle of blood comes out—not enough. A snakebite can be treated by bathing the wound in warm milk, but

Higgenbotham doesn't have any warm milk; he has encroaching dusk and not much else.

He pinches the skin again—nothing. He breathes in. He knows what must be done.

He bends forward, takes the wolfdog's wound between his teeth, and sucks through the fur to get at the poison. He spits and sucks again, repeating the act several times.

Scout goes completely still. He has never been this close to a human being, has never experienced such intimacy.

His fur, Higgenbotham notices as he spits out a stray hair, is coarse and spiny, as wiry as a boar's bristle. He draws in what he hopes is the last of the poison and spits again, twice for good measure. This is a wolf's coat, not a dog's, not even a half-wolf's.

Without a doubt, this coat belongs to a wild animal.

He gargles creek water to rid his mouth of any remaining venom. Scout waits with head lowered, trembling, in the twilight.

—All this time, Higgenbotham says, standing, wiping his mouth on the back of his hand. —All this time, you were more one than the other. That coat's pure wolf, my friend.

Scout's head lifts, a little.

That night, his last before this chase will reach its end, Higgenbotham sleeps in the woods between two streams, far from the camped regiment and the lone travelers' roadhouse he has seen. He cannot abide the thought of sleeping near other human beings. He misses his mare Mandy. He misses the pony Pistol. He has no whiskey and no tent, just a single blanket and a bedroll; his stolen stallions are tethered to a chestnut tree, close enough that when one of the horses sneezes, Higgenbotham says —*God bless.*

He lies on his back in the small forest clearing. He gazes up at the night sky like a star that has fallen and cannot right itself. His palms are open, his eyes wide. He tries counting stars but gives up—thousands of them up there, winking off and on. A silver streak flashes across the sky, then another. He hopes Barker sees it from where she's lying. A meteor shower? A meteor trickle. He hears raccoons in the brush behind him disputing something, a defiant rustle, the never-ending battle over territory.

Then, overhead, from a nearby tree, he hears a new sound and sits up. Bobcat? Could it be a panther? *Please let it be a panther*, he thinks. It has been a lifetime since he saw one. Scout is deep asleep beside him, dreaming of jackrabbits, copperheads, pared apples. Higgenbotham peers up at the darkness. It's not a panther. It's an opossum, crossing the heavens on the branch of a chestnut tree, and her three joeys following. When Higgenbotham coughs, the opossum and her triplets freeze.

He pounds his forehead with his fist. What he wouldn't give for a drink. If he cannot have a panther in the trees or a friend waiting for him at the end of an evening, he should be allowed a drink. Whiskey is one of the few respites God gave the human race, one of the few sacraments remaining.

He looks over at his companion. Scout's paws are twitching; he's attacking marauders in his dreams. In sleep, he's reversing time, extruding the great intruders, sending them back the way they came. And the wolfdog bears within himself the same agonized dissent as this assaulted land, the same throttled bewilderment.

19

HERE IT IS, then. Here it is, lay it down and be done with it. Yes, lay this burden down; let it reside elsewhere, let it dwell somewhere else. Your father can't hold it. No man can hold it. No man can hold what a woman holds, not when it comes to these things.

But you, you're another story. So here's your task: Stop carrying it. Or stop carrying it while pretending you're not carrying it. Stop carrying it long enough to say the words. Give your tale back to God; hand this moment back to Him—to He Who Stood By, He Who Allowed It. Remember how the two of them merged, your father and the Heavenly Father? If they merged for the good, they stay merged for the not-good also.

That's him across the way there, isn't it? You've finally made it, finally reached your destination. Across the rise, on a lookout point high over the Tallulah River canyon, so far away he doesn't see you yet, he's there—Lorenzo's right there, near the same rim trail where you found him more than two years ago, that day you hopped and danced on the edge of a cliff to make him smile, and, for reply, he chastised you.

Your father was not at the farm the day you needed him the most. You have held this tale by yourself. You will hold it by yourself in the future also.

But you need to get it out, to yourself, if no one else, to yourself and to He Who Allowed It. Time to speak and not speak, both at once; time to exorcise this day while simultaneously sealing it in its vault.

In other words, time to become a preacher.

Here, then.

After Higgenbotham rode away from the farm that Maundy Thursday, you met your uncle in the doorway to the dogtrot. You asked him what he planned to do now. Wiley held an open bottle of spirits in one hand and the lottery papers in the other.

He said: —What business is it of yours what I do. Move out of my way, girlie.

But you didn't. You didn't move. Those papers were in your name. You were like popcorn steaming in a pan, bursting through unstarched skin. You were just so fed up with him.

When he wouldn't give you an answer, when Wiley raised that bottle of gin and took to it like he hadn't had a drop in days, you stood and blocked his way inside his own cabin. Higgenbotham was barely out of sight, barely down the road on his old gray mare, when this fight with your uncle started.

—That land ain't yours, you said. —It's in my name.

—It's not yours, he said. —I'm your uncle; I'm your guardian; that land's mine to do what I want with. Move—you're in my way.

He tried to push you. He listed sideways. He'd drunk too much already.

—No, you said, and stood your ground. —You ain't my guardian. What you are, Uncle Wiley, it don't have a name.

Then he exploded.

Much of what happened next, you can't remember clearly, though you do recall him taking another swig before setting the bottle down and grabbing you by the shoulders. He shook you until your teeth knocked in your skull.

—Don't you contradict me; don't you speak to me like that in front of visitors—

—I wasn't contradicting you, you said right back. —I was *correcting* you. And that messenger agreed with me, Uncle Wiley.

He spun sideways, grabbed you by the neck, shoved his way inside the dogtrot with you in tow, latched the door behind him. He seized the neck of your dress and pulled your face close. He reeked of homemade gin.

—Let me go, you said to him. Then you said it again because it felt good, standing up to him, speaking back, even as your knees threatened to give way. —Let me go, Uncle Wiley!

For reply, he clapped his hand over your mouth, then released it long enough to slap you so hard, the inside of your lip opened against your tooth. He covered your mouth with his palm again.

—Don't you start telling me what I can and can't do, he spat. —Don't you keep yapping at me. Be quiet. Be quiet like a woman should.

That's when you scratched him. You reached up and scored two long marks along the side of his face, opening the skin, raked him temple to whiskers. Wiley reared back, cursing. Where his hand had covered your mouth, you tasted clay, salt, man. Of course you were going to pay for all this.

He dragged you over to the bed. To his bed this time, not the loft. You prayed he would take you up to the loft;

you prayed for a measure of familiarity. This was not a Wiley you knew. Garbled sounds issued from his throat. This was not even Belligerent Wiley. Someone else had come through.

He half shoved, half threw you onto the mattress. The back of your head struck the bedpost, and down you went, him heaving on top of you, misshapen, making a strange lowing sound like a bison, that's what he sounded like; it's what he looked like, too, his head like a bison's, oversize, shaggy, wounded.

—Lay still, the bison said, swiping at his bleeding temple. You had cut him; you had cut him good.

Aunt Elma! you thought in a whirl. *Help me!*

But she was nowhere to be found.

The room flickered and fogged. Wiley pulled up your dress, your petticoat. He tugged at your shoes, your underdrawers. His free hand circled your neck again, throttling. You gagged and kicked; he held you down. Saliva collected in the corners of his mouth. He pushed your legs apart, and the room went white; your ears filled with a new sound.

Then—all at once—he withdrew. What was this?

For an instant, you thought you might be spared; for the briefest of seconds, you thought your prayers had been answered and the better angels of Wiley's nature had landed on him.

Your prayers hadn't been answered. No better angels had landed on him.

Your uncle had withdrawn merely to change position. He adjusted himself, spat into his hand, adjusted himself again. Then he grasped your hips, rocking you up, too high—what was this—and thrust in again.

Different, this time. Not like a man with a woman.

In that moment, the night table and the bedcover and the rope ladder and the window leading to the vegetable patch and the latched rug leading to nowhere all gave way to color. They dissolved, and color swooped in to take their place. Florid cherry, burned cinnamon, flame orange. Gold is the color of pain, you learned. Tighter and tighter he drove, into your inmost world. He kept you pinioned. When he loosened his grip on your neck, you cried out; you called out for your dead mother. —Mama, you cried. —Mama.

—Shut up, he sputtered. —Shut up, you dumb whore.

Your thoughts floated upward, ascended to the rafters, hovered far up, above the bed. The scent of your shit couldn't follow you up here.

It went on for a long time. But it wasn't happening to you anymore; you were no longer part of it. Poor Barker down there—well, that was another story.

Afterward, he fell asleep, spent and snoring within seconds, arms flung wide across the bed, every exhalation a plume of gaseous liquor. The bottle on the floor lay on its side, nearly empty.

Someone else took over then; someone else sprang into motion. Some other Barker.

You watched from on high, from the loft and rafters. You kept vigil as the girl down there picked herself up, stepped over to the washbasin, and cleaned herself, scrubbing frantically, thighs, buttocks, legs. Just as she was finishing, a noise stopped her short. Her head lifted. That squeak was the door opening. How was the door opening? Wiley had latched it. But someone knew how to enter anyway, to get around the closure; someone had learned, over many years, how to sidestep the obstacles Wiley Wood placed in front of her.

And all of a sudden, the girl wasn't alone anymore.

Elma Wood stood in the open door, weaving like a swaybacked horse. She wavered there in that doorway, her sleeves rolled to her forearms, still aproned, a ball of cooking twine in her hands from whatever meal she'd been preparing. You saw that she wanted to run away, but she wouldn't; she was as afraid as any creature hunted or whipped has ever been, but she was not going away this time; she was not leaving you to him any more.

She was here.

Elma looked at you, then at the bison in the bed. Her gaze traveled back to you again. You were beside the bed now; you had come down from the rafters. You were here too. Not a word came from your aunt's mouth. It didn't have to. You read her eyes and grasped their message. You saw her silence as observation, as attention, as intent.

Elma moved. She strode over to her sleeping husband, climbed onto the bed, and straddled him. Wiley murmured and shifted, stuporous with drink. A bubble of saliva formed between his lips and evaporated. Elma thrust the twine at you and mouthed: *Tie him.*

So you did. You took that same ball of twine your aunt used to tie the legs of plucked hens, and you grasped Wiley's hands, carefully lifted them, and knotted the string around his wrists. He slept on, unmoving, though his lips smacked a couple of times. When he was good and bound, you stepped back, and Elma leaned forward from her straddled position. She took a hunk of his hair in her right hand and twined the locks around her second and third fingers. She got a good grip on that hair, just as he used to say he'd done to his opponents the many times he'd bragged about his rough-and-tumbling days. Elma hadn't missed the lesson.

Wiley began to stir. The same gin that knocked him out could also wake him up prematurely. But just as his one eye threatened to flutter open, Elma tore it out of him. She jammed her thumb in at the bottom, at the base of his socket, and she pressed, digging and screwing and gouging. Her thumbnail wasn't long or tallowed; it wasn't primed for the deed. But it was strong; it would suffice; it came with rage attached.

It was an ordinary woman's thumb, after all, a thumb marked by servitude to a very bad husband, a thumb with a chipped nail belonging to an overworked hand, to a hand freckled and calloused from long days and longer nights, hours and years spent wringing out washing, stirring pots, pulling up weeds, clapping out rugs, praying to a moon that would not rescue her.

Blind him.

When he roared, Elma did too. Coming from her, the sound was so surprising, you nearly started squalling yourself, even as you helped hold your uncle down, even as you helped her do what she was doing. She roared an ungodly howl that didn't sound like the Aunt Elma you knew: *No more.* She kept it up the whole time she dug that organ out of its socket; it looked like she was pitting a peach. The eye landed on the bedsheets.

And the fluid—gelatinous, blood and tissue—quilt and pillows spattered, the scratch you'd administered to him earlier suddenly nothing, suddenly sophomoric. All while your aunt roared above him, as afraid as anything alive, yet not relenting; she overpowered him like that tale you had always loved from the Old Testament, the one about the female judge, the only truly angry woman in the Bible, in your opinion: Judith preparing to take the head of Holofernes. That was what Elma Wood looked like. She looked like Judith rearing up over a tyrant, preparing to decapitate him to save a nation. She *was* Judith, in that moment. A woman doesn't have to be fearless to do what Judith did. She just has to be brave enough to render a judgment.

Wiley pitched up, flailing and screaming, hands still bound. He never saw his judge. He never knew his wife had come into the room. He never knew it was his wife who had attacked him.

Elma sprang away, leaving him and that cavernous socket, scrambling off the bed before he could grab hold of her, before he could reach out and feel her apron or her worn-out body and realize his wife had done it to him.

But he should have thought of that possibility a long time ago; he should have been ready. You can't push someone's face in the dirt forever and expect nothing will come back in the other direction.

Elma turned to you, trepidation in her gaze, fear and alarm but also something new glimmering around the edges, something like satisfaction.

Run, she mouthed. Then she was gone.

What else.

Tie on your bonnet. Snatch the lottery papers from where he dropped them when he loosened his trousers.

Those stupid golden acres, that lucky draw that started everything.

Find your shoes: Where are they? You're alone again, except for Wiley; your aunt has left the premises. You can't find your boots. Take his instead; time's running out.

Retrieve your coat, unlatch the door, fling it wide; the day is cold, the air so cold it scalds. Don't look back, just get out. Get out and shut the door on him. Maybe hand him what he lost before you leave; maybe hand him that eye, press it into his palm, and say *Good riddance*.

You can't remember if you did that part or just imagined it afterward.

Find your aunt, rocking herself behind the barn, hugging her knees, squatting in a patch of dead garden. She's hiding once again, returning to herself. Her hands cover her face even when you try to peel them away.

—Come with me, you beg her. —Come with me, Auntie, we'll run together. We'll find a place that's safe.

But she wouldn't leave him. She will never leave him. She had the one act in her, and the one act only. She gave all she had, and now she must sit back down again, wait for the moon to return, resume her lunar vigil once again.

She didn't believe the moon would follow her if she ran.

—Go, Elma said to you hoarsely. —Go, and don't you come back here. Hurry.

And a final admonition, her face lifting, briefly, from her bloodstained hands, her gaze upon you steady.

—Live, she said. —Live your life, Barker.

She sees her father the same moment she hears the roar of the cataracts. They have rounded a bend on the rim trail, and the afternoon fog has lifted just enough to reveal him up on his lookout point. Light rain has started falling.

Lorenzo McRae sits alone on a boulder jutting out over the canyon, the Tallulah River thundering through the gorge below. The scene is so vast and wild, Barker notices everything that is *not* her father first—silvered canyon; white falls, a vertical forest descending from the rim trail down to the river floor. A black vulture circles rising steam from the falls. Wet wind riffles Barker's hair as Kerchief's horse moves up the trail. Barker is back on the palomino as of this morning. Her last rider wearied of her, gave her back to her original captor. Kerchief didn't protest; Barker didn't either. The canyon below them is an ocean of spray and fog.

For a moment, she feels absolute lightness, a pure quiet like no other.

When he sees the men of the 221st District advancing below him along the trail, Lorenzo stands up. He watches the company's procession, waits for them up there in his somber black coat with his hands clasped behind his back and his head bare. He has been waiting for something to happen for a long time now. He thinks maybe this is it. He's been seeking a sign, asking God to shine His face on him again.

Tallulah, after all, is the canyon where he lost the witness of the Spirit more than two years ago. He lost his wife not long after. Since then, he has been preaching dry, preaching without lubrication. He has little trust anymore in what his sermons are saying.

He has returned to this site in desperation; he has begun to think God dwells not in the heavens but in the canyons. This lookout point that he has chosen for his daily meditation received its nickname from the tourists—they call it the Pulpit. When he heard that name shortly after his arrival, Lorenzo knew God was leading him to this very spot, to wait and pray as long as the Holy Spirit required.

And Lorenzo has been busy since Sarah's death, frantically so, too busy. He has preached without ceasing, up and down the goldlands, advocating repentance, conversion, sanctification, fair treatment for the least of these, the release of the captive, aid to the vulnerable.

He has remarried too.

Yes, it's true, Lorenzo married his cause just a few months ago. He hasn't told many people yet; he finds the situation slightly embarrassing, if he's honest. But he isn't the first preacher to fall in love with the object of his advocacies, and he won't be the last either.

Initially, he thought the new marriage would help him, would catapult him out of his spiritual desert. But to date, it has not altered his dilemma. It has not relieved his exiled state. Lorenzo cares for his new wife, but she is a stranger to him in every way. She makes him nervous with her long, unfathomable gazes, her silent appraisal of everything he, a white man, does and eats and says. He recently caught her probing the contents of his chamber pot with a stick, trying to determine if his insides operated the same way hers did. He has not brought his Cherokee bride to Tallulah with him.

For her part, Barker cannot breathe as she looks at him.

A thousand feet down, the river winds through its basin, surrounded by walled rock, inverted mountains, knobs and sheets of quartzite granite that have carved out the canyon's spine.

Closer now. The nearest cataract is deafening. The trees at the canyon's base are thimble-size from where Barker looks at them. A few hundred yards more, and she'll be within range of her father's rocky lookout point; she'll be able to walk from this trail up to where he stands, throw herself in his arms if they'll let her, if she wants to be held by him.

She does and she doesn't. Spend half your life yearning for someone, and when you find him, the reality can be somewhat disorienting.

—Don't lean so much, Kerchief says from behind her in the saddle. —Lean any further, and you'll topple into that river.

A hundred yards now from the base of the lookout point. A pair of peregrine falcons rocket past, dipping below the rim trail before soaring up above the company men. They fly all the way up to Lorenzo on his elevated rock before lifting beyond him, disappearing into the fog. Barker calls out to her father, raises a hand, waves up at him. But he doesn't recognize her. Or he does and he doesn't; he's squinting and staring; he's not sure. It's been two years, after all; she's fourteen now, not twelve; she's not the same girl. Barker drops her hand. She can hear Wiley's wagon rattling behind the riders, behind Kerchief, and hear her uncle inside, calling out to Scissors, asking if they've reached the preacher yet, demanding to know if the men believe him now. —I knew where he went, he keeps saying. —I always knew it! The other horsemen ignore him.

Barker looks again at her father. She blinks away rain, which is also river. The sky is silver. Everything is damp—her face, her hands, the butterfly weeds sprouting from the rocks, Kerchief's shirt, the back of his neck, his palomino's coat. Kerchief slows his horse and looks back at Barker, his brown-eyed gaze steady, a hint of understanding in those eyes, understanding and maybe pity.

—You ready? he says. —Time to do this.

20

HIGGENBOTHAM WILL BE the witness.

Ten men converge on Tallulah Gorge, high on the rim trail that overlooks the Hurricane. Or is it L'Eau d'Or, or the Tempesta, names assigned to these waterfalls by European tourists? He doesn't know and he doesn't care. He leaves the stolen stallions tied to a horse rack outside a tourists' inn, takes a minute to compose his thoughts, to gather up this plan that is no plan, this venture that amounts to announcing himself before a group of armed militiamen and trying to talk them into releasing Barker to him.

He'll walk the remaining way. He'll walk in the misting rain, with Scout beside him.

When he sees Kerchief and Barker riding up the trail, instinct tells Higgenbotham to wait a little longer, to watch for what comes next. Off the trail he scurries, ducking into a grove of hickory saplings girdled with early blackberries. Those blackberries are mere flowers now, but by July, if he were a bear, he could feed himself for days here. He has a partial view of the canyon and a full view of a rocky lookout. He can see the regiment men on the rim trail, a covered wagon following them. When Scout sees the militiamen, a low rumble rises in his chest.

—It's all right, Higgenbotham tells him. —They aren't your masters anymore.

The wolfdog stays close beside him.

That's Barker's father in the flesh, isn't it? At long last, waiting up there on that rocky outcropping, ignoring the rain. Lorenzo with the leonine mane, Lorenzo with his preacher's coat and his bleak apostolic face. And Wiley's here too, good Lord; there he is. Higgenbotham hasn't seen him since that day at the farm, the day that started everything. Barker's uncle climbs down from the wagon with the help of his driver, then steps toward the boulder's base where the other riders have gathered. He uses a walking stick, and he wears two eye patches. His driver does not walk beside him.

Higgenbotham can hear most of the words Wiley bellows up at Lorenzo but not all of them. He catches snatches:

Look at me, Preacher.

This is what your offspring did.

Did you know you raised a savage?

Love those Injuns so much didn't know your daughter was one.

Tell me how you plan to recompense my sufferings.

Barker breaks in from her position on Kerchief's horse, craning her body around her captor to call out.

—Pa! she shouts. —It's me!

When he hears his child, Lorenzo freezes. Wiley swivels around, hearing the same voice; Wiley hears Barker better than her father sees her. He has words for his niece as well; his speech tumbles out, taking over, lines he's been waiting to say to her:

Where'd you go off to, girl—

I been asking for you—

I been telling them to bring you over here—

Where did you hide yourself, you little—

Higgenbotham, crouching in the thicket, blackberry thorns jabbing at his buttocks, feels queasy as he listens.

Why'd you hide from me all this time—

Where were you, where did you go—

This isn't the Wiley Wood with whom Higgenbotham exchanged words on Maundy Thursday. This is a different man. It's Besotted Wiley, clotted with yearning, interrupting the long-delayed reunion between father and daughter. If Besotted Wiley had another eye, he might well let it be plucked out too if he could put his arms around this child afterward.

Why did you go away from me, my little Barker—

All at once, Higgenbotham understands. He comprehends what has happened to her. It's as bad as he had tried not to speculate. As bad and worse.

He passes a hand over his eyes. He hears the supplicant in Wiley's voice, slick and needy. He hears the silence coming back from Barker—a quiet beyond bearing.

As someone who has no child, or, more accurately, who had three children for a total of six hours, Higgenbotham is clear about one thing: Wiley Wood has committed a sin unpardonable, a sin that has no forgiveness in this life.

And Lorenzo's sin falls close behind it. Lorenzo's failure to keep watch over his daughter made Wiley's trespass possible.

Higgenbotham reaches down and checks his watch. It's four o'clock. Of course it is. Four o'clock is the hour this whole thing started back when he gave Wiley the papers. It's also the worst hour of the day in general. At four o'clock, there's not enough time left to mend whatever has gone wrong, but there's too much time left to abandon the day altogether, to succumb to the numbing rituals of night.

He snaps his timepiece shut. He watches as Kerchief guides his horse to the base of the overlook, ignoring Wiley's beseeching words, Barker still in the saddle behind him.

But if Higgenbotham's going to indict a man for his sins, his own are right up there as well—and committed for the most selfish of reasons: to earn enough money to flee Georgia, to leave a land whose ruin he has, by his messengering, accelerated.

And Barker's forty acres are tucked into his coat now too, that property grant he can't seem to get rid of, the duty he can't discharge.

—McRae, Kerchief calls out. The young militiaman swings himself down from his horse and tugs his hat against the weather. He looks up at the preacher on his rock pulpit. —We have someone who belongs to you. And we've been told you have something that belongs to us.

He pauses, looks at Barker, then back at Lorenzo. —We're here to collect the forty acres that was deeded to your child. We're here for the lottery papers that she tells us are, or will soon be, in your possession.

He turns again to Barker, but she's in motion, sliding off the palomino. She doesn't have time for negotiation, for bluster or positioning. She certainly doesn't have time to stand around arguing over forty acres. She hits the ground running, bursting past Kerchief; he didn't bother to tie her wrists this last ride. She races toward her father, scrambles up the rocks to the lookout point. She's agile; she could have been a mountain goat. But twenty paces from the summit, something stops her short.

Higgenbotham, watching this moment, has the same thought Barker appears to be having. And it's not about the lottery papers. Higgenbotham, in his mind, stops halfway to the lookout point too, right alongside Barker.

Lorenzo should be running toward her. He should be hurrying down from his solitary plateau now that he finally sees her, now that he grasps it's his daughter before him. He should be frantic to reach her; he should be meeting her halfway or more. Why is he just standing there? Why is he making her climb all the way up to him?

Barker catches her breath, chest heaving. Bewilderment is etched across her face. She shouldn't be doing all the work. It's a father's responsibility to narrow the gap, to step toward his child, as difficult as that might be, as complicated as his own life might remain.

What's wrong with him? Higgenbotham and Barker both think.

When he sees the truth, when he realizes the identity of this half-grown stray dressed in boy's clothes who has stopped below him, this daughter he has not laid eyes on in over two years, so much older and ganglier than he remembers, Lorenzo briefly sags forward, as if someone punched him in the stomach. When he straightens, his eyes find hers.

—Barker, he says. —Oh, Barker—

—Pa! she calls out again. —Where've you been? Why'd you leave me so long?

Lorenzo lowers his head.

They demand he hand over the lottery papers. Lorenzo doesn't have any lottery papers. He bristles, defensive, grows resistant. —I have no idea what you're talking about, he says.

They ask again. The more he flares, the more agitated the company men become. Barker misled them. Of course she did. They're fed up with not being paid. They dismount from their horses.

Lorenzo can't decide whom to look at, ten milling militiamen or one confounding daughter. He settles on the militiamen. County troops and their demands he can handle. His own child is another story.

She's a gouger, wanted by every able-bodied man in Clarke County.

Forty acres, Wood's name on it, hers first, though.

Near three weeks we been chasing her.

She said you had 'em, the lottery papers, either that or you'd have 'em shortly.

Fair, innit? A trade. You're her father, ain't you? A father will do what he has to.

Don't piss us off, Preacher.

—But I don't own forty acres, Lorenzo calls down, looking from one man to the next. He has not left the Pulpit. —I don't even own this coat I'm wearing.

They ask for the papers again, calling up to him, ask if he's had a visit from any Moravians; they tell the preacher to consider his answers carefully.

—*Pa*, Barker says. —I can explain—

—I don't have to consider my answer, Lorenzo says, bridling, speaking over her. —I have no lottery papers on my person. And even if I did, I wouldn't give them to you all.

His hands are on his hips. Righteous anger is starting to brew. —Those lots belong to the Cherokee Nation. Any white man in possession of such papers ought to burn them.

—Pa. Barker tries again. She's just a few yards down the rock from him.

He frowns quickly over at her. —Where's your aunt? She was supposed to keep you. Where's Elma, and why aren't you with her?

Barker blanches.

—I'm trying to tell you. Pa, Uncle Wiley, he—

But Lorenzo is fully inflated now; he doesn't need other people's explanations; he doesn't need facts to interfere with a good sermon. Too many details will hobble a message; he learned that lesson a long time ago. Just one burning issue is enough; it's all he needs, just one thought, one point, one passion. It's all about the energy, the back-and-forth, the flow of language around a single flame. That's preaching.

And if these men are here about the Cherokee land lottery, he'll give them something, all right. He'll give them a piece of his mind, forty acres of moral outrage.

—Gentlemen, he says, directing himself to the company. Barker's hands have balled into fists. Lorenzo doesn't notice. —Allow me, if you will, to speak.

Yes, he possesses *it* today, whatever *it* may be; today is one of the good days, one of the days he doesn't have to slaver and beg for it. He can preach; he *feels* something; he can love and condemn simultaneously. The sight of his daughter has left him both joyous and ashamed and, because ashamed, overcompensatory.

—I will orient my brief remarks, he says, around the plight of the Cherokee—

—*Pa!* Barker cries again. —Listen to me—

—Daughter, he says sharply, all ministerial now, intolerant of interruption, the circuit rider reviving. —Can't you see I'm speaking?

Can't get his attention? Do it again, then, do what you did that time before, even if he yelled at you for it. Dance on the ledge of this rock, hop-skip into his frame of view. Panic him—force him back into his fathering role.

Race up the remaining feet of this lookout point; that's it, that's how you do it; jog to the edge of this boulder stone leering over the canyon. You're not afraid; falling's not your fear. Dance and jig until he's forced to notice you.

Aunt Elma told you to live. She said it twice. But she never said don't call your father to account while doing it. She never said don't bend backward over the cliff's edge in the process, don't tempt fate, don't pretend to be a plunging falcon, that bird of prey that—look!—just shot by you—

Higgenbotham scrambles forward, but he's late, ridiculously late; he waited too long to present himself, and now he can't free himself from these blackberry canes, thorns hooking his breeches. He pulls and tugs, tearing fabric, thorns piercing his hindquarters. Finally, he breaks away. The nerve along the back of his leg is spasming again. Scout has sprung to his feet, tail up, alerting. But both Higgenbotham and the wolf-dog are too far away to stop what's happening.

When Barker falls, she doesn't fall straight. She's too agile, too quick. Her reflexes are instantaneous. *Grab something.* She twists around, catching rock; her chin clocks against granite. She scrapes the boulder as her hands find stone, grit, sand. Her hands have a hold now, but her feet have no purchase, legs dangling. She'll fall into the canyon as soon as she loses her grip.

Lorenzo howls forward. Forgetting his speech, forgetting the militiamen, he bounds toward her, shouting. Barker's over the ledge, or nearly. *Hold on*, he cries, reaching out, hands high, like he's answering his own altar call. *Hold on, Barker, I'm coming—*

He reaches the Pulpit's edge and seizes her by the wrists. In a second, he has her. He lifts and drags her to him, pulling painfully. The pain travels from her shoulders up to his hands; they both feel it. He keeps pulling until she's on the rock again and he has hauled her to safety. Both the fall and the retrieval take place so fast, the soldiers below can't quite track what's happening. Higgenbotham limps through the clearing, pushing toward the scene, racing as best he can. Wiley alone caws a warning.

Wiley, crow that he has become, hears, feels, divines something. The heightened signals he has started to receive from his remaining senses now torment him. —Look out, look out, he cries belatedly, arms flapping, and again, until Kerchief tells him to be quiet, to shut his mouth or he'll do it for him.

Gingerly, Barker stands up from the rock. Lorenzo seizes his daughter by the shoulders. He searches her face intently; he's saying something to her; Higgenbotham can't hear what. Higgenbotham can't hear anything but his own heartbeat. He can only watch. And that look in Lorenzo's eyes isn't relief, or it isn't relief alone. Something else is in the water also.

Don't you dare, Higgenbotham thinks, breathing heavily as he hitches toward them. *Don't you dare dole out any words to her right now but loving-kindness.*

Too late.

—What were you thinking, Lorenzo cries, the universal fatherly chastisement. —What in the world were you thinking?

Barker shoves him away. She won't have it. She won't have another male admonition, not today, not after everything. Being told what you've done wrong shouldn't be the only way to be loved by someone.

—Child, he says. —You need to *think*.

She shoves her father again, harder, tears starting; her strength surprises him. Lorenzo wasn't expecting this drama today. He was hoping God might talk to him. Instead, here is his daughter, with whom he is *not* well pleased, his daughter whom he loves but who is strange to him, even mildly frightening. And odd-looking too, dressed like a boy, albeit beginning to take after her mother also, her mother whom Lorenzo still misses, whom he still grieves.

Beside Higgenbotham, Scout emits a whine. The wolfdog has shifted his attention to Lorenzo. He has locked his sights on Barker's father up there, tracking him as Lorenzo grips his daughter's shoulders. Lorenzo shakes her gently at first, but when Barker tries to wrestle free, he shakes her again, more forcefully.

—Don't take such risks. Don't fling yourself into harm's way like that, he shouts.

Scout whines again. Only it's not a whine this time, it's lower. It's a warning. Higgenbotham is approaching the base of the boulder, the company men looking on, the wolfdog a half a breath behind him.

—Listen to me, Lorenzo calls out. —Barker. I know you've been lonely.

—I'm not lonely, she cries back. —That's not what I—

—I know you didn't want me to leave, he says. —Watkinsville. I know you didn't want to go live with your aunt and uncle. Well, I didn't want it either.

The rain is steadier now, seems never-ending. Lorenzo still grips her by the shoulders. —These past two years have been tremendously difficult, he says. —But I had to do what the Holy Spirit asked of me.

—How do you know it was the Holy Spirit? she hurls back. —What if you was just talking to yourself this whole time?

Lorenzo makes a garbled sound—fury, admission, both. Barker pulls away again, but he won't allow it. She's his daughter, after all; she's his catastrophe to resolve. He wraps his arms tightly around her.

—Enough, he says as he draws her closer. —Enough, Barker. It's me. I'm here. It's Papa.

She starts sobbing.

—I'm here, he says again, hugging her tighter, relenting, softening. —I'm right here. Hush, now, it will be all—

But he will not get the chance to tell her it will be all right. That reassurance will never leave his mouth.

What Higgenbotham sees next, what he observes from fifty paces out, makes no sense at first: A blur of legs and tail, silver-gray crashing forward, bounding up the Pulpit, a cannonball of hackles and fur. He doesn't recognize the animal as Scout until he looks down and realizes the wolfdog is no longer behind him.

The regiment's horses rear up, whinnying and sidestepping. To them, this beast is a wolf, no less and no more; they know a predator when they smell one. But Scout's not interested in horses.

He surges up the rock, snarling, his ears so flat, they're part of his skull. One of the horses loses her footing, starts scrabbling backward. Kerchief calls out a warning, steps forward to grab her lead, looks up in time to see the wolfdog flying up the lookout point. He whistles sharply, a call to *Come here*, a command from the boar hunts Scout used to dread going on.

The militia know this animal. They know his type too: the runt of the litter, the outsider. They train these creatures for two commands and two only: *Come here* and *Go kill it.* Scout learned only one of them.

—What? What is it? Wiley shouts. —What's happening to me?

He fears another punishment, another bottle of gin or female rage emptied out on him. But this judgment is not coming for Barker's uncle.

Scout leaps. Briefly airborne, grace in motion, pure wolf once again. He will save the one who fed him grits when he was hungry. He will not let anyone lay a hand in anger on her again.

Kerchief draws his gun but a clear shot at the wolfdog is impossible. Barker and Lorenzo both cry out; Barker scrambles backward, away from her father. Lorenzo raises his hands, instinctively protecting his neck. It's not enough. Scout lunges for the throat of the preacher.

A single cry, a last revelation, and Lorenzo McRae finally sees God's face.

The collision sends the pair flying backward, past Barker, man and wolfdog entwined, tumbling. There's not enough rock left to hold them, not enough Georgia left for them both. Over the cliff they plunge, Scout's jaws locked on Lorenzo's throat, clamped as tight as the copperhead that bit the wolfdog the day before. *What goes around comes around,* Higgenbotham mutely, numbly thinks as he begins scrambling up the Pulpit, as all the company men start forward, shouting.

The pair fall in a long arc toward the cataract. They fall as one, through the mist and steam, man and dog, man and wolf, toward the waiting river. One of them hits a tree on the way down, but they keep falling. Scout does not let go of him.

21

ON YOUR KNEES now, at the edge of the canyon. Sink to your knees right here, on the rock where he went over. Peer through the rain and steam and spray, that plunging forest, bird's-foot violet lining crevices of stone. He might be on a ship, that's how seaborne this air feels; he might be sailing into a suspended sea. Look for any sign of him.

Rain is in your eyes, your hair, your life, your face. You cannot see him anywhere. As your father went over, you glimpsed his final expression. His countenance held neither fear nor shock but something beyond both, something of awe, otherworldly. His white shirt fluttered, and that long red hair whipped like a cat-o'-nine-tails as he fell. The wolf-dog did not lose his grip on him as they vanished into the waterfall.

You turn, rise, and stumble away from the ledge, fleeing the overlook, back to the rim trail. You pass the regiment men on their way up as you descend the rock; they're swarming, surrounding the plateau, peering over the Pulpit's edge, shouting, pointing. *Do you see him? Do you see anything?*

Lorenzo is not returning.

Wiley Wood paces at the lookout's base, cane tapping, asking what has happened. His driver has absented himself, retired to the mules and the covered wagon. Nearby, the horses rear and backstep, still spooked. Kerchief leads two of the horses away from the canyon rim, talking as he walks backward with them, motioning with his head to the other men: *Go. Look for him, go, go, go!*

Find the preacher, or what's left of him.

So that's it, then? All those years your father spent preaching and praying and bearing other people's burdens? All gone in an instant? And all those days you and your mother spent bearing his burdens so he could bear others'?

Never once did he take a rest; never once did your father say, *I should step aside; I have earned a natural human vacation in the natural human world.* That way was not open to him. That way is not the circuit rider's.

And always praying, always fasting, giving away whatever someone gave him, giving it away even when it hurt. You learned to be like him, didn't you? You learned your calling from him. Give it all away; give comfort away as well; accept suffering for yourself, accept discomfort, but do not tolerate it for others. Speak up for the underdog, unless the underdog is yourself.

Find Christ in everyone but the person in the mirror.

You cannot think of a day you didn't worry about Lorenzo McRae, not one single day you didn't feel your own heart would break if your father was sad or sorrowful. All that now gone.

The militiamen look for a path to the river. They won't climb those thousand feet down to search for the preacher until they find a navigable trail. One of the men points to an indentation, a shadow against the canyon wall; another shouts that there's no way down, no use searching—the path can't be that steep.

—*Go*, Kerchief bellows again, and the men comply with their new leader's orders.

Wiley, adrift and sodden, totters around the Pulpit's base. —Where's Barker? Tell me who fell, tell me it weren't—

Kerchief, again, tells the captain to shut his mouth, and the other men, pushing him aside as they head to the gorge floor, order Wiley out of their way; they have no more use for him.

And a new problem: A man walking up the rim trail, a man with a wide-brimmed hat and a stumping gait, his advance slow but resolute. One step, then another, headed toward you.

He removes his hat, tucks it under his arm. He has silver hair. Silver on the way to white. An older man, advanced in years, almost old enough to be Matthew Higgenbotham.

Wait.

You peer through the rain. You wipe the back of your hand across your eyes and peer again.

Kerchief strides forward, one hand on his holster. —Another step and you're a dead man, he says. —State your business.

Higgenbotham lifts both hands. He's unarmed. You should know: You liberated him from his pistol five days ago.

—I didn't come for trouble, he says. —I believe I have something you're looking for.

Then he gazes right at you. His eyes are so blue, they make your heart hurt. His eyes are the one young and hopeful thing about him.

—Mister, you say. Rain drums on the top of your head, your shoulders. —You came.

He holds your gaze and says not a word. Kerchief watches the two of you, waiting.

You glance back at the canyon, at the place where your father and the wolfdog fell.

Lorenzo never came after you. He never came back. You loved him anyway. You might love him more for it. That's something else you will have to wrestle with one day.

You open your mouth. —It weren't enough, you tell Higgenbotham. —It weren't ever enough. No matter what I did.

He shakes his head. —I don't know what's enough and what's not, he says. —But one thing I do know, Barker McRae, you are a born preacher.

He glances over at Kerchief, then back your way. —I figured someone ought to tell you that once in your life, in case you didn't know it already.

A sob bursts out. You clap your hand over your mouth, but another comes behind it. And another, until somehow, without moving toward him, without walking a single step, you find yourself in his arms, enfolded, properly grandfathered. Your face is pressed against his chest. He's not your father and never will be. But he smells of blackberries and rain; he smells of pine cones and the road and safekeeping.

The negotiations go quickly because there are none. Kerchief has what Higgenbotham wants—the girl. Higgenbotham has what the men scouring the river basin want—the rights to lot number 96, forty acres on pristine Blood Mountain Creek, in Lumpkin County's first section, fifteenth district. Relief lights up Kerchief's face when he realizes what Higgenbotham comes bearing. No Moravians needed.

Higgenbotham has four more lottery grants too, of course, tucked away in his saddlebag, those final plots he was supposed to distribute to other lucky drawers. But he doesn't mention those grants to Kerchief. He's done handing out stolen acres in Georgia.

Kerchief pores over the Blood Mountain grant, reading every word. The rain is lightening. Shouts in the canyon from the regiment men: They found the preacher's hat in the shallows, but nothing else, no circuit rider and no wolfdog either. The river has taken them.

Kerchief's face as he scans the lottery papers is his uncle Thrasher's—regal, calm, deliberate. Yes, Higgenbotham decides, the innkeeper's imprint is on this young man; it's in his steadiness, his flint. He feels a twinge of fear for young Johnny Thrasher, for all that's coming toward him.

—Do what you will with those papers, Higgenbotham says. —But don't ride with those militia fellows anymore. Time for you to stay out of trouble. Go back to your uncle; he'll be wanting to see you.

Kerchief's eyes flicker up to Higgenbotham. —Maybe, he says. —But these boys need me.

He's barely more than a boy himself.

Kerchief looks over at Barker next. She stands apart from both men, by the rim trail, watching the searchers as they start their long climb up from the river basin. The afternoon is waning. Her hair is loose, blowing across her face, her features grave. For several seconds, Kerchief studies her.

Finally, he turns. —She's your charge now, he says to Higgenbotham with a short nod. —We'll be gone within the hour.

By the time the regiment men have hiked back up to the top of the canyon, they're tired and hungry and still have their captain to deal with. Wiley is sickening; his infection isn't improving; he's not a well man. He's barking out commands, talking to Scissors, or at him. For his part, Scissors stays in the wagon, doing his best to ignore him.

Wiley tells his men they're all useless. He demands a doctor, his wife, his niece's ministrations.

Kerchief steps aside and confers with the company men. After a few minutes he approaches Wiley and relays their decision. They'll do their captain the courtesy of taking him to Toccoa—it's the nearest town with a doctor. But that's all they'll do. They won't wait with him, won't escort him back to Clarke County if he survives his infection. If he does survive, he will need Elma. He will be wholly dependent on his wife the rest of his life.

But maybe he was already.

Wiley's strength is considerable. Even now, in his fevered state, it takes three men to drag and shove the captain into the wagon for the trip ahead. He's out of his mind with delirium. When Scissors tries to tuck the blanket around his lap, Wiley grabs the youth by his hair, twines his fingers through the thick coils, and prepares to go for his eye, just like he did in the old days. —I can take it out blind, Wiley bellows.

And he could, he truly believes it; most of life is lived by feel anyway.

Scissors rears back and tries to pull away, but Wiley has him locked in; he's poised and ready.

Kerchief steps forward once more. Without a sound, he presses a blade to Wiley's throat, shoving the captain against the wagon sideboard. He digs the point in a little so that it tickles the jugular. Wiley goes stock-still.

—He's one of us, Kerchief says. —He's militia now. Let him go.

Wiley releases his hold. Scissors steps away, cursing and sputtering. Wiley leans over the side of the wagon and retches. Higgenbotham, waiting at some remove, looks away, averts his gaze. He's not so far out of his cholera that he can't recall what fever feels like, what that kind of heat frying the brain does to a person. Across the gorge, the sky is changing, a hint of crimson threading through the clouds, a streak of color so striking, he forgets to breathe for a second.

Scissors steals a glance at Kerchief as the militiaman sheathes his knife. Johnny Thrasher meant what he said; it's a genuine offer. The 221st Company's a mess. It's doomed, if they're forthright about it. But they'll take a man they can rely on; they'll take a man who's not afraid of a bully and who has demonstrated mettle.

Barker steps forward. She takes final stock of Wiley Wood in that wagon, appraising her uncle one last time, her gaze measured. When he calls her name once more, she turns and walks away from him.

22

TO VERMONT, THEN. It's not a good plan. It's a terrible plan. But it's better than no plan.

They can't head south. Higgenbotham will not see Milledgeville again, will not collect his final payment. Minter Templin will have spread Higgenbotham's name far and wide by now, into Alabama as well, telling every uniformed man or bounty hunter he can find about the lottery messenger turned horse thief.

The only direction left to them is north. And Barker will go with him.

—We can't slow down, he says as he taps the four stallions with the reins, Tallulah Gorge receding behind them. —We have a thousand miles in front of us. That's two months' riding, if we're lucky, if nothing happens.

Someone else in his situation might head to the port at Savannah, purchase a fare, sail to Cape Cod without shoeing a single horse. But Higgenbotham promised his Ruth many years ago that he wouldn't follow her to Savannah when she left him, that he wouldn't travel to his wife's hometown. He has honored his promise this long; he's not going to stop now.

Also, the seasickness might be the death of him.

In the past couple of days, Higgenbotham's heart has started ticking strangely, poor syncopation followed by fluttering. A passing phenomenon, he hopes, a temporary disruption. He will not mention the development to Barker.

—Once we get there, he says, I have the house in Brattleborough, the home I grew up in. There are schools nearby too, good schools, I hope, for young women. You'll have more freedom to pursue an education. He pauses, chews at his lip. —Not as much as you might want, but better than in Gainesville. Better than pressing wax flowers.

—I don't need school, Barker says. —All I need's the Bible.

But then she falls silent, contemplating the possibilities.

She stays quiet for another mile, well after the canyon has disappeared and daylight is fast disappearing. She's quiet for so long, Higgenbotham begins to worry.

—You said you wanted to come with me, he says. —Have you changed your mind? You can stay in Georgia if you'd rather. Though I'm not sure who'll take you. You'd have to go back to your aunt. That's assuming your uncle doesn't make it home, and I wouldn't place money on that.

Barker shakes her head. —I can't go back. Elma wouldn't stand for it.

—Smart woman, Higgenbotham says.

Their route will take them through the mountains. The four horses gain strength and speed as they turn onto the Unicoi Turnpike. This toll road is wide and level and well maintained; it's the best road in Georgia, by Higgenbotham's lights. And he should know; he's ridden every road this state has built, every trade path that ever saw a traveler.

They stop for the night near a burial ground with slot-and-tab tombstones, and Higgenbotham finds a roadside spring to water the horses. While the stallions drink, he pulls the four remaining lottery grants from his bag. He produces a flint, strikes a spark, and lights the pages, one by one. He holds each page up in the twilight as it burns.

Barker watches in silence. He's doing what Lorenzo told the regiment men they ought to do—burn those property rights as reprehensible. When he finishes, Higgenbotham blows the remaining ashes into the creek. It's not much, as far as resistance goes. It's not enough. It's the equivalent of spitting into a long Georgia wind. But it's what he has.

He glances over at her. When Barker nods, he steps back from the creek and starts laying out the ground covers.

From their campsite they see a man traveling south, riding an old mare with a gray coat, the man's torch held high, lighting the road. When Higgenbotham sees that grizzled mare passing, for a second he thinks she's Mandy, his faithful companion, miraculously making her way back to him, finding him from the stables where he left her.

It's not Mandy, of course. He will not see his mare again. He has left the past miles, the past years, littered with abandoned friends, Scout only the latest casualty among them; Scout, whom Higgenbotham misses but doesn't want to speak about, doesn't want to mention, because of what the wolfdog did. And Barker's loss so much the greater.

But his heart hurts at the thought of him.

Higgenbotham glances over at Barker. She's whispering to herself on her pallet, lying on her back, snatches of words and prayers visiting her, battling their way forward. When she catches him looking at her, she scowls.

She's going to have to get all those words out soon enough, one way or another. By sermon or hymn, by exhortation or pamphlet. She's not going to be able to keep herself to herself much longer. And preaching will be a hard life for her; it will be almost impossible, even in the north. She will never feel at home there. She will miss her parents and the Blue Ridge Mountains always.

Again, Higgenbotham thinks of Scout, and briefly he falls into a reverie, a half-dream, another impossibility. In this dream, he sees the wolfdog alive, having survived the fall, heaving himself out of the Tallulah River onto dry ground, shaking his coat, a thousand flecks of foam flying off him. His cheek is still swollen from the snakebite, but he's wagging his tail, pleased with himself. Someone is coming up the road toward him; someone is waiting for him on the bank. Higgenbotham can't see who it is, but Scout can.

What next? the wolfdog asks, panting with mad gladness. *What adventures shall we have now?*

Higgenbotham opens his eyes. A phrase from the Psalms comes to him, out of ancient childhood. *The sun shall not smite thee by day, nor the moon by night.*

He says it under his breath; he says it several times over. *A good prayer for the road*, he thinks.

—If we're going to travel together, he says to Barker the next morning, a few ground rules are in order.

—What're those, she asks, shifting on the buggy seat.

Higgenbotham is at the horses' heads, adjusting their gear, checking their traces. —I'm in charge of what I drink, not you, he says. —I promise to be reasonable and temperate. In turn, *you* promise not to comment every time I uncap a bottle. I'll not be henpecked.

Barker frowns. —I don't henpeck.

He's trying to distract her with trivialities, with humor and quibbling. He wants to keep her mind from vaulting over that canyon ledge after her father. Above the mountains, the sunrise is a sweep of rose and violet.

—Your turn, he says, and hauls himself into the driver's seat. A flock of blackbirds lift from the field behind him. —It's not just me setting the terms here.

—All right, Barker says. —We go to church. Every Sunday, we find one and we go. Or I do, anyway, and you don't march off and leave me.

—Last I recall, you were the one doing the leaving, he says.

—That was because you was rude, she replies, brightening slightly. —That was because you kept saying terrible things to me.

—Well, institute a no-rudeness rule, Higgenbotham says, taking the reins in hand. —Institute a no-terrible-things rule. State the terms you require. You want to be a preacher, you need to speak up; you need to say your piece.

A hint of color appears in her cheeks. The road is draped in pale light. In his chest, Higgenbotham feels that curious fluttering, that metronome gone awry again.

Hurry, he tells himself.

Thrasher might come up one day if he invites him, once the innkeeper has had his fill of Georgia. Maybe Thrasher's nephew will venture north too, if he can stay alive until then. If he can keep from one of the million deaths that await a young man like Kerchief in the goldlands.

Or maybe Barker will find her way just fine without any of them. Maybe it's time the world stopped underestimating girls.

She reaches out and pokes him in the shoulder. Just once, but it's enough. He understands the directive; he knows the order of the day.

—Let's be on, then, he says, and touches the reins; the stallions fly forward. —Time's wasting.

–THE END–

Historical Note

The Deliverance of Barker McRae takes place at the height of the Georgia gold rush and the Cherokee land lottery, two interconnected events that have not received sufficient attention in our collective understanding of the United States in the decades leading up to the Civil War. I also drew from literature on Methodist circuit riders and female evangelists across post–Revolutionary War America. I took inspiration for Barker's father from Lorenzo Dow, one of the most colorful and challenging itinerant preachers of his day, and I imagined what life might have been like if a man like Lorenzo had had a daughter—and if she felt called, amid extreme personal circumstances, to pursue the same vocation as her father.

I then complicated matters for poor Barker by placing her in the state of Georgia during the middle of one of the biggest land grabs in American history in the years immediately prior to the Trail of Tears, the genocidal exile of Native peoples to regions west of the Mississippi. The Georgia and western North Carolina gold rush started in the late 1820s and marked the first major gold rush in the United States—these prospectors later became known as the twenty-niners. By 1830, over twenty thousand miners and rushers had poured into the goldfields. They contributed sizably to the nation's gold stock, with some estimates placing antebellum southern gold at approximately forty million dollars. When Georgia began distributing plots of Indigenous land—some of it laden with gold deposits—to white settlers through a lottery system, the chaos increased. Claims and property rights were disputed on all sides and often had to be settled by attorneys. In some instances, white orphans were eligible to receive land in the lottery, though their guardians often took charge of the details.

The Georgia gold rush didn't make the fortunes of impoverished men—or at least, not many of them. Those who already had money tended to benefit the most, those men who went nowhere near a stream, who never bent down to pour silt and water into a pan or shovel mud into a cradle rocker. Those who benefited financially from the gold that poor and enslaved laborers extracted included attorneys, who made money off disputes over land; northern banks and bankers, who helped fund large mining operations; mine-company owners, who often used a combination of poor white and enslaved labor; and southern plantation owners, who rented out that enslaved labor in the offseason. European financiers also got involved. As recent scholarship has documented, gold from placer operations wound up serving the interests of New York stockbrokers and traveled through the financial and commodity markets. These purchases sought to ensure that the federal government could pay foreign bondholders and keep American banks solvent. While my novel has a narrower focus on Barker and her imagined journey, these larger events inform the story and the moral dilemmas with which Matthew Higgenbotham in particular grapples.

I also placed Barker in the context of rising militia groups and guardsmen operating in Georgia during this period. Every county had its own militia, and in December 1830, Governor Gilmer authorized the statewide Georgia Guard to drive intruders from the gold mines. The Georgia

Guard existed in tense relation to the federal troops who occasionally made their way into the region. The federals initially tried to slow the tide of gold seekers who trespassed on Cherokee sovereignty by arresting anyone who entered the vicinity of the mines, whether white or Native. But when federal soldiers turned this enforcement over to the Georgia Guard, all bets on behalf of the Cherokee were off.

Nineteenth-century southern-backwoods brawling has a history all its own, and one that also deserves more attention. Eye gouging seems to have been unfortunately common in frontier circles in the late eighteenth and early nineteenth centuries. An 1837 article in a Georgia newspaper provided a description of the aftermath of such brawls so vivid that I borrowed from it for Wiley Wood's story: "This [tavern] used to be a 'torn down' place, to use our Georgia phrase. It was reported in the mornings after drunken frolics and fights you could see the children picking up eye-balls in tea-saucers! i.e., there was so much gouging going on." An earlier report, from 1802, noted that men of the region took care never to cut their fingernails, letting them grow long and hardening them into weapons by smearing them with hot tallow. When fights took place, brawlers often went for the eyes of their opponents. "Since these fights occur often," the witness reported, "it follows that you meet in this nation few men who do not have one eye put out in this manner."

How southern frontiersmen fought during this period—what tactics they used, what codes of justice they did or did not follow—tells us something about the social values and cultural requirements that shaped Georgia and the southern Appalachian region. Allowing Elma and Barker to step briefly into a space claimed by men—and dominated by a very particular vision of masculinity—was a leap of imagination that I took while writing.

The impact of the Georgia land lottery and the gold rush wasn't just financial and racial. It was also environmental. In addition to accelerating the criminal dispossession of the Cherokee, the state survey of the gold region and subsequent land grab opened the door for well-funded mining companies to buy up large swaths of land for exploitation and development—and environmental destruction. I live in Dahlonega, a town where the signs of the old gold rush can be seen to this day, both in the mines that still offer visitors historical tours and in the long ditches that can be spotted along the sides of hills and mountains; these ditches supported massive hydraulic mining operations in the later years of gold mining. Decades of unchecked mining plus rapid settlement meant the loss of old-growth forests, wildlife habitat, and rare species. It meant the transformation of Indigenous lands into settler farms, towns, and, eventually, in more recent years, a shift toward corporatized industrial agriculture, which characterizes towns such as Gainesville today. I wanted to craft a story that invites the reader to imagine what north Georgia might have looked and felt like in the final days before Cherokee removal and unfettered white settlement—the last days of an older and surprisingly diverse frontier age, even as I know the word *frontier* remains complicated.

While I did my best to capture what this world could have looked and felt like, the final product is still unapologetically fictional, a work of imagination in conversation with historical materials—and in conversation with my own history as a relatively new resident of this complicated region, which is today marked by small-town charm, economic harship, the loss of farms and blue-collar livelihoods, and the gradual gentrification of the area as wealthy Atlantans buy up land and property that long-term residents and rural families can no longer afford. Dahlonega has become a destination for wineries, for high-end weddings, for Porsche owners who want to take a drive with fifteen of their fellow Porsche owners on the county's switchback mountain roads on the weekends. A land grab of a new sort is underway now in northeast Georgia, and its implications for the Chattahoochee-Oconee National Forests, for wildlife management, for water and housing and the people who call these small towns home will be far-reaching.

In Georgia resident George Paschal's biography of his mother, Agnes Paschal, a leading figure in the boomtown (now ghost town) of Auraria during the gold rush, he describes the "Indian issue" of the 1830s and admits that the whites of his and his mother's day were wholly culpable. "We wanted the land," he confesses. He acknowledges that his own family was in favor of the land lottery "and not very nice about the moral aspect of the question." But, he adds, the immorality was so infinitesimally divided among many thousands of white Georgians that no one at the time felt responsible.

Paschal's observation raises a question that I've tried to explore in this book—what it means to do one's duty as an individual during a profoundly immoral collective historical moment. What are we responsible for and what are we not? What counts as a trespass? And if we observe a trespass committed against another person, even if that person is a stranger, how are we called to respond?

In addition to Lorenzo McRae, several characters and scenes in this book were inspired by—or at least named after—real historical figures and events. I wish I could take credit for it, but I didn't come up with the name Wiley Wood; a man named Wiley Wood is listed in the *Western Herald* in 1833 as one of several settlers with unclaimed mail waiting for them at the Gainesville post office. Mary Franklin was a real widow and mine owner during this period and accrued significant wealth from her operation, though unlike the Mary in this novel, she had children and brought them with her to gold country. She ran her mine with the expertise and oversight of at least two enslaved women, and she lost a team of enslaved male workers during a mine collapse. The experience of Higgenbotham's wife, Ruth, losing triplets early in their marriage, comes from the biography of Auraria resident Agnes Paschal. Her son George recounts that Agnes gave birth to triplet girls who "lived but one day" and were buried in one coffin. His mother was deeply affected by the loss and used to say that she would give much for "wax figures representing these little beings," though he doesn't say if anyone ever gave her such figures.

The character Jethro Scudder is loosely based on Jacob Scudder, a wealthy mine owner, enslaver, and war veteran during this period. The *Cherokee Intelligencer* and the *Southern Banner* both reported a violent fight between thirty Cherokee and numerous white settlers in late April 1833 at Scudder's inn. The *Southern Banner* explained that the brawl had erupted over a land dispute and then declared (in a tone of satisfaction) that after two hours of fighting, "the whites are still in possession." I should also note that most of the poems, hymn excerpts, and sayings that appear in italics, such as *All I want in this creation / Is a pretty little wife and a big plantation / Away up yonder in the Cherokee Nation*, are taken directly from early nineteenth-century source materials.

The minter Templin with his four fast stallions was inspired by the real-life Templeton Reid, a watch repairer turned coiner during the gold rush. I have no idea if the real-life Reid was as unlikable a fellow as the Templin in my story; I hope not, for the sake of his friends and family. Last but not least, the character Matthew Higgenbotham received his name after I read a brief mention in the historical materials of a man named Higginbotham (no first name given) who was once employed by the Jefferson Mining Company. This historical Higginbotham was apparently tasked with traveling to Milledgeville whenever a particularly coveted land lot was drawn in the lottery, locating the winner, and bringing him back to the company owners so they could purchase the rights from that person. As the historical record indicates, in one instance, the lottery winner chased down by Higginbotham was a cautious farmer who accepted the money the company offered—ten thousand dollars—and used it to buy or pay off his existing farm rather than trying his hand at gold mining up north. He was probably better off for it.

Resources for Further Reading

Anthony, J. S. *The Life and Times of Rev. J. D. Anthony: An Autobiography with a Few Individual Sermons.* Atlanta: C. P. Byrd, 1896.

Brekus, Catherine A. *Strangers and Pilgrims: Female Preaching in America, 1740–1845.* Chapel Hill: University of North Carolina Press, 1998.

Coulter, E. Merton. *Auraria: The Story of a Georgia Gold-Mining Town.* Athens: University of Georgia Press, 1956.

Daly, Ann Marsh. "Every Dollar Brought from the Earth: Money, Slavery, and Southern Gold Mining." *Journal of the Early Republic* 41, no. 4 (Winter 2021): 553–85.

Dow, Lorenzo. *The Life, Travels, Labors, and Writings of Lorenzo Dow: Including His Singular and Erratic Wanderings in Europe and America.* New York: C. M. Saxton, 1859.

Estreicher, Justin. "'Unoccupied and of a Valuable Kind': The Georgia Gold Rush and Manufactured Cherokee Savagery." *Georgia Historical Quarterly* 105, no. 2 (2021): 87–119.

Gorn, Eliott J. "'Gouge and Bite, Pull Hair and Scratch': The Social Significance of Fighting in the Southern Backcountry." *American Historical Review* 90 (February 1985): 18–43.

Harris, Cora. *A Circuit Rider's Wife.* Philadelphia: Henry Altemus, 1910.

Hill, Sarah. *Cherokee Removal from Georgia: Final Report.* National Park Service and Georgia Department of Natural Resources, 2005.

Longstreet, Augustus. *Georgia Scenes, Characters, Incidents &c., in the First Half Century of the Republic.* New York: Harper and Brothers, 1850.

Moyer, Paul B. *The Public Universal Friend: Jemima Wilkinson and Religious Enthusiasm in Revolutionary American.* Ithaca, NY: Cornell University Press, 2015.

Owens, Sheldon Ben. *The Dogtrot House Type in Georgia: A History and Evolution*. Master's thesis, University of Georgia, 2009.

Ownby, Ted, and David Wharton. *Georgia's Old Federal Road*. Department of Transportation, Center for the Study of Southern Culture, 2007.

Paschal, George W. *Ninety-Four Years: Agnes Paschal*. Washington, DC: M'Gill and Withrow, 1871.

Pecina, Jozef. "Eye-Gouging in Antebellum Popular Fiction." *American and British Studies Annual* (December 2017): 24–32.

Sant, Claudio. *Unworthy Republic: The Dispossession of Native Americans and the Road to Indian Territory*. New York: W. W. Norton, 2020.

Seymour, Dexter C. "Templeton Reid, First of the Pioneer Coiners." *Museum Notes* 19 (1974): 225–66.

Starbuck, Richard W., ed. *Records of the Moravians Among the Cherokees*. Vol. 9, 1830–1833. Tahlequah, OK: Cherokee Heritage Press, 2018.

Warren, Mary Bondurant, and Eve B. Weeks, eds. *Whites Among the Cherokees, Georgia 1827–1838: Written by the Participants*. Athens, GA: Heritage Papers, 2014.

Western Herald. Auraria, Lumpkin County, Georgia, 1833. https://gahistoricnewspapers.galileo.usg.edu/lccn/sn89053249/.

Williams, David. *The Georgia Gold Rush: Twenty-Niners, Cherokees, and Gold Fever*. Columbia: University of South Carolina Press, 1993.

Acknowledgments

The writing community in Georgia and the Southeast is as vibrant and deeply supportive as anywhere on the planet, and I feel lucky to be a part of it. Special thanks go to Katy Carroll, Brett Chloupek, Julia Franks, the late Richard Gess, Liza Nelson, Jonathan Rabb, Tracy Roe, Michael Rudin, Rob Voss, Daren Wang, and all the regulars at Writers' Happy Hour in Decatur. Historian Ken Akins volunteered many hours helping me navigate north Georgia history—I was fortunate to have him as an expert guide. Fulton Arrington provided wise counsel as well, and I want to thank him. I also want to thank the many Georgia state park employees and local courthouse museum curators who answered questions and provided insight as I researched north Georgia in the early 1830s.

Marc Jolley and the staff members of Mercer University Press are a historical novelist's dream team, and I'm thrilled to work with them.

I want to acknowledge my parents, Gordon and Marion Brown; my sister, Candace Brown; and my beautiful stepdaughters, Bella and Saba—thank you all for your ongoing support and loving encouragement.

Writing a book is a long and lonely endeavor, people say, and that's often true. But I wasn't alone. My partner, Mark Pelletier, was by my side every step of the way. Over the past few years, as I've experienced multiple ups and downs as a writer (that's a nice way of saying I'm prone to staggering from exhilaration to despair and back again), he helped me to be kinder to myself, stay present, and allow joy into each day, even, or especially, when anxieties and uncertainties loomed large in the broader world.

I'm writing these words on January 1, 2025. None of us knows how the coming year will play out, let alone the rest of our lives. Almost everyone I know is uneasy about the future for one reason or another. But fear doesn't get to have the last word. To borrow from theologian and writer Frederick Buechner, "Joy is at the end of it, after all."

Joy to you, my fellow readers, and my deepest gratitude for the time you've chosen to spend on these pages. Onward!